MW01167415

Anonymity

ANONYMITY. © 2003 by Margie Gosa Shivers.

Published by MGS Publishing, Calumet City, IL
www.mgspublishing.com

ISBN 0-974-40661-9

Library of Congress Catalog Number: 2003096301

Printed in the United States of America

Book design by Keith Saunders
MARIONDESIGNS

Anonymity

Margie Gosa Shivers

Publishing Company

While many things are too strange to be believed,
nothing is too strange to have happened.

- Thomas Hardy

In loving memory of my mother

Annie Robinson Gosa
July 31, 1924 – April 17, 1997

The legacy of your strength, and a loving, giving heart
shall continue to guide my life

I love you and miss you dearly

ACKNOWLEDGEMENTS

Giving my eternal thanks and all the praise to God for leading me to this point in life, for without Him, none of this would be possible.

I want to thank my son, Patrick Cook, my sisters, brothers, nieces, nephews, aunts, uncles, cousins, schoolmates, and friends. Your love, support and admiration for my accomplishment during the first release of my debut novel, was overwhelming.

To Joan Burke Stanford, my editor/publicist; Pearlie Greer Westbrooks, my high school classmate for line editing services, Keith Saunders, my graphic designer and L. Julie Torrey Parker, copy editor. Your professional expertise and friendship have helped to move this edition to a new and exciting level!

To all of my author friends for their support and encouragement: C. Kelly Robinson, Kimberla Lawson Roby, Linda Dominque Grosvenor, Maxine Thompson, Denise O'Neal, Heather Covington and the Disilgold Network, Natalie Darden, Sheila Goss, Kenneth (Kanko) Bowens and Hope C. Clark, MsSammie, Idella Phillips, Francine Yates, Yvette Stewart, Adrienne Pickett and all of the rest of my colleagues in this industry.

Thanks to my schoolmates all across the country, and Carol Ann Adams of Dancing Rabbit Bookstore in my hometown of Greenwood, MS., friends, and supporters at my alma mater, Mississippi Valley State University, for your friendship and support.

To my schoolmates in St. Louis: Thelma Redmond Clark and Mable Lakes; and, Tommie Galloway, my schoolmate and sister friend in Chicago. You rendered serious support by going out of your way to purchase books for several other classmates.

To my cousin, Brenda Robinson and friend Jean Pryor Knight (Delta Sigma Theta Sorority), and Sherita Shunn, President of the Sophisticated Souls of Learning Book Club of Memphis, TN, for helping me deplete my inventory at Afro Books and Davis-Kidd in your fabulous city.

My deepest gratitude to Roger Bethel, Brandy Tate, WREG television co-anchors Alex Coleman and Mary Ruth Conley of Memphis, TN for their support in garnering local publicity.

To Arance Brooks Williamson, Deborah Quinn, Paul Brooks, Ernestine Epps, and my sisters: Shirley and Barbara Gosa of Greenwood, MS., for the lovely book reception you helped to sponsor in my honor.

To my cousin, Teresa Cosey and Charlene Parham for the extraordinary work in setting up my book signing at Barnes&Noble-University of Chicago Bookstore.

And words simply cannot express my gratitude toward all of the book clubs situated throughout the country. Your support plays a major role in building my reading audience.

A special thank you to: the Sophisticated Souls of Learning Book Club of Memphis, Tennessee, the Mahogany Book Club of Albany, N.Y, SistaGirl Book Club of Chesapeake, VA; Let's Talk Book Club, Just Us Book Club, Ya-Ya Sisterhood Book Club and Go On Girl Book Club of Chicago, IL, James and Toni Waller and friends in Flossmoor, IL, and Harith Razaa of Cincinnati, OH; Sarah Hinton Miller, Rebecca Brooks Carr and Lovie Tabor of CA; Queen Brooks Stinson and daughter Monica Stinson of Grenada, MS; Joseph Collins (Howard University), Orlando McDonald, Thelma Gosa of Detroit, MI; Sonny and Carole Gardner, Joe and Sandra McCaster of St. Louis, MO; Jeanette Archie

Washington of Jackson, MS; Jessie and Joyce Gosa of Richton Park, IL; Arick Streater and Renita Streater-Rhodes of Chicago, IL; Kim Dates of Memphis, TN; Rev. Dr. Jeremiah A. Wright Jr., Rev. Dr. Delores Johnson, Rev. Barbara J. Allen and S. L. Allen, Mr. and Mrs. Blaine DeNye, Dr. Iva Carruthers, Attorney Patricia Eggleston, Dr. Sokoni Karanja, Rosalyn Priester, Pamela Jackson, Gus Bowers, Marie, Denise and Patricia Cary, Leola Washington Boyd, Betty Mayes, Nathaniel Riley, Armando and Walter Palmore, Iva Robinson, Youlanda McCarthy, Denise Conway, Cynthia Lowe, Anita Ross , Leslie Junkins and my sister, Mary Gosa Streater of Chicago, for lending your support early on.

To all of my readers everywhere who have been kind enough to pick up this book, you are the most important of all, and please know that I will always remember that. I'd love to hear your thoughts on *Anonymity*, and of course, I personally respond to every one of my e-mails.

All my love and appreciation
Margie Gosa Shivers

E-mail: margegosa@aol.com
Website: http://www.margegosa.com

Chapter 1

Chicago, Illinois
April 2000

There was no question about it. Cara Fleming loved her husband from the day they met in 1991 at Tennessee State University and she knew he still loved her. She was nineteen and he was twenty. Neither grew up with siblings, a circumstance that helped to bring them closer throughout their courtship. As many expected, the college sweethearts married and later had a child.

And now, at twenty-eight, she still had the figure of a young girl with fresh, exuberant looks to go with it she couldn't understand why sex between them was never again hot and intense. Neither did she ever complain that he was the one satisfied and that she wasn't! Playing tennis with his friends and going to Chicago Bulls games seemed to occupy Mario's interest more than ever. Even more unsettling were his sudden mood swings and over-possessiveness for no apparent reason. He even had a problem with her being on the computer for extended periods of time. It was as if he wanted her all to himself. Other than her church friends and coworkers, Mario was it.

More than ever, she wanted to rekindle the romance and passion their six-year marriage once had. Oh sure, her faceless friends on the Internet had given her plenty of advice, but they didn't know Mario! Two weeks ago, she'd bought tickets for them to see Luther Vandross perform at the Rosemont Horizon Center. Since Mario had always been enticed by her style of dress, Cara decided to let that be the first step in her plan of action - A *to die for* outfit.

While shopping major stores in the Loop, she remembered how loving and attentive Mario had been right after they moved to Chicago. Although he found reasons not to go to church with her, she appreciated that he took her out to dinner every Friday night, and he never missed an opportunity to surprise her with fresh flowers, or to take her to see a play or a concert once a month. And, he was always willing to go with her to museums or to take romantic walks in the park.

Two hours later, she arrived home with the most perfect outfit - a flowing sleek golden duster pant set with sparkling white embroidery and bugle beading. It was sensually feminine and showed off her honey brown skin. She took a long hot bath and rubbed a peach-scented lotion all over her body, leaving no area untouched. Then she applied a medium beige foundation to her Alicia Keys look-a-like face, slipped her five-foot-six slender body into the new outfit and brushed her long dark brown hair as far as her arms could stretch. To set the mood, she selected a Barry White CD and poured chilled champagne into two flutes. When the last song played, she checked her watch. Darkness would soon claim her private view of the lake. *Where was he? He had promised to be home an hour ago. Had he been in an accident?*

She tried to calm her nerves by watching a popular game show, but that didn't help.

She walked to the full-length window and peered into the darkness of the night. It was a little after seven. Suddenly, she heard keys rattling at the door.

"Cara Slater!" His voice was loud enough to wake up a dead man. She knew something awful had disturbed his goat. The last time Mario called her by her maiden name was on their wedding day.

Eager to greet him, she rushed down the hallway toward the door and stopping abruptly, she gazed at Mario fearfully as he wobbled his five-ten, athletic body closer to her. He wore an orange T-shirt, and matching white shorts and gym shoes. But mostly, she took notice of the evil look on his face and wondered for the first time in their marriage, if she should fear for her life.

Instinctively, she stepped back and put her hands against the wall for support. "Mario, what is wrong with you? You're late. We're going to miss the concert."

"Forget the frigging concert," he shouted, throwing his keys on the glass-top table in the foyer. "You've been cheating on me Miss Angel, Miss Goody Two-Shoes."

Cara's breathing shortened and she tried to swallow, but her mouth was dry. Mario walked toward her, eyes watery, eyebrows furrowed and thin moustache slanted in a frown. Without looking at her, he headed straight to his liquor cabinet in the corner of the living room. He poured a shot of Wild Turkey and almost fell over when he tilted his head back to toss down the golden fluid. He stumbled to the sofa and plopped down. "So, the lady wants to know what's wrong? I'll tell you, Miss Lady. While you were out, an anonymous caller gave me the sordid details. From all he said, one thing convinced me he wasn't lying. Oh, and the jerk explained why he wanted me to know." Mario sprang from the sofa and walked toward her, stopping to sip his drink. "The evidence speaks for itself, Miss Lady."

"What evidence?" Cara screamed. Tears trickled down her face. "What did the caller tell you?"

"Enough," he said bluntly.

"Enough about what?" Cara stared at Mario and remained silent.

"Why should I tell you what you already know? Anyway, you want to know what ripped my heart out? That the two of you are planning to get married."

"I have no idea what you're talking about. That is ridiculous!" Cara cried.

"You're lying. I can't believe anything you say," Mario said with disgust. "And you know what else Miss Lady? I don't believe Ashley is my child."

"First of all, stop calling me Miss Lady. I have a name, remember?" Cara said with authority in her voice. "And, you could never be more wrong about our daughter. You were the first and only man I've been with and you know it."

"I'm not so sure about that," Mario said.

"I can't believe you just said that." Icy contempt flashed in her eyes, as she shook her head, trying to ignore the sting of pain that knifed through her. "I know you're sleeping with another man. So just stop lying to me."

"I am telling you the truth," she spouted the words slowly.

Suddenly, he put his glass down on the bar and stormed off toward their bedroom. Taking short steps, she quietly followed, and watched him remove his gun from the drawer. Without waiting around a second longer, she dashed out into the long hallway. She took off her heels and fled with all the speed she could rally. Realizing the elevator would slow her down she opened the door leading to the stairway. Taking two steps at a time, she was in the lead, at least by four floors.

When she reached the fifteenth floor, she realized the silence behind her. Still running like a bat out of hell, she started to think he'd stopped to rest or he was too drunk to continue. *Maybe he went back to the apartment. Worst, maybe he would take the elevator down and catch me on a lower floor.*

As she quickened her pace, she slipped on the tenth floor. Whisked in a surge of energy, she got up and ran some more, ignoring the pain that writhed through her tired body and aching feet. It wasn't long before she saw the sign on the back of the door below that told her she was about to reach the first floor.

Breathing hard, she quickly slipped on her shoes and walked slowly into the lobby. To her left, voices drew her attention to where people sat in the lounge watching the big screen television. A lady stood alone peering through the window.

She took a deep breath and crossed the lobby. Cara walked toward the circular desk guarding a paneled wall with closed doors. Her high heels pierced the marbled floor, alerting the tall and muscular security guard who looked like he could be Aaron Neville's twin. He was wearing a matching dark blue shirt and trousers and a shiny badge. *That's it,* she thought. *He can protect me, hide me in the back room, and call the police.*

Without his permission, she walked behind the security desk and kneeled to the floor.

"Hey lady, you can't play hide-and-seek here," the guard chuckled.

Index finger over her lips, she whispered, "This is no game. I can't let my husband find me. Help me, please!"

At that moment, Mario rushed through the lobby calling her name. He ran outside, looked up and down the streets and didn't see her.

"Humph, stay down and don't move." The guard's lips compressed. He watched Mario run back inside the building and head toward the security station. He got up and stood at the entranceway, shielding Cara.

Mario nodded a hello to the guard and edged closer until he stood directly in front of the guard. He looked down at the floor.

Doggone it! Cara thought, as she looked up at Mario.

"I looked all over for you," Mario said, holding both hands out to her. "It's okay. I'm not going to hurt you." His tone was civil.

Cara stood, looking briefly at the guard. It wasn't the time nor did she feel comfortable making a scene for the public to know that she was scared of her husband and while she believed he wouldn't harm her, she prayed that her instincts were right. "This is my husband, Mario."

Reluctantly, she stepped toward him and walked with him to the elevator as if nothing was wrong.

Mario pushed the button and she looked back at the guard as the elevator door opened. The guard removed his hat and scratched his head. Once they were inside, a thirty-something black couple got on the elevator, flirting and holding hands. When the door closed, Mario stared at Cara, which made her wonder if he would lose it once they were behind closed doors. The man and woman tried not to stare. Afraid to say anything that might rouse his anger again, she pressed her lips closed and breathed deeply.

When the elevator stopped on the twenty-seventh floor she let him lead the way to their apartment.

Inside, she sat on the sofa and quietly thanked her guardian angel for sparing her life.

"We need to talk about this," Mario said, sitting down in the love seat facing her. "I'm sorry. I was so angry. I wanted to shoot myself, not you.. Don't you know I'd never harm you?" He held his head down and she started to sense his regret.

For a moment her brown eyes darkened. "Read my lips, Mario. I was scared," she demanded. "Just what did you expect me to do? Stand around and let you put a bullet through me?"

"You're right, I shouldn't have done that," he said in frustration.

Cara didn't want to hear anymore. She stood up and walked out onto the private balcony. She held onto the iron railing, body still flushed in warmth, undaunted by the coolness of the night. Dappled light fell across the plants hanging from the balcony. Sounds of water splashed against the cement wall bordering the lake. She stared at the sky, black and dotted with millions of sparkling stars. The night view was spectacular. Even that couldn't erase the desolation that swept over her. She just couldn't understand why he wouldn't reveal to her the evidence that made him believe she'd been unfaithful. Not to mention that he practically knew her daily routine; the time she left home, where she was going and what time she would arrive home. Did he ever stop to ask himself when did she have the time to have an affair? None of it made any sense to her. Cara let her mind drift back to the allegations and the insults. The more she thought about it, the angrier she got and she could physically hear the thumping of her heartbeat, which was racing a hundred miles per second. She even wondered if he'd made the whole thing up. *Oh sure, in the past Mario lied and cheated on me, but never has he lied about something like this. He was immature, extremely jealous, self-centered and easy to anger. But this time he has gone too far,* she thought.

"I need the truth," Mario said, walking out to the balcony. "You hurt me. Can't you understand that?" he said in a pleading voice.

Looking around at him and filled with disgust, she brushed past him and went back inside. He followed her inside to the living room.

Slowing her steps to turn and face him, she said, "Considering your track record, I find what you just said amusing."
"Throwing mud in my face again?"
"Not exactly," she said, without a blink of the eye. "After what you just put me through tonight, it was the perfectly logical thing to say."
"How many times do I have to apologize for cheating on you?
"Whatever," she said angrily.

Mario rushed over to his white, gold-trimmed bar, poured another shot of bourbon and stared at her. The longer he stared, the more he poured. Once the liquor took effect, there was no telling what Mario would say or do.
She walked toward him and stopped. "You can believe this so-called anonymous caller if you want. But I don't do adultery; that's your style, not mine!" She turned around and walked to the guest bedroom and locked the door. Not long after, she heard him stomp down the hallway and shut his door. After long moments of thinking and nursing her emotional wounds, finally she slept.

At exactly eight o'clock the next morning, she woke up. It took more than ten minutes to move her body out of bed. Instantly, she realized it was Sunday and she got up and showered. Mario had left the apartment. It was his regular day to be on the tennis court.

Two hours later, she was dressed in a two-piece oyster white suit and her hair was perfectly styled in a french roll, held in place with a sparkling hair clamp. She grabbed her long, black leather coat from the closet and quietly shut the door behind her.

Cara arrived at church an hour later. Sitting on her favorite pew, she prayed and recalled the life she and Mario had back in Memphis. She had been honored with the teacher-of-the-year award. As one of the best coaches in the region, Mario had received numerous track and field awards for his outstanding coaching. However, the low wages, combined with Mario's spendthrift habits, forced them to pursue a better life in Chicago.

She found herself standing and singing the opening hymn. She thought about their daughter, Ashley. She missed Ashley and she wanted to feel her daughter's short arms draped around her. Her parents, motivated by fear and concerned about the safety of their almost three-year-old granddaughter living in the big city, had pressured Cara to let them take care of Ashley in Memphis for a little while longer or at least until she and Mario were firmly settled into their new life. Just three days ago, however, Cara decided since the public schools would close in June for the summer and Mario had opted not to work the summer session, he had the time to go to Memphis and bring back their daughter.

When services ended she eased past everyone, not in the mood for small talk, and greeted those she recognized with only a friendly smile. She got into her car and drove home. It was a sunny, cool day and there was little traffic on the streets.

Arriving home, she opened the drapes and sat on the sofa looking around the living room. Lots of mirrors were on the walls facing the balcony door; their reflection gave extra daylight for all the plants and made the room look even bigger. Ceiling high plants rested on both sides of the large window. A hand woven basket in between the sofa and loveseat was filled with *Ebony, Jet, Essence* and *People* magazines. She reserved the top of the floor model color television for displaying brass-coated frames containing colored photos of her, Mario and Ashley. Realizing that Mario wasn't due to arrive for another three hours, she undressed and changed into a sleek leopard caftan and matching ballerina shoes. She opened the drapes, checked her phone and e-mail messages, watered the plants, paid the household bills, and baked a cake.

Cara returned to the guest room and took a nap. An hour later, she awoke thinking she heard Mario come home. She got up and pushed the master bedroom door open hoping to talk to him. She checked the kitchen, the bathroom and the balcony. He must have come in and left again.

———

The next day, Mario was stuck in rush hour traffic on the Ryan Expressway hoping to get home before Cara. He reflected on the way she had talked to him, intimidating his male ego. *How could she do this to me? What a fool I've been,* he thought.

Then he remembered when they lived in Memphis and how badly he felt when Cara found out about his affair. Her words still rang in his head. "The hotel clerk said you checked in under the name of Mr. and Mrs. Mario Fleming. Since I didn't go with you, it's obvious you had another woman at the hotel." Her eyes were set ablaze like cackling wood burning in a fireplace on a cold winter night. She spent two weeks in their guest room until he broke the ice and begged for her forgiveness.

Somehow he believed the magic would work this time. It didn't. Now, the shoe was on the other foot. He started to think: *She's in the hot seat now and won't admit her guilt like I did. Maybe she just forgave me and didn't forget.*

Soon he parked his white Thunderbird in the underground garage. Feeling completely worn, he walked into their semi-dark, quiet apartment. Mario's thoughts had left a bad taste in his mouth, so he headed straight to the liquor cabinet.

He lit a cigarette and turned the television to Channel 7 Eyewitness News. The male reporter was interviewing an alderman about a good deed he'd done for the people in his ward. Mario barely caught the name, Alderman Giles Bennett. He lowered the volume and sipped the rest of his drink.

He looked at his watch thinking Cara would walk through the door in an hour.

Fifteen minutes later, relaxed, though still not at ease, he heard the door open. Cara placed a basket of clothing on the kitchen floor. *Did she take the day off? Maybe, she called in sick again, like the caller said.*

"Hello Mario," she said without expression.
"What happened? You and lover boy get your signals crossed?"

Here we go again, she thought. She knew it was best to keep quiet and not respond. If she didn't respond with one of her smart remarks, maybe he'd leave her alone.

He got up and walked to the bedroom.

She breathed a sigh of relief and put the neatly folded clothing away. Then she started preparing dinner, pepper steak with steamed rice and a tossed salad. As she washed the tomatoes, lettuce, and cucumbers, she thought about how it was going to be nearly impossible to get along with him if he continued to believe that she was having an affair. *If I leave him, how will I support myself?*

An hour later, Cara stood outside their bedroom door. "Mario, dinner is ready."

He slowly came out a few minutes later and sat down at his end of the table. He acted hungry and didn't wait for her to bless the food. The silence was unbearable until halfway through the meal.

"So, how was your day?" he asked.

"Not so good," she replied, looking at him. "How was it for you?"

"Same here," he answered, without looking at her.

Cara sipped her white zinfandel. "Have you called your parents?"

"Just my father."

"How're they doing?"

"Fine. They're doing just fine," he spat, eating the rest of his food like he had to get somewhere in a hurry.

"Spring is here. I suppose Bradley's going to be busy," she said, trying to fill the silence with small talk. Mario's father had owned a successful landscaping company since he was a young child. He'd expected Mario to keep his promise and take over the business when he passed on.

"You got that right," he replied, checking his watch. He dropped his napkin on top of his dirty plate. "Thanks for the food."

She watched him stand abruptly. "I made a pound cake yesterday while you were out. Can I get you a slice?"

He walked away from the table without removing his plate, grabbed his light jacket, and left through the front door.

Still fearful, but without intimidation, she got up and locked the door behind him. She wondered what the anonymous caller told Mario that was so convincing? Who was this man that called her husband? Why were the facts a big secret? How will she defend herself against such blatant allegations?

Cara dashed into their bedroom and located his gun. She walked to the guest bedroom. Mario had left her with only one option.

Chapter 2

Mario drove away, heading to his favorite watering hole, the *Due Drop Inn*. Thunder roared like a rumbling disaster in the sky. Raindrops covered the windshield. He slowed down, started the wipers and decided to call his tennis buddy, homicide detective Lester Miller.

After several attempts, Mario left a message: "Hey, Lester. I'm at the end of my rope. Meet me at the Inn."

At thirty-seven, Lester stood six feet tall and was ruggedly handsome with light skin, dark wavy hair and perfectly straight teeth. Considered by some to be Chicago's best-looking African American cop, he had compelling dark brown eyes and a generous smile.

Lester entered the lounge at 7:20 p.m. Mario appeared to be mesmerized by the bubbles that moved gracefully in his glass. Lester tapped his buddy on the shoulder and sat down on the high-legged bar stool.

"What's up? You look like hell has run over you, twice."
"Yeah, right," Mario replied and finished his beer. "Glad you could make it." He wiped drops of moisture from his forehead.
"Your message sounded urgent. What's wrong?"
Mario stammered, "I...I've got major problems at home."
"Hate to hear that, Buddy. What's this about?"
"Cara is sleeping with another man."
"Whoa! Come again." Lester demanded. The bartender placed a beer in front of Lester and quietly disappeared.
"You heard me. Don't make me repeat it!" Mario snapped.

"Well, how did you find out?"

"I got a call from the guy; he wouldn't tell me his name," Mario uttered. "But whoever he is, he had his facts straight. I got madder than a junkyard dog. I wanted to grab him through the phone and kill that son of a bitch." Then he told Lester the caller knew about Cara's birthmark on the left side of her butt that resembled a strawberry. "And if that wasn't enough,"

Mario filled Lester in on the rest. "He had the nerve to leave a brown envelope for me at the security desk of my apartment."

"What was in it?"

"Three pictures of my wife standing close to a dark-skinned man with curly hair. They were smiling and looked like they were happy. How do you think knowing what I knew and seeing them together made me feel?" Mario slammed his empty glass on the counter.

"Hey, calm down," Lester said. Before he could continue, Mario rushed to the men's room.

With his mind still heavily on Mario, Lester remembered a snapshot of Cara that Mario showed him. He thought she was a very beautiful woman. Not once had Mario introduced them. Lester had come to believe that Cara was a good woman who mostly stayed home and out of the streets, unlike some women he knew. According to Mario, she wasn't the type who would cheat on her man. Now, he wasn't so sure. *What went wrong with the model couple?* Lester wondered.

Mario returned to the bar.

"Feeling better?" Lester asked.

"Hell no!" Mario paused for a moment. "Are you ready to kick it up a notch?"

"Sure. Count me in. I'm off duty," Lester joked and ordered bourbon for them both.

Mario gathered his thoughts. "Man, once I saw those pictures, I had to confront her."

"Well what happened?" Lester asked. Mario took a deep breath.

"I'd had way too much to drink before I got home. She was

expecting me to take her out to a concert. I walked through the door and blew off like a nuclear missile. She saw me take out my gun, but it wasn't meant for her. Before I knew it, she ran out the door and down the stairs faster than a track star."

Lester stared without blinking.

"Don't give me that look. I was mad enough to shoot me, not her."

"What the hell were you thinking?

Mario didn't say anything, so Lester continued the conversation. "Well, I'm glad nothing happened," Lester replied. Wouldn't want to be the one to take you to jail," he added, and sipped the rest of his beer. "So, what did you do?"

"I'm ashamed to tell you." His brows set in a straight line. He realized that Lester was keenly attuned to everything he'd said thus far. Then, he decided to tell Lester everything about that night.

———

"So, you let your anger get the best of you again. Obviously, she thought you were chasing her with your gun."

"Yeah, I can see that now. I said some awful things to her and I feel badly about what happened. Half of it I don't remember."

Lester shrugged his shoulders and put his arms around Mario's shoulder. "If she's having an affair, my heart goes out to you. If not, then you better get on your knees and pray she forgives you."

Toni Braxton's "Un-Break My Heart" blared from the Inn's music system. A few of the people got up to dance and soon the crowd grew larger, as did the noise. Moving his body rhythmically to the music, Mario sipped some of his drink wondering how he was going to make things right with Cara again.

He started to hate himself and at the same time he realized this had been the first time he'd let his anger cause him to behave like a total ass.

Suddenly he decided to change the subject. "How're you getting along with your girlfriend?"

Lester glanced at the ceiling remembering his date with steady girlfriend, Barbara Rhodes and how angry she'd become when he cancelled their last two dates. He didn't have the heart to tell her the relationship wasn't going anywhere. "I have yet to find a woman who has everything all wrapped in one package," Lester said.

"Oh, so, you're still on the prowl, huh?"

"Hey, I'm not like you. You believe in love and following your heart, right?"

"True. I came from the good old birds and bees country. It doesn't take much to fall head over heels in love in the South. In my case, it took just one beautiful woman and a colorful butterfly. Before I knew it, I was up and away in love. Out of all the women on campus, I knew Cara was the woman for me," he said forcing a smile. Now, I hurt and I feel sick inside knowing that she has let another man make love to her. I guess I lost it when she kept saying she wasn't doing anything wrong."

Lester leaned back and shook his head. "As your friend, let me put a few things on your mind. I know how much you love her, but you can't do what you did and say the things you said to her and expect to keep your marriage together. In other words, don't hurt the one you say you love. Don't throw away what you have with your wife. Maybe, you should seek professional help with controlling your anger. Lighten up on the drinking, too. Go home and talk to Cara. There's still a chance that you can work this thing out with her," Lester added, giving him a pat on the back.

"Thanks. I guess I needed to hear that. You're the big brother I wished that I could've grown up with."

"You and me both. I had to talk to male friends older than me for advice about life. Especially women. Some things I learned well, and others, I'm not so sure."

"Thanks for listening."

Still Mario knew he'd messed up big time and that his marriage would never be as good as it was. Still believing the anonymous caller, he wondered if there was a limitation on guilt.

———

Cara had removed the bullets and put the gun back inside the third drawer underneath a pile of sweatshirts. She hated that he had it, but went along with the idea for their personal safety. It was so like her to go along to get along in order to please him.

Mario unlocked the door shortly after ten o'clock that evening and entered the living room as though he feared what she'd do or say. "We need to talk." His voice was almost a whisper now.

Looking up at him, she said, "Sure. You go first." She sat up and closed the book she was reading. Bourbon reeked from his body. She regarded him with coldness. Not in the mood to talk to him about anything, she studied his face leisurely.

"Why can't you admit you've done me wrong? Haven't we always been honest with each other? You forgave me for that affair with Paula. Now, I'm prepared to forgive you," he said.

Cara stood up, held her two index fingers together and pointed at Mario. "I want you to listen and listen good. For the last time, I'm telling you that I'm not having an affair. Realize it, Mario, someone framed me."

Suddenly, he spun around, turned away from her and looked at his liquor bar as if he couldn't decide whether to respond or pour himself a drink.

Before he came home, she'd picked her dignity up from the floor. She'd thought long and hard about her decision. She knew it would be a struggle to divorce him and there would be hardships, but she was up to the task. She believed she could make it on her own the old-fashioned way. Remembering her modest southern upbringing she thought, Even if *I have to eat black-eyed peas and cornbread for the rest of my life, I'll do it*. Quickly, she walked around him and grabbed his attention. "A few minutes ago, you wanted to talk. Well, good, because there's something I need to say to you."

The room got quiet. Cara was in charge, which was evident by the beads of sweat that began to drip from Mario's forehead.

"All right. Talk to me," he blurted, standing a few feet from her. The look on Mario's face told Cara that he believed he was finally going to get a confession out of her. His tension-filled jaw began to relax, as he thought that he would once again be in control of the situation. That was not going to happen this time. Cara held firm and maintained her innocence.

"It seems we've found ourselves on a dead-end street. The No Detour sign is staring us smack in the face." Her voice had depth and authority. "Sometimes it's harder to close a door than it is to close a window," she breathed heavily. "By your actions and behavior, you've somehow made it easy for me" she paused to take a deep breath. "This time, it's really over!"

"Oh, I get it. You want to go and be with your other man. Is that it?"

Cara looked at him, blinking away the tears.

"Answer me! Is that what you want?" Mario demanded as he walked closer to her.

"You know what? Believe what you want. Nothing I've said up until now has mattered anyway. One thing's for sure. I can't live with someone who demands I confess to something I'm not guilty of. Clearly, you haven't made this easy on either of us. You wouldn't even tell me what the caller said. Aren't I entitled to know?"

Mario slammed his hand on the wall and his voice raised an octave. "Bullshit! I want your ass out of here! The sooner the better!"

Cara was stunned. She couldn't believe her ears. "All right, then. Your wish is my command. I'm out of here. Count on it!"

With tears streaming down her face, Cara paced back and forth two times until Mario decided to say something.

"Hey, I'm sorry. I never should have said that. So, you're really leaving me, huh?"

"Have you lost your mind or what? You made your intentions

very clear. You can't say you want my ass out of here and not mean it."

Mario stared at her for a little while and then he headed straight to the bar and poured a drink. *Yeah, go ahead and drown yourself in the stuff. It's where you seem to find all your answers when things don't go your way,* she thought.

Refusing to look at him one minute longer and still frozen by his harshness, she managed to retreat to the guest room. She'd had it up to her ears with his anger and how he always let his ego fool him into making snap decisions. This time she'd called his bluff as soon as he'd presented it to her. She locked the door and sat down in the chair to think. She needed a game plan. There wasn't much time to pack and move. Maybe, just maybe, after tempers cooled, they could come to a harmonious solution, giving her time to save enough money to start over.

———

By nine o'clock on the first Saturday in May, Cara had packed everything that wasn't nailed down and was ready to go. Mario was on the tennis court but he knew she was leaving. After a few days of the silent treatment, they had agreed to split everything equally, including the money. She'd withdrawn half of the joint savings, a mere three thousand dollars after moving expenses. Realizing that it took both incomes to pay the rent on their apartment, she wondered what he'd do. Would he look for a roommate to help him pay the rent or move? She figured he'd do the latter because living together without the benefit of holy matrimony wasn't his style.

She took her final cup of coffee and walked out onto the balcony to capture a last look. The sun gently streamed down on the perfectly blue water of Lake Michigan, rendering a peaceful warmth and calmness. She started to feel sick inside, wondering what could've been if this dreadful lie hadn't come between them. She loved her husband and would never dream of having sex with another man. But what was a woman supposed to do in a situation like this?

It occurred to her that she was leaving without parting words between the two of them. Not once since he had told her to get out had Mario tried to get her to change her mind. She went back inside and wrote him a letter.

Mario:

Believe it or not, I've been framed. I have no clue why anyone would do this. What I do know is that I'm innocent. I've been totally faithful since the day I met you, and you were my first. Even though I've stood by you through thick and thin amid all of your flaws, you have put me through hell because of this mess. You couldn't even give me the benefit of the doubt and trust me. If you don't believe Ashley is yours, get a paternity test. Obviously, you know more than you're willing to tell me. But, somehow, someday, the truth will come out. But then, it'll be too late. Life goes on, and so shall I.

Cara

Chapter 3

Cara's two-bedroom unit located on Seventy-seventh and Exchange was, if nothing else, affordable. Here and there, windows were boarded up and cars were parked bumper-to-bumper along the curb. It was not uncommon to find used condoms, broken glass, and discarded litter resting on street corners. At best, Cara's new abode was merely minutes away from large grocery stores, fast food establishments, and public transportation.

She woke up on the first day in her new apartment, showered and dressed in black leotards and a white baggy T-shirt. Her hair was pulled in a ponytail. Taking a sip of her coffee, she walked to the large bay window in the living room. She felt blessed to have a roof over her head. She paced the living room floor some more and glanced at her surroundings: the sofa, two lamps, the floor model color television, a brass floor lamp, a tall weeping fig tree, a bushy spider plant and several philodendrons that amply filled the octagonal-shaped living room. A portrait of Martin Luther King and Harold Washington and two of her favorite oil paintings graced the living room walls. Glancing at the windows, she thought, *I hate not having curtains or blinds, but white shades will have to do for now.*

As if touring the place for the first time, Cara walked slowly into the smaller bedroom, which she turned into a workspace and play area for when she would bring Ashley to live with her. The walls were bare so she looked around and focused on the only things in the room, her desk and computer. *My good old Compaq Presario will be my friend. At least the computer won't break my heart, cheat or lie on me.* Sitting down at the computer, she decided to log on and create a new screen name, **Current Wife**. After checking her e-mail, she quickly logged off.

Finally, she entered her bedroom and eased her body on top of the peach and green floral comforter that draped the queen-size bed and stared at the bare walls thinking that if she could afford to stay in Chicago, Ashley was still small enough to share her bedroom for at least another year or two. Suddenly, she realized, *I must call my parents. They need to know where I am in case they need to reach me. But, how am I going to break the news to my mother?*

Naomi, fifty-five, half Cherokee and half African American, was a woman who believed in staying married for better or worse, richer or poorer. Open and honest communication between them had ceased when Cara turned fifteen. She often thought about her mother's brand of sex education and took delight in the humor. She knew her mother had done the best she could. The words still rang inside her head: "Every month, Cara, you're going to bleed for a few days. Remember to never let the boys ride on you like a horse or else you'll come up pregnant with a baby." Cara was forced to learn about her body, sex and babies from reading library books.

She reached for the phone and dialed her parents' number. "Hi, Mom."

"Hello, Cara," Naomi said. "It's about time we hear from you. How're you doing?"

"I'm okay. I miss my daughter," she said in a low tone. "How is Ashley?" Cara had tormented herself daily over leaving Ashley with her parents. Considering how things were between her and Mario, and how at the present time, she could barely live from paycheck to paycheck, she believed it wasn't the right time to bring Ashley to Chicago.

"She's fine, and looking more like you everyday." Naomi boasted. "You sound different. Is everything okay? How's Mario?"

"I don't know."

"What is that supposed to mean?"

"I've left Mario." Cara's voice broke. Momentarily pausing, she bit her lip to stifle the sobs that threatened to come out.

"No! You left Mario? Why?" Naomi screamed. "Where are you staying, for God's sake? Are you okay?"

"I'm fine, Mom." Cara said. She slowly gave her mother the details.

For a few moments there was complete silence on the other end of the line.

"Mom, are you still there?"

"Barely," Naomi replied, pausing for a moment. "We talked over the phone two days ago. Why didn't you mention that you were having problems? Why did you leave?" Naomi asked.

"Baby girl?" she heard her father's voice call out for her. Frank Slater, fifty-eight and a master carpenter, had called Cara by that name since she was six years old. "What's this I hear about you leaving Mario?"

"Daddy, he accused me of cheating on him. Can you imagine that?"

"I swear before chicken gizzards. If that don't beat all I've ever heard!" Frank, a normally mild-tempered man yelled out the words.

"What would make him believe such a thing?" asked Naomi, joining them.

"Oh, good. You're both listening. Hope you're sitting down. It's a long story."

Cara told them everything. What she didn't do was repeat the words Mario hurled at her: *I want your ass out of here.* The sting lingered in her heart. It had been awful to hear the words and difficult to repeat, even to her parents. *What will they think about me? That I've been a bad wife and deserve to be thrown out by my husband?*

"The nerve of that man, thinking you would cheat on him. What's gotten into him?" Frank asked, spacing the words evenly. "Well, I've got one better than that. Mario will answer to me if he hurts you."

A heartbeat of silence followed in which Cara could almost hear the thoughts spinning through her father's mind. He wouldn't lift his hand to hurt a fly. For her, he'd kill and regret it later. "Luckily, Daddy, that didn't happen. I ran for my life that night."

"Still, I don't like it one bit. I wonder what his father would have to say about the way Mario behaved?" Frank asked.

Cara had wondered the same thing. She heard a click.

"It's just you and me," Naomi said, after a long pause. "Your father has heard all he wants to hear."

"Is Daddy okay?"

"Yes. Try not to worry about us. It's you we're concerned about now. You're a Slater woman, a tough cookie. I'm glad you didn't compromise your principles."

"I can thank you and Daddy for that. A marriage based on deception and infidelity can't thrive on such shaky grounds. All your hopes and dreams for a peaceful, secure life become impossible expectations," Cara preached.

"That-a-girl! Listening to you talk such wisdom at your young age is remarkable. I couldn't have said it better," Naomi said proudly.

By that response, Cara was relieved to know that she could finally talk to her mother. Her parents had lived in pursuit of relatively few pleasures: living decently, owning a house, having good friends and great Southern food, and going to church. "I want you to promise me," Naomi paused.

"Yes, Mom?"

"Promise me that you'll be careful up there. You're alone and don't have a husband to look out for you anymore. For God's sake, keep your cellular charged and with you at all times. Get a motor club card in case you have car problems. Just be careful."

"I promise." Then Cara remembered the rest. "Oh, I forgot to tell you; he's disowned Ashley," Cara blurted, scarcely aware of her own voice.

"What?" Borrowing one of Frank's southern sayings, Naomi blurted, "I swear before baking powder. Has Mario lost his mind? Why does he think that he's not her father?"

"Would you believe because she looks like me and nothing like him?"

"He actually said that? Well, he's not the same man you married." Her voice was heavy with disgust.

"He's not, Mom. It's like I don't know him anymore. Can you believe it? The man I vowed to live the rest of my life with has really changed for the worst."

"I'm disappointed your marriage couldn't have turned out differently. But I do applaud your decision," Naomi said. "I'll pray that he'll come to his senses, and soon. That child needs her father, even if he doesn't want her. Now that you've left him, what are your plans?"

"I'll take one day at a time, Mom. I'm no quitter."

"Good girl. Remember, when it comes to Ashley, she's in good hands. Just take good care of yourself. Remember, you have a home here with us."

"I'll keep that in mind if all else fails. But, Mom, I'm going to make it the old-fashioned way. I'll work hard and earn my way. You'll see," Cara said, and hung up.

Cara's career was very important to her and being in control and being able to make choices about her life had always been a priority. She loved her job as a director of the *Parent Child Care Agency*, but it offered neither room for growth, nor an appreciative salary in the near future. Government-funded programs were low on the totem pole when it came to paying employees, and giving employees considerations for their dedication and services. The paperwork required to document compliance had enough rules to fill a book. Yet, she could reach out and touch the lives of the less fortunate. Being able to help others meant a lot to her.

Panic welled at the thought that whoever framed her was lurking around somewhere in Chicago. Also her savings would soon be gone, but she let the determination to make it on her own give her courage. *I need someone to talk to before I go crazy.*

The only girlfriend she had in Chicago was Jennifer Tate, whom she met at a church function. Right away, they became friends. Until now, neither of them talked to each other about their marital problems, which was what they liked the most about their friendship. It was hard to find a friend who wasn't consumed with being in your business. Genuine concern was one thing, but being downright nosy was another.

Jennifer was a high school math teacher on the South Side, and she worked out regularly to maintain her size ten figure. She was married to Duncan Tate, Assistant Comptroller for the city. They owned a modest three-bedroom home in Pill Hill, an affluent, South Side neighborhood and were childless.

Cara reluctantly dialed Jennifer's number.

"Hello?" Jennifer answered.

"Hi, it's me."

"Hey, girl. It's been awhile. How're you doing?"

"So-so." Cara's voice dropped two octaves.

"You sound different. What's going on?"

Cara could hear Jennifer's rapid breathing. "Well, let's say it's something I'm not proud about. I've moved out. Mario and I are separated."

"No. Please tell me you're joking."

When Cara had finished giving Jennifer the details, she broke down and cried.

"Oh, my God. I'm so sorry. How could Mario possibly believe you'd cheat on him? Damn him! The nerve of that man!"

Cara's crying eased some. "I was framed."

"Oh no. You've got to be kidding."

There was a long silence as Cara gathered her composure. "What's worst is that I don't know who framed me or how to prove my innocence."

"My goodness! I hate this happened to you. Are you all right?"

"Yes, I'm okay, for now."

"Good." Jennifer paused. "Think about it, girlfriend. Maybe, it was someone who had a score to settle with you."

"Actually, I don't have a clue. I've tried so hard not to make enemies."

"What if Mario lied? It's a possibility. He refused to tell you about this so-called evidence. Why? Cause there isn't any. Sounds like some intelligent, cooked-up shit on his part, if you ask me."

"I don't know what to think anymore. Right now, I'm tired of thinking about what happened and the reasons why."

"I know. I'm sorry. I'm just mad as hell for you," Jennifer declared. "Living all alone has got to be rough. Do you need anything?"

"Right now, just be my friend and most of all, keep this to yourself. Just lend me your ears and shoulder when I need to cry."

"Sure. I won't breathe a word," Jennifer promised. "Remember, I'm here for you. All you got to do is pick up the phone."

Chapter 4

Surprisingly, another weekend had come and gone too soon and for the first time she realized even though she was alone, she wasn't lonely. The best part of about yesterday was that Ashley had wished her a happy Mother's Day. Hearing the words from her daughter's young voice over the phone made her even more determined to find a way to make it. She vowed that it would be the last Mother's Day she would spend without Ashley.

Dressing for work hat morning, she suddenly sensed a chilly ache in her stomach: *I want your ass out of here.* His words wouldn't go away. If only she could find a way to block them from her mind.

Cara checked her watch. It was 8:15 a.m. exactly. She grabbed her brief bag, the packed lunch consisting of a can of tomato soup and a ham sandwich, her keys and locked the door behind her.

During the drive to her office, Cara's imagination forced her to consider another possibility: *Mario met another woman. He fell in love with her - someone who is satisfying him like I no longer could. He needed to be free of me. Divorce was the logical answer; however, I was a good wife and he had no grounds. He labels me the adulterer this time. Bingo! That gave him sufficient grounds for divorcing me. Only he didn't have the proof, like I did about his affair. He knew I loved him and was in the marriage for keeps. He got drunk and staged a vicious argument, hurling enough allegations to make me hate him. He added fuel to the fire, stomped off saying he was mad as hell, and frightened me with that gun.*

She felt so strongly about her theory that she was steaming like a pot of water about to boil over. Slowing down in the far right lane at the intersection of Seventy-first and Stony Island, suddenly she felt her body jerk forward and a sharp jolt to her neck. Her heart was racing, blood rushed through her veins and a nervous sensation overtook her. She thought she was going to regurgitate her breakfast, "Oh, no! My car!" She looked at the driver who had hit her. He shook his head back and forth. Instantly, she imagined that he was thinking, "Dumb slow-driving broad."

Onlookers suddenly stopped along sidewalks. Traffic slowed. She just wanted it to be over and to get out of view of gapers eager to see the ruins of an accident. Physically, she seemed all right. Nothing was broken, and there were no bruises or blood visible. Worry about her dwindling savings account swirled throughout her body like sand tossed about in a storm.

Minutes later, lights flashed and police officers converged.

Anxious to see how much damage had been done to her car, she got out and took a long look. Soon the other driver approached her. He was a dark-skinned gentleman of medium height, and he wore expensive sunglasses, brown slacks, and a crisp white shirt that was large enough to cover his pot-belly.

"Hi. I'm sorry about this. Are you okay?"

"I seem to be. How about you?" Cara replied, heaving a sigh.

"I'm fine. The name is Joe Michaels." He slowly removed his sunglasses, riveting her with his liquid dark brown eyes that were hooded like a hawk.

"I'm Cara Fleming. What happened, Mr. Michaels?" She clamped her jaws firmly shut, making no protest as he gave her a flighty gesture.

"To tell you the truth, I had a lot on my mind."

Cara thought, *you and me both.*

"Well, at least neither of us is hurt," she said.

"Thankfully," Michaels replied, turning around to face his car.

They exchanged the required information.

"Well, Ms. Fleming, take care of yourself. Again, I'm sorry for the damages to your car. My insurance company will take care of everything." Joe Michaels sauntered to his car.

Returning to her car, she used her cellular to call her office and leave a message on the secretary's voice mail: "I had an accident on my way to work. I'm okay, just a little shaken. I'll return to the office tomorrow." Expecting a visit from Jennifer any day now, she stopped at the Walgreens store on Seventy-First and Jeffrey and bought two bottles of wine, white and red zinfandel.

Twenty minutes later, she parked at her building and noticed the first floor neighbor peering out the window. She waved a friendly hello, grabbed the mail and went inside her apartment.

By eleven o'clock, Cara had accomplished a lot over the phone. She had reported the accident to her insurance company and settled on taking her car that afternoon to Turner Auto Collision & Repair. To her surprise, the owner was thoughtful to offer her a ride back to her apartment and to pick her up when the car was ready.

Afterward she wondered, *what else can go wrong? I've got to be strong and not let my problems, as great as they might be, get the best of me.*

With nothing else to do that day, she relaxed and reflected some more about her life. Sitting on the sofa, she had a flashback of her storybook wedding six years ago. The wedding was perfect, but the honeymoon left her unsatisfied as a woman. Funny thing though, she was always glad when it was over.

She finished the wine, picked up the daily *Sun Times* newspaper, and turned to the jobs section. The doorbell rang. It was three o'clock. She looked through the peephole and saw the first floor neighbor whose face was a strong likeness to Della Reese. She was obviously someone who cared about her appearance and she seemed friendly. She was of medium height, carried just the right amount of weight, and she appeared to be over sixty-five. She wore a pretty, aquamarine polyester pantsuit. Her partly graying hair was wrapped in a thick ball on top of her head. Right away Cara felt relieved. *It's about time someone broke the ice. It's so unlike me to be unfriendly and shy away from people,* she thought when she opened the door.

"Good afternoon," Cara said, greeting the lady with a smile.

"Hello. My name is Thelma Walker. I'm your downstairs neighbor. It took me awhile to stop by for a visit, but here I am."

"Hi. It's nice to meet you. I'm Cara Fleming. Please come in for a while."

"Well, okay, but not for long." Mrs. Walker sat down in the chair facing the kitchen.

"What happened to your car? "Are you okay?" she asked, taking little peeks at the surroundings.

"A man in a bit of a hurry hit my car as I was about to turn right on red." *She's not so bad, a little nosy maybe, but mostly concerned about me.*

"Well, I'm glad you're all right," Mrs. Walker said.

Cara got an overview of everything from the building to the neighborhood. An even mix of singles and married folks lived there and they stayed mostly to themselves. Of course, there were a few strange ones, but they didn't bother anybody. She made sure Cara understood the rules for staying safe as much as possible. Keep your door double locked and check before you open it to anyone you don't know.

Cara got up and walked to the kitchen. She returned with two glasses of cold lemon flavored tea she'd made the day before.

"Thanks," Mrs. Walker said and sipped her tea. "Let me tell you about Louis, the guy above you. If you haven't met him, you will. Anyway, every time I turn around, Louis is packing or unpacking."

"Why is that?" Cara remembered bumping into him on her floor a day ago. He'd spoken to her and kept walking.

"Well, he has a place down in Florida. People like Louis do that sort of thing when they retire. Not me, I like it here. I never go down for the winter like some people do. Oh, sometimes, his lady friends come to visit him, young and bony looking. They all dress like they're hustling him for money."

"I see. Good for him." Cara said without thinking. Her mind was busy trying to figure out if Mrs. Walker was as nice as she appeared friendly.

"I hope you like living here," she said.

"So do I," Cara replied. She pulled out Ashley's photo album and showed it to Mrs. Walker.

"One thing I want you to know about me is," Mrs. Walker said, as she thumbed through pages of pictures, "I'm very independent and never ask nobody for nothing. So you don't have to worry, I won't bother you. Just want to be neighborly."

"Oh," Cara threw her a warm smile. "Well, in that case, you'll find me to be the same."

"Good," Mrs. Walker replied.

Afterwards, Cara talked about her little girl, but she was careful not to bring up Mario, where he was living and why he didn't live with her. Then, they exchanged phone numbers.

"Call me if you need anything or if you're feeling lonely. Believe me, I know what it's like to be alone. In your case, you're too young to suffer like that."

"Well," Cara thought, raising her eyebrows inquiringly, "She's done her homework."

"It was nice to meet you. I'm sure we'll get along just fine. There's nothing like a good neighbor," Mrs. Walker said, putting her glass on the coffee table.

Following the brief visit, Cara closed the door and returned the glasses to the kitchen. Her thoughts were still on Mrs. Walker. She was friendly and she seemed protective. *She's a bit gossipy, but she's someone I believe I can count on,* Cara thought.

In the past, Cara had been friendly and open with others about her personal life. She got stabbed in the back with gossip that never seemed to quit. She remembered that day in the ladies' room over a year ago at the school she worked at in Memphis. She was in the right place at the wrong time. While she was in one of the stalls she overheard another teacher say, *If she and Mario are so happy and in love like Cara claims, you would think he wouldn't find other women so interesting.* Another one said, *I don't quite understand how a man can play around on a wife as pretty as she is.* Then a third voice spoke, *Seems to me, men need more than a pretty face and a pencil thin body to keep them satisfied.* When her silly coworkers had stopped giggling they walked out. Cara was left in tears. She got wise and learned to deal with folks who put her down, especially, those who couldn't get their own lives in order.

Her memory had brushed back over mistakes she'd made as a result of sharing too much of her personal life with so-called friends. She didn't have any male friends outside her marriage. She became a social recluse, living her life on her terms. It wore on her like a habit that she hadn't been able to break. *Now, more than ever*, she thought, *I need to keep to myself. No character assassination, probing questions, or opinionated advice.*

It was around five-thirty that afternoon and she was hungry. She opened the brown lunch bag, poured a glass of skim milk and ate the lunch she had prepared to eat that day at the office.

Later, she went online and e-mailed Jennifer. Then she clicked on her favorite places, and searched Monster.com for potential jobs. Realizing her chances for getting a better paying job were slim to none, she felt like screaming. Instead, she decided to do the crossword puzzle in the *Sun Times* newspaper.

By six thirty, she'd finished the puzzle when the phone rang. She started to reach for the phone. "I won't answer another hang-up call." But, after four rings, she answered.

"Hello."

"It's Bradley Fleming calling." His voice was unusually cold. At fifty-eight, he was a proud, leading businessman in Memphis, respected by important people, including the mayor. Since the day Mario introduced her, she'd felt adored and considered as a daughter, rather than a daughter-in-law. She even remembered how Bradley would often say nice things about her to his friends, that she came from a loving, Christian family and that he was glad Mario had chosen her. He boasted about how she'd worked hard to earn a college degree on a student loan and a part-time work-study program.

"Hi, Mr. Fleming. How are you?" Cara asked, trying to sound upbeat.

"I'm disappointed in you." His tone was low and he paced his words. "You had me and everyone else fooled and now I think you are immoral and unfit. I feel sorry for my son. You've ruined his life. I promise you that I'll see to it that you lose custody of my granddaughter. You are unfit to raise that child," he said, as his mood veered sharply to anger.

She felt like the scum of the earth and all she could do was close her eyes, trying to gather her thoughts. "You're so wrong about me," she answered, struggling to get the words out. "There's another side to this story."

"Don't even try to deny it. Mario told me everything."

At that moment, she realized that as far as Bradley Fleming was concerned, she was shit! Trying to hold it together, she said, "I'm sorry you feel that way about me, sir. I'm not like that. One day the truth shall be told." After a long pause, he sill hadn't come back at her with more of his wrath.

Consequently, she couldn't figure him. Feeling nauseated and fed up to her eyeballs, she lacked the words to continue. "I can see you're unhappy with me. Perhaps, it's best we end this conversation, so, I'll say good-bye." She hung up no sooner than she said the words.

Well, she thought. *This call lets me know where I stand with Mario's parents.*

She leaned back in the armed chair, hands shaking. *Oh, God, what have I done to bring such misery upon myself? When will it end? Could it be that it's my turn to be the victim of what goes around comes around?*

Chapter 5

Bradley's eerie phone call was still on her mind when she woke the next day. *That* she could manage to put aside. What she couldn't understand was that a month had passed since she left Mario. *Did he care at all as to how she was doing on her own? Was he moving on with his life?*

She felt excruciating pain in her neck and shoulders, but somehow she managed to shower and dress for work. After that, she went to the kitchen to make some coffee and remembered she had only instant coffee in her cupboard. The gas stove hissed at her, and she finally had to light it with a match. She put a pot of water on to boil and thought about what she wanted to eat. More ravenous than ever before, she cooked two strips of bacon, scrambled two eggs, and browned a slice of wheat bread.

She sat down later at the table, poured a glass of orange juice and savored the harmonious flavors. Suddenly the pain in her neck and shoulder lingered, making it difficult to continue. She decided to take a sick day.

Jennifer called around eight that morning. "Why don't I come by later to check on you?" she asked, in a bit of a hurry.

"That would be nice. When shall I expect you?"

"I'll come by right after work."

"Sure, I'll see you then." Cara hung up the phone, flushed down two Excedrin capsules with a glass of water, and slowly drifted off to sleep on the sofa.

An hour later, the doorbell woke her.

She looked through the peephole. A gentleman wearing a beige and brown uniform stood with a grim face and his body still.

Cara slowly opened the door. "Yes, may I help you?"

"Are you Cara Fleming?"

"Yes," she uttered. She let him in and he handed Cara the thick document and a clipboard.

She flipped through the document and at first glance, the words **DIVORCE PETITION** jumped off the page. Her thoughts were jagged and painful like an old wound that ached on a rainy day. *So, he actually filed for the divorce? The grounds for the divorce were there, as clear as day and night: Adultery. At least I know where I stand. He wants it over and right now. But why am I not surprised? Mario has not cared enough to call to check on me, yet he has managed to find out where I moved and to get a lawyer.*

Motionless, she just stood and continued to read.

The officer interrupted her, seemingly in a hurry to get out of there. "I need your signature," he said moving his fingers down the sheet of paper on the clipboard. In her state of disbelief, she forgot that she didn't need to read the document before she signed the delivery confirmation papers. She signed the form and handed him the clipboard.

"Okay, you have a good day," he said, and turned around to walk out as calmly as he'd entered.

She locked her door and scanned through the petition. Mario had taken the upper hand and had wasted no time. *This changes things, now more than ever. I've got to defend myself, but how? Hiring a lawyer will be costly. Should I tell my parents about Bradley's call? Now what? If I get one more piece of bad news, I'm going to scream my fool head off.*

Still in pain and ready to explode into a zillion pieces, she forced herself to get busy making the apartment look presentable for Jennifer's visit.

Slowly, she made the bed and pushed the vacuum over the living room carpet. According to the weather report, the temperature was around eighty-five, but the humidity was vicious. She turned the control up one notch on the air conditioning. Afterward, she sprayed a cinnamon flavor air freshener around the apartment. Then she brushed her hair into a ponytail, swerved it to the right side of her head and held it together with a yellow cloth band. She slipped into a pair of yellow pants cut just above her knees and a white pullover baggy shirt tucked at the waist. She hoped that seeing Jennifer again would brighten her spirit.

While she waited, Cara got busy on the computer. First, she played *Free Cell* for about an hour. Just as she grew tired, she clicked on *Statistics* and noticed she had six hundred wins versus two hundred and ten losses. Winning was very important to Cara, no matter what she involved herself in doing, and there was no question that *Free Cell* had become an easy target for stress relief and accomplishment. Besides, it helped to pass the time away ---time that she would spend thinking about how much she missed Ashley.

———

Around three o'clock that afternoon, Alderman Giles Bennett finished writing a speech for his friend, Alderman Horace Tucker. Bennett, thirty-seven, was a light brown brother, and slightly heavy at five foot-eight. He'd replaced the incumbent two years ago.

His office had a masculine aura to it. There were ultra modern lights in the ceiling, glass front bookcases, and leather chairs around a granite-topped table. The huge space on the third floor was where he spent most of his time. The walls were papered with an earth tone striped paper, tapered from top to bottom and set off by oak baseboards. On one side of the room, the walls were lined with books and art objects. Three dieffenbachia trees thrived in large hand-painted clay pots. He kept a small refrigerator stocked with diet sodas, beer, bottled water and wine to share with his friends. Those who knew him didn't comprehend the absence of pictures of his family. Neither did his visitors mention the subject to him.

He was holding a soda pop when his deputy chief, Joe Michaels, appeared at the door.

"Hi, Joe. Come on in and pull up a chair."

"Good afternoon, Alderman. How's it going?" Joe Michaels remained standing, belly thrust out for balance. He took a pair of glasses out of his pocket, shook them open, set them on his short nose, and sat down. He'd had a full day helping to solve problems ... trash pickup, meetings, and organizing a picnic for the people in Bennett's ward. He wanted this day over and quick.

"I'm finished," Bennett put the papers inside a large brown envelope. "Take this to Alderman Tucker on your way home."

"Sure."

"By the way, how did it go with the church member?" Alderman Bennett asked.

Michaels boasted, "Oh, yeah, that went quite well. All that's left is to wait for the lady to take the leap."

Bennett's eyebrows raised a fraction. "Good. I'll need you to keep an eye on that situation. Remember, it's really important that it doesn't get linked to me."

Chapter 6

"Hi. Come in," Cara said after she opened the door and embraced Jennifer with a sisterly hug. Jennifer, now twenty-nine, had the face and body of Debbie Morgan. Her long thick brown braids showed off her cute face. Her white sandals displayed her toenails, painted bright red to match her sleeveless dress. Gold looped earrings swung from her ear lobes. "It's so good to see you," Cara said, and stepped aside so Jennifer could walk in.

"I'm glad to see you, girlfriend. It's times like these that good friends have to stick together. I feel bad that I haven't kept in touch like I should have. Especially, now that you've left Mario and you have to live by yourself. So, how're you doing?"

"Okay. It's not so bad, living alone, that is. Anyway, what choice do I have?" Cara said and wrinkled her nose. "How've you been?"

"Can't complain," Jennifer said gazing at the freshly painted off-white walls and finally at the beige carpet on the floor. Then slowly, she walked ahead of Cara and helped herself to a tour of the rest of the apartment.

"It's small, but nice and clean. I like it," Jennifer said returning to the living room.

Cara smiled at Jennifer as much as she could. "Hey, it's a far cry from where I once lived, but you won't hear me complain. The only thing missing in my life now is having Ashley with me. I saved some space in the second bedroom for her toys. She and I will bunk together. But, if my finances don't improve real soon, I'll be joining her in Memphis."

She excused herself to the kitchen to get the bottle of chilled wine, but Jennifer followed her.

"Care for something to drink?"

"You know me. It's the best way I know how to unwind after work."

After Cara poured the wine, they raised and clicked their glasses together.

"Cheers," Jennifer said, taking a good sip. "Wish I could be so brave. I envy you."

Cara remained silent as they walked back to the living room and sat down on the sofa.

"I'm only that way because I have to be," Cara said hesitantly. "Lately I'm starting to expect to be surprised or startled by some unpleasant event."

"Really? Why you say that?" Jennifer lifted the glass again to her lips.

"Other than getting rear-ended in traffic by some strange man yesterday, would you believe that my father-in-law called me hours later? It wasn't pleasant. He called me unfit and he threatened to help Mario get custody of Ashley. Can you believe that?"

Jennifer relaxed her back on the sofa and shook her head. "Seems Old Man Fleming doesn't know that Ashley is a disclaimed member of the family." She grinned at her words and looked at Cara. "Joking aside," she asked, quickly wiping away her smile. "How did you manage listening to that man?"

Cara took another sip of her wine. "I got through it. What he doesn't know is that I'll fight to keep my daughter." Cara suppressed her anger.

"I'm sure. Have you heard from Mario?"

"Funny you asked that. I was served with divorce papers today. As you can see, I have a lot on my plate. If one more crisis erupts, I'm going to call it a platter."

"What's his hurry? Seems to me, he's got other plans, don't you think?"

Cara shut down on her and got quiet. It was difficult to imagine Mario cooking up plans of deception.

As Jennifer put her glass down on the table, she noticed a business card. Picking it up, she said, "Joe Michaels? How do you know him?"

"He's the guy that hit my car."

"Joe Michaels hit you? He's the alderman's top man. He's worked with Duncan on a few projects."

"Really? The alderman is a member of my church," Cara said, sitting up straight. She sipped some more of her wine.

"Girl, you should sue him for some whiplash money."

"No, that's not my style." Cara sighed. "Besides, I'll be all right."

"Just a thought."

"With all due respect, I thank you for your concern. One thing's for sure, Mr. Michaels needs to slow down or one day he'll hit the wrong person, someone who'll take him for all he's worth."

"I heard that." Jennifer downed the rest of her wine and she darted off to the kitchen for a refill.

A few minutes later, she returned holding her filled glass and the half empty bottle. It had surprised Cara that Jennifer drank a lot. Putting that aside, she figured Jennifer had something heavy on her mind.

Cara said, turning the heat on Jennifer, "I'm curious. What have you been up to lately?"

"Oh, nothing much," Jennifer responded quickly. Her eyebrows flickered a little. "Oh, you should come by and see my flower garden. It's simply beautiful this time of the year, if I may say so," she added, and finished another glass of wine.

"I'd love to," Cara replied. Some of your red peonies would work well in my living room."

"Great! I've got another great idea. Come work out with me at the YMCA. I get one free pass each month."

"Sounds like fun. When?"

"How about this Saturday?"

"It's a deal," Cara said.

"I'll come by around nine o'clock if that's okay."

"I'll be ready."

"Now tell me, how does it really feel to be single and free?" Jennifer probed.

"Girl, please. At first I felt lonely a lot, but I'm getting used to it. Sometimes, I feel like crying. When I'm not feeling sorry for myself, I find so many other things to do."

"Have you considered getting out and meeting new people?"

"At times, but I'm not ready. A new man in my life is the last thing I need right now. Besides, I'm still married."

"I'm not saying you've got to go to bed with a guy. I just thought it might be good to talk and laugh and do fun things together," Jennifer suggested.

Cara grinned. "Sounds appealing, but not now."

"There's something I've learned about you tonight."

"Really? What's that?" Cara asked.

"You not only respect your privacy, you know how to return the favor. I like that about you."

"Thanks. You know me well. And, thanks for being my friend," Cara replied. She sensed something was wrong with Jennifer, but couldn't put her finger on it. For the moment, she had enough mess in her own life to work through.

Suddenly, the exuberance in Jennifer's face swiftly died. She checked her watch and quickly turned to Cara.

"Hate to leave like this. There's something I've got to do."

———

Jennifer sped away in her maroon Lexus knowing she'd been partially dishonest with Cara. She was going to check out something, but that something was Duncan's whereabouts. She knew her husband was up to no good. She needed to prove it wasn't just her imagination. His excuse for not coming home for dinner tonight was a political meeting.

Fifteen minutes later, she drove past Alderman Horace Tucker's ward office.

Just as she'd suspected, Duncan had lied again. The area looked like a ghost town.

Lately, Duncan had begun to shower before going to work and afterward, he splashed on new cologne. Before that, a shower the night before seemed sufficient. It was apparent that he was cheating. Now, he created reasons just to get away during the evening.

Chapter 7

Cara lifted the divorce petition papers from the kitchen counter and sat down at the table. She read the six-page document twice. Uncertain about how things would turn out in the divorce, pain and isolation resurfaced. *It's difficult enough to handle Mario's accusations concerning Ashley, so I will not let Bradley's threats concern me. The one thing I want from Mario is child support for Ashley.*

She went to her computer, clicked on Notepad and started to write, in prioritized order, her immediate goals: *Find a lawyer. Find another job. Prove my innocence. All are equally important, and yet more than ever I've got to find another job. The attorney must be paid.*

Then, as Cara always did before bedtime, she signed on to America Online under her master screen name, **CaraNchgo**. She clicked the mouse once, twice, three times and the icons on the computer screen opened and departed at her command. Junk mail was deleted before she began reading her messages.

Seconds before she switched screen names, she heard, "You've Got Mail!" The message was from someone with the screen name, **Green Lawn.** Opening it, Cara read:

Just got a personal computer at home. Seems like everyone has one. I know that you left Mario. It's hard for me to believe any of the crap he told Bradley and me. I care about what you have to say. This is my private e-mail address. Call me when you get this message."
Mary Lee Fleming

Around two o'clock the next day at work, Cara ended her meeting with Teresa Peyton, a twenty-one-year-old mother desperately looking for her birth mother. Raped when she was sixteen, Teresa abused drugs and prostituted for a living. Cara's heart wept for Teresa and she pledged to search the Internet to help her. *Helping others is definitely the antibiotic. No one will know the despair I feel.*

The phone rang, interrupting her thoughts.

"Good afternoon. Parent Child Care Agency, Cara Fleming speaking."

"Hi. This is Barbara Rhodes."

"Hello, and how're you doing?" she asked, thinking how odd it was to get a phone call on the job from the pastor's secretary.

"Oh, I'm fine," Barbara cheerfully responded. "Can you come by the office on your way home? I need to talk to you."

"Okay." Cara wondered if it was church related or what. She didn't belong to a church organization and was satisfied with being a bench member. *Maybe she wants to ask me to join the usher board.* "Can you tell me now?"

"I think it would be better not to talk about this over the phone."

And on those words, Cara panicked, hung up, grabbed her purse and tote bag, and hurried out the door. Although Cara and Barbara saw each other at church, they weren't exactly friends and they really didn't know much about each other.

Still, Cara wondered if it had to do with her marital situation. Her spotless reputation meant a lot to her.

Thirty minutes later she parked her car in front of the church. The sun was still high in the sky, streaming through the windows. It seemed more like high noon than 3:15 p.m. Before entering, she stopped to say hello and shake hands with the church custodian and security guard. She walked up to the second floor slowly. Barbara's office was the corner one. She stood, took a deep breath, and knocked once on the door, dreading the thought of what she'd learn.

———

For the past twenty minutes, Barbara's thoughts had been on Lester Miller, the man she'd been madly in love with for more than a year. She had believed he was Mr. Right. But twice she'd seen him on dates with other women. She had come to realize that he was the type of man who couldn't commit to one woman. A week ago, she had finally broken off the relationship.

Suddenly she remembered that she'd heard a knock at her door. *A good hour too early for it to be the deacon,* she thought. She opened the door and saw Cara Fleming who wasn't expected to arrive until after five.

"Oh, hello Cara. Come in." They gave each other the customary church-member hug.

"Hi, Barbara. I'm early. Do you mind?"

"No, don't be silly. Come in. Make yourself comfortable."

"It's good to see you." Cara sat down in one of the chairs facing the desk, hands folded. "How've you been?"

"Really well, and you?"

"Busy. Thanks for seeing me. I'm sure you're busy," Cara said, sounding apologetic.

"No problem. My next appointment is less than an hour from now. What I want to share with you is not earth shattering."

Involuntarily, Barbara recalled Joe Michaels' visit to her office yesterday. The look in Joe's eyes screamed serious business. "Make sure that a lady named Cara Fleming knows about the job opening at Human Services. Do not mention the source of this information. Urge her to apply by August 15," he had demanded.

That a politician had gone to such trouble to help Cara caused Barbara to want to know more. Was she married? Not once had she seen Cara at church services with a man. Lester cancelled a date to help a friend in trouble. His name was Mario Fleming. Could there be a connection?

Cara sat motionless. "Am I in trouble or something?"

"No," Barbara replied, pondering how she'd handle the matter with discreetness. "Someone who knows your credentials and work ethics asked me to tell you about a top-level job opening at Human Services. You should submit a resume right away."

Cara's eyebrows lifted. "A job with the city? You're kidding me?" Cara realized she'd been wrong about Barbara's urgent phone call. She didn't know any powerful people in Chicago. She racked her brain and couldn't think of anyone who'd want to do her a favor. *Maybe, this is the blessing I've been praying for. With God on my side, how can I lose?*

"As elated as I am about this opportunity, who shall I thank?"

"I don't believe you know the person." Barbara reached for the ad Michaels had left with her and handed it to Cara.

Still stunned, Cara quickly scanned the paper. "I …I thank you." She had wanted to, but couldn't tell Barbara the real reason for her jubilation, that she'd left her husband and needed to make more money. This job opportunity could be the answer.

"If you're wondering who your benefactor is, don't ask. Some things are better left unknown. Besides, what does it matter anyway? Be happy and go for it."

"Yeah, maybe you're right," Cara said.

"Try not to think about the messenger. Focus on the message. It's not everyday that the chance of a lifetime falls in your lap. I hear that the city pays really well, not to mention the benefits," Barbara said.

"I suppose. But since it's no secret that only a powerful politician can get someone a city position, do you honestly believe I'll get the job?" She shrugged. "Your chances are probably 50/50, but don't let that discourage you."

"All right, I won't. Tell you what, I'll give it my best shot and then say a big prayer. Prayer changes things, you know," Cara said.

"Hallelujah! You go girl. By the way, mind if I ask you a personal question?"

Feeling the pressure, Cara asked, "What do you want to know?"

"I'm preparing invitations for our pastor's anniversary. It just occurred to me that we don't have your husband's name on the records."

Why am I not surprised to know you weren't finished with me? Cara thought. "Oh, he's not a member," she replied, thinking Barbara would've known that. "His name is Mario."

"Good. Now the invitation will be addressed properly."

"I forgot to give you the new address and phone number," Cara said, covering her tracks.

"Well, I can update the information now." Barbara turned on the computer and updated the information. Then she faced Cara and said, "I'm glad you remembered to tell me. Otherwise, the invitations would've come back here."

"Right," Cara said, checking her watch. She stood up. "I've taken up enough of your time. Thanks a lot for the information."

"Sure, and God bless. Please keep in touch, okay?" Barbara said, as she walked her to the door.

"I'll do that, and thanks again."

After Cara left, Barbara's thoughts drifted back to that night Lester had to meet his buddy. As small as the world had seemed at times, she figured that this person had to be the same Mario Fleming. Lester postponed their date because of him. Cara and Mario aren't together anymore. Now, a politician is helping her anonymously, she concluded.

———

While driving, Cara noticed a man in a white sedan following her. Later on, he vanished. Relieved, she reflected on how well the day had gone for her. It was a good day. Barbara gave her reason to be hopeful.

She stopped at the Food Basket on Seventy-ninth and Yates. Just as she stepped out of her car, she watched what looked like the same white car stop along the street. The driver, whom she couldn't recognize, continued to sit inside the car with the engine running.

Cara's heart seemed to beat in her throat. *For some reason, someone is following me.*

Chapter 8

It was a quarter to seven that evening when Mary Lee Fleming sat staring at the welcome screen on America Online. The home computer and private lessons had been a gift from Bradley. Worrying about Mario, she shut down the computer she called *Sweet Pea* and reflected on a phone conversation she had had with Mario a week ago.

"Hello, Son. I've been trying to reach you."

"Hi, Mama. Just walked in the door when the phone rang. How're you doing down there in Memphis?"

"I'm fine. Your dad's fine, I suppose. So tell me what's going on? I worry all the time about you."

"Not much to tell. What's up with Dad?"

"Funny you asked. He's not himself lately. I suspect it has to do with your breakup with Cara."

"Oh, really?"

"Does your father know something I don't?"

"Can't keep nothing from you, can I? Dad knows all about Cara's affair. I told him the day after I discovered the truth," Mario said.

"I don't believe that she'd do something like that. Not the Cara Slater-Fleming I know."

"The caller told me things that he could only know if he'd seen her naked. What do you think about that? Still think she's an angel?"

Mary Lee remembered closing up on him and didn't respond.

"Did you hear anything I said?" he asked.

"Yes." Her voice drifted into a hushed whisper. "I need to ask you something. Did you think to check out this man's story? Or, whether she took off sick from the job, when and how often? Did she change in anyway at home and with you? Things like that?"

"Well, now that you mention it, no, I didn't. There wasn't time. I was angry. I was hurt, and I just exploded. I did offer her a way to save the marriage."

"Really? What was that?"

"All she had to do was confess and apologize. I gave my word that I'd forgive her."

She remembered how they had spoiled him with enough material things and not enough common sense. She began to wonder what else the Fleming men were hiding.

"Seems to me you didn't do enough to prevent this breakup," she said.

"You want to know the truth? She can't admit she's wrong because all her life she's been Miss Perfect. Why would she admit to her wrongdoing?" Mario squawked.

Mary Lee realized then that trying to get through to him was useless. "As usual, you're letting your anger rule you and not your heart. You should get professional counseling. I hear that it can help."

"No way. I don't like the idea of talking about my situation with a stranger. Anyway, how're you getting along with Cara's mother?" he asked, changing the subject.

"Naomi and I are still friends. A friendship like ours is hard to come by. She's a good woman and someone nice to talk to. Your father, on the other hand, has cooled his relationship with Cara's parents. Wish I knew why."

Realizing the damage her son had caused, Mary Lee had decided to salvage her losses and call Cara. Besides, she loved Cara like a daughter. And, now she needed to convince Cara of that.

"Hi, Cara. How are you?"

"Hi, Mother Fleming. I'm doing fine and you?"

"I'm all right. It's been too long, I couldn't let another day go by without talking to you."

Mary Lee announced that she had a new computer and that she

was trying to learn how to operate it. From there, the conversation veered to Cara.

"All I need to know is, were you involved with another man?"

"Absolutely not. Not then and not now."

"Did you mention your birthmark to anyone other than Mario?"

"No. Something personal like that? No way," Cara replied, with a slightly raised voice.

"According to Mario, the caller knew about it."

"But how? Who would've told a stranger about my birthmark? Mario is lying. I'm starting to believe he actually wanted out of the marriage."

"I hate *not* to believe my son; however, you make an excellent point."

"Mario didn't tell me what the caller said. It was like I didn't need to know."

"My dear, know that I'm in your corner. Okay?"

"Thanks. It helps to know that." On the tip of Cara's tongue was the temptation to tell Mary Lee that Mario had actually ordered her out of the apartment. But she couldn't. "In case you don't know, he's filed for a divorce."

"He didn't. I'm so sorry," Mary Lee stammered. After a short pause, she continued. "Call me if you need help, okay?"

"I will, and thank you," Cara said.

———

Cara thought about her promise to help Teresa Peyton.

She signed onto AOL and entered Family.com. She browsed chat rooms and read message boards and she downloaded snippets of information on finding biological parents. Then she noticed the icon, "Chat Room Host" and clicked on it. The first host had done community social work for fifteen years. She had worked with hundreds of people from all over the U.S. and internationally. The second host, whose life experience had run the gamut from single mom to online chat host, was the mother of two adopted grown sons. Cara became impressed and e-mailed them.

With a mostly nonexistent social life, Cara knew that she had plenty of time. Helping lost children would become her main cyberspace agenda. It was then that she decided to become an advocate for lost children.

Later, she checked the main page on Family.com and found helpful information for Teresa. She printed addresses and phone numbers of agencies and organizations in Illinois.

Twenty minutes later, she joined a chat room called *Wayward Friends*. There were fifteen roomies. The conversation proved interesting. Scrolling up and down, she viewed screen names, searched for profiles, and, to her surprise, several had created bios.

Then she heard the Instant Message chime. The small screen magically appeared in the top left corner on her monitor. It was from someone named **MattIwas**. "Hi, **Current Wife**. You're awfully quiet. A few minutes ago, I saw you in *Lost Children* and then you left. Looking for your folks, too?"

"Hi, Matt. No, I'm trying to help a young woman find her birth mother. What are you up to?" she typed.

MattIwas responded, "When I was five years old, a strange man and a woman took me from my mother's car. We were parked at a gas station. My mother had gone inside to pay for the gas. That's when the strangers took me away. My daddy had stayed home with my baby brother. That was over thirty years ago. I'm looking for my birth family."

"Why don't we meet in a private room?"

"Why not? I can use some advice," MattIwas responded.

"I'll name it ***Lost Children00***. Give me a minute to set it up. Watch for the small screen inviting you to come in and click, *Enter*."

Within a few seconds, it was done and **MattIwas** entered the room.

"Okay. This is better. Can you tell me more?" Cara typed.

"Sure. The man who called himself my father physically abused me until I ran away at the age of fifteen. I lived on the streets for a few days until I met a former prostitute named Odessa Grant. She let me live with her. I stayed there and worked after school until I graduated from high school. By then, I had saved enough money to leave her abode."

"I'm so sorry. You must be really anxious to find your real parents. Do you remember their names? Where you lived at the time?"

"Vaguely. Mother's name was either Martha or Margaret. Don't have a clue about Dad's or my brother's name. That's the thing I've struggled with for so long."

"It must've been awful for you to have blocked out such details."

"Yes. No one can imagine what it was like. At first the people who took me were nice, trying to get me to like them. When I realized that my real folks weren't going to find me, I got angry with them and the world. Most of the time I was depressed and in shock. I took my anger out on the folks who abducted me. I never really accepted them. I could write a movie about my life; it has been just that interesting."

"I'm sure," Cara typed.

"Enough about me. What about the young woman you're helping?"

"When she turned twelve, she accidentally discovered her mother gave her up for adoption the same day she was born. At sixteen, she was raped and gave birth to a son. Secretly she tried to find her real mother up until she finished high school. Her life has been difficult. Unable to maintain a steady job, she has been forced to live an unsafe life in the projects. In spite of repeated arrests for prostitution, she has continued to sell sexual favors in order to pay the bills. Her son is in day care and he has developmental and emotional problems."

MattIwas responded, "Gee! That's terrible."

"Tell me about it," Cara typed. "Can you imagine what it's like having to sleep around with all sorts of men just to eat and pay a few bills?"

"I suppose. No, I just told you a lie. I *do* know what it's like. It's a long story, but I can give you the abbreviated version. After all, we're talking anonymously," he responded.

"True. It's what I like about chat room talks. You can share your darkest secrets. No one will ever know who you are," Cara typed.

MattIwas responded, "Well, I had this idea that I could get rich quick running an escort service, not like any other. I secured the clientele, arranged the fees up front and provided the love nest in my four-bedroom apartment. It kept the girls off the street and out of jail. We split the money equally. When one of them had saved enough money to move on to a better life, I allowed it. The girls were runaway teens. I kept no more than three at a time. It wasn't a pretty life. But they were safe and I took good care of them. So you see, I do understand, and I hate the fact that the young mother you're trying to help has to suffer like that."

"How long were you in business?" Cara typed, wanting to ask if he had sex with them, too.

"Three years. I got caught. It's another long story, but this one I'll spare you. Anyway, I went to prison. While serving my time, I realized that I wasn't cut out to do that sort of thing. Maybe it's family genes handed down to me from a heritage I know nothing about. So I got a job selling cars. I was good at it, too. Luckily, I stashed some money from the business and worked by day and took college courses at night. I got my degree and a new career. Now, I need to find my birth family. It's the only thing left for me to achieve, and then I'll be truly happy."

"I'm so proud you turned your life around in spite of the obstacles dealt you," Cara typed.

"Thanks. You seem to like helping folks like me. That's good. I could use your help, too."

"I'd love to. Where should we begin?"

"The basics. I just bought my computer. I'm still learning how to get around on AOL, let alone the Internet," he responded.

"No problem. I'll e-mail you something soon, maybe tonight."

Cara left their private room and clicked on links to other websites. Sympathizing with his plight, she decided to help him, and she believed he felt her compassion toward him. *We've established a secret cyberspace bond. Nothing said shall reveal our identity.*

Chapter 9

On Saturday morning, Cara was dressed in a light blue jogging suit and looking forward to working out at the gym with Jennifer. Shortly before nine, Jennifer called and canceled their workout without any explanation. She promised to call back later. Somewhat baffled, Cara decided to make good use of the extra time and took care of her outside errands.

She arrived back home that afternoon and put away the groceries, folded laundry and read her mail. Soon her thoughts drifted to Jennifer. *She's hiding something. If only she'd talk to me.*

Then she started to think about her own situation with Mario, and as much as she missed the good times they had together, the memories of their last argument danced in her head. *Why couldn't he tell me what the so-called evidence was?*

Putting that aside, she turned on her computer, checked for e-mail from **MattIwas** and searched the Internet for information on marriage and adultery.

Finding nothing from her online buddy, she entered iVillage.com. The article for today appeared in a large blue icon: ***How Women Feel About Adultery***. All she had to do was click it on. Once on the page, she moved the mouse down, slowly letting her mind absorb interesting messages: *The betrayed person feels terribly. But he didn't listen to the distress signs. A relationship is like a fire. You can let it go down, but you can't let it go out. Even though you're in another part of the house,* *you have to go back every once in a while to stoke the coals.*

Reflecting on those words, she knew she had been on the right track to rekindle the passion between her and Mario. She remembered his affair, but never understood why he broke his marriage vows and hurt her dearly. She read on: *Men are actually more likely to have extramarital affairs – because they split sex and affection. There are the nice girls you marry and the wild girls you have sex with. The double standard is alive and well.*

Then she clicked on the message board to find out what other people thought and had to say about the subject of adultery.

Subject: Why do women stay with men who have affairs?

They don't want to be alone. Children are involved. They lack the means to make it on their own. To sum it all up, they stay because the price is right.

Subject: How do women feel about adultery?

(1) Affairs are often a chance to try out something new.

(2) When someone starts confiding things to another woman it creates an emotional intimacy that is greater in the friendship than in the marriage. An affair can begin quickly when a man confides negative things about his marriage. What they're doing is signaling: I'm vulnerable; I may even be available.

Cara found it all interesting and yet disturbing, particularly the last one. *If I live to be a hundred and ten, I'll never accept the reasons for being unfaithful in a marriage. Color me old-fashioned, color me anything, I just can't stomach sleeping with another man while I'm married.*

———

At noon on Monday, Cara arrived at Human Services.

"Good afternoon. May I help you?" the polite middle-aged receptionist looked up and asked.

"Hello. I'm Cara Fleming." She gave her the brown envelope containing her updated resume. "This is for Mr. Dunlap. Will you see that he gets it?"

"Sure, Ms. Fleming."

"Thank you very much. Have a good day."

On the elevator, Cara thought, *I've taken a bold step to help myself. After all, nothing comes to those who sit and wait for a miracle to fall into their laps. I need this job like I need a head on my shoulders.*

When she arrived home it was almost six o'clock in the evening. She contacted a divorce lawyer that Jennifer had recommended. No sooner than she hung up, the phone rang three times. Each time she answered, the person hung up. When she checked her Caller ID, it showed that all three calls were from unknown callers. She wondered if the anonymous calls were from Mario.

———

Two days later, Cara walked into the law offices of Jesse Garnell and Associates. She wore a two-piece beige summer suit that she had bought at Marshall Fields a year ago. According to Jennifer, the lawyer was the best on the South Side and was affordable. In her mind, the office looked more like downtown Chicago than a neighborhood law establishment. It was well decorated, combining contemporary and afrocentric themes, and displayed some very fine paintings. The attorney's wife had hired a young aspiring black interior decorator that had been recently featured in *Ebony* magazine.

"Come in, Ms. Fleming. I'm Jesse Garnell." He wore a gray suit, appeared to be in his forties, was of average height, slender build, and wore sparkling jewelry on his hand.

They shook hands, and she sat down in a blue and white striped club chair. Fresh coffee permeated the air.

"It's nice to meet you," she replied handing him the divorce petition.

"Good. Same here." His smile was comforting.

He offered her coffee while he read the document. Later he pounded her with questions. Tired of reliving the ordeal, she forced herself to tell him what he needed to know. This time, she didn't omit the humiliating demand made by Mario: *I want your ass out of here.*

"Your husband has put you between a rock and a hard place. Can you prove your whereabouts during that time period?"

"Yes. We're required to maintain daily time records at work. My secretary can pull the files at your request."

"Oh, good. Were you absent much?"

"I took a sick day a few days ago because I was in a fender bender and suffered from whiplash. She gave him the details.

Attorney Garnell presented Cara with options for how he could get the child support she was seeking for her daughter. He promised to contact Mario's lawyer right away and get the show on the road. She signed a bunch of papers and wrote a check for five hundred dollars to cover one-half of the attorney's costs.

"I'm not sure how this could've happened to you. I'll admit, it'll be hard to disprove the adultery allegation, but I can guarantee you that I'll get support for your daughter."

"That's a relief. It's all I want from him."

Chapter 10

It was the middle of June and Cara was pumped up about her interview with Human Services Director, Earl Dunlap. She was dressed to impress in a beige three-piece suit and matching shoes. Her hair was freshly shampooed and full of bounce.

She arrived in the Loop around ten o'clock that morning and she parked her car at a parking garage four blocks from the building. *Any other time, I'd stuff coins in a meter and walk as many as twelve blocks just to save some money. I don't mind it this time. The nine dollar rate is a sound investment toward the job I need,* she thought.

Ten minutes later, she appeared at Mr. Dunlap's office door.

"Come in," Dunlap said. He gave her a professional, but impressive smile. His square, light-skinned face was handsomely set off with his thick, black curly hair and a matching moustache.

For a moment, she questioned his ethnic origin. Cara moistened her semi-dry lips to get the courage to speak. "Good morning. Thank you for seeing me." She spoke and sat down quickly on one of the black-and-white striped chairs facing his massive oak desk.

"So, how're things at the Parent Child Care Agency?" Dunlap asked, shifting around in his chair.

"Really good, actually," she replied.

"Talk to me about why I should consider you for the curriculum coordinator's position."

"Besides my credentials and work experience, I believe I can make positive changes for preschool children on the south side." She sensed that she'd gotten his attention.

"Sounds good. Please continue."

"I view the role of curriculum coordinator to be that of a leader, someone who can teach and motivate the adults… managers, teaching staff and parents. In less than a year, I've been able to make a lot of progress in that area."

"Yes. I'm aware. Word gets around, you know, and you're to be congratulated. I'm curious. How would you achieve such a goal here?"

She thought for a quick moment. "During the past five years I've learned that employee attitude makes a difference in job performance. Employees need to know they're appreciated. If they do, they'll work harder," she expounded, taking a moment to gather her breath. "What seems to work well for me is a philosophy I brought from the South."

"Oh yeah? What's that?"

"To be fair, firm and friendly and not necessarily in that order," she replied.

"Cara, I must say, your philosophy is definitely one to model. Don't believe I've heard anyone, man or woman, put it so simply."

"Thank you," she replied.

"Now tell me, how has it worked for you?"

"Well, for one thing, it helped me to win the respect of the people with whom I work. Actually, they trust me and they know, among all other things, that I'll be fair."

"What has been your greatest reward?"

"The achievement of a true team spirit. We hardly ever hear people saying things such as, "That's not my job, you do it, or I've done my part; now you do yours."

"I see," he said, looking down at his notes. "However, this job involves working with more people than you're accustomed. Why do you believe you can change varying institutional habits and attitudes of people in decision-making roles?"

"Mr. Dunlap, with all due respect," she said, with a smile and gleam in her eyes, "I can be elastic like a rubber band when it comes to dealing with people. But on the other hand, I can be a fierce fighter when it comes to a worthwhile cause," she told him. "Children, particularly the younger ones, are definitely worth the effort."

"And I agree with you, Ms. Fleming. Somehow that cause seems to always get pushed aside. I see it all the time, even in this department,"

Dunlap replied, as the intensity in his voice lessened.

"Adults are the most important educators in a child's life," she continued.

"Good point. Is there more?"

"You bet, Mr. Dunlap. When the community-at-large is successful, the department looks good, and so do you," she pointed out. At that moment, she didn't know if she won him over or turned him off completely.

"Amazing. Just amazing," he replied. "There's one last question. Are you aware that working for the city sometimes means having to deal with things that require more than your ability to motivate and inspire?"

Think positive. He might be trying to ruffle your feathers just to see what you're made of.

"If you're referring to the game of politics, yes, I'm aware of that element of the job." That was not a question she expected, but she was hoping she had scored. "Such an influence can be a barrier, but it's not one that would stop me. Besides, I love a challenge. It'll just make me work harder," she added.

"You have certainly done your homework," Dunlap said, with a smile and a trace of laughter in his voice.

Taking the expression on his face as a compliment, Cara smiled and waited for him to speak. He didn't move an inch and suddenly offered her coffee. *Perhaps, my answers exhausted him.* After a few minutes of chatting more about the department's goals, and people-relation issues, he thanked her and promised to give her application a thoughtful review.

They shook hands and said good-bye.

She drove home thinking she couldn't ever remember having a single job interview exhaust her as much as the one with Earl Dunlap. *He shot questions at me faster than the speed of a bullet. Maybe he will or maybe he won't consider me for the job. Without political support, I doubt it,* she thought.

She decided not to fret much. She'd done her best to impress him.

Chapter 11

Three days later, Cara walked into her office hoping her situation would change for the better. On her desk was a message from Earl Dunlap. She rushed to pick up the phone to dial his number, knocking over the cup of hot coffee onto the floor. "Doggone it. What a mess!" she yelled, just before he answered.

"Dunlap speaking."

"Hello, Mr. Dunlap. This is Cara Fleming returning your call," she spoke in a tone that was as professional as she could manage.

"Oh, yes. How are you Ms. Fleming?"

"I'm fine, thank you. How're you?"

"Terrific," he said and paused. "How does forty-one thousand a year sound?"

"Oh, my God!" She paused for a moment. "I got the job?"

"Yes, you got it."

"I'm so thrilled! Thank you Mr. Dunlap." She could barely get it all out, trying not to sound like a bumbling idiot. *That means I'll make fifteen thousand more per year*, she thought.

"Well, it wasn't easy. There were two other strong contenders, with a great deal more experience," he admitted. "But, that's all they had over you. What they lacked was something that you have, and a whole lot more."

"That being?"

"Let me put it this way, you can see ten thousand miles down the road, while some people I know can only see as far as they can spit."

"I'm overwhelmed, but especially pleased to be thought of like that," Cara said, thinking he was one who spoke his mind without hesitation. And, for the first time in her life, she was almost speechless, filled with a tremendous sense of accomplishment. "If you'll excuse me, Mr. Dunlap, I feel the urge to shout for joy."

He laughed, and she started to laugh, too.

"I can see this means a lot to you."

"Yes, more than you'll ever know. And, Mr. Dunlap, I promise to work hard to get the job done."

"I'm sure you will. Now, will you be able to come to work on July 15th?"

"Absolutely."

Dunlap advised her to keep the orientation appointment.

"Ms. Fleming?"

"Yes?"

"Welcome aboard. You're in the tough lanes now!"

Around noon, the cadence of his words still rang in her head like a nonstop drumbeat. She could picture herself standing before a large audience of teachers and administrators saying, "I'm Cara Fleming, curriculum coordinator for the South Side. I want to take you on a new journey. I invite you to join me."

She put the In-Conference sign on the outside of her office door, locked the door and fell down on her mahogany, executive style chair and closed her eyes. She prayed and cried tears of joy, undisturbed for a few minutes.

Then she thought about her parents and dialed the number.

"Hello," Frank answered.

"Hi, Daddy. I've got something good to tell you."

"My Lord! Tell me before I burst open."

"I've been hired by a major city department, earning a hell of a lot more money."

"For real?"

"Yes, it's true," she exclaimed.

"I'm proud of you. Congratulations."

"How's my little girl? I miss her, Daddy." Cara quickly muttered.

"I know you do. She's doing fine. Right now she's taking a nap."

"Is Mom home?"

"She's out to lunch with Mary Lee."

"Okay. Tell her my good news. I'll call back later to talk to her and Ashley. Make sure you give my daughter a great big hug and tell her that I love her and that I miss her so much."

"I will. But before you go, remember to be careful. Work hard and get your life in order. Ashley will be just fine down here with us," he said, haltingly. "Another thing, don't forget to check your gas meter often. Never let your car get past a half tank of gas. In case I haven't already mentioned it, carry a can of mace in your purse. I don't want to think about you running out of gas on a street somewhere all alone."

"Okay. I promise to do all the things you've taught me."

Cara breezed through two brief staff meetings, ordered supplies, completed two reports and signed out to go home.

Thirty minutes later, she drove home, and, as she turned onto Columbus Drive, a black Infiniti darted into her lane. The driver followed her.

It was not until she'd reached Fifty-seventh and Lake Shore Drive that she knew he was tailing her. By then, another vehicle had merged between them preventing her from getting a closer view of his face and license plate. The lanes were jammed with rush hour traffic. Even if she had tried, she couldn't have escaped him. Her palms became sweaty and her heart began to race.

Why would someone be following me? She quickly thought of Mario. *Maybe he actually believes I'm seeing someone else and needs to get more evidence? It would definitely help his case against me,* she concluded. Suddenly she became irritated. "Mario took away my joy and damn near ruined my life trying to be free of me. But he won't take away my spirit."

Thirty minutes later Cara reached the Seventy-first and South Shore Drive juncture. She glanced in her rearview mirror and saw that the driver turned left on South Shore Drive. Relieved, she remained on course and drove home. She had started to watch everyone. *Daddy will be proud,* she thought.

When she parked her car at the apartment a few minutes later, Cara checked and didn't see any sign of the black Infiniti. She quickly entered her apartment and tossed the mail on the sofa. Still nervous, she peeked between the blinds to make sure no one was outside her window. Relieved that nobody was lurking outside, she took three deep breaths and began to relax. She needed something to take her mind off of the black Infiniti driver, so she decided to get online. She had thought all day about her newfound buddy, **MattIwas**, wondering who he might be, what he looked like, where he actually lived, and what type of person he was. Questions, she knew could never be answered. "One thing I do know, **MattIwas** is a man," she said.

After she finished eating, she left e-mail messages for Mary Lee and Jennifer telling them about her new job. She didn't tell them how much she would earn.

Then, she read Matt's e-mail. *"Hi, **Current Wife**. I've been busy following through on your suggestions. Got booted offline a few times. Back to square one. Meet me in our private room at nine o'clock tonight."*

Cara checked her watch. She had three hours to kill. After she fixed a peanut butter and jelly sandwich for lunch the next day and rolled her hair, she soaked in a hot tub of fragrant bubbles. Listening to slow jams on V103 FM helped her to pass the time quickly. *Too bad I can't share this moment with someone special.*

Promptly signed online, she waited for **MattIwas** in their private room and thought, *I will tell him my secret. He thought it was safe to tell*

*me things about his past. There's no way he could possibly know who I
am. It'll be okay,* she thought.

Suddenly, he entered the private room.

"Hi, C'Wife. How was your day?"

"Fine. I've got something to share with you," Cara typed.

"Lay it on me," he responded.

"It's complicated, so, I'll be brief. I've left my husband.
Someone told my husband I was having an affair. It's possible he created this lie. I believe he's in love with another woman. He refuses to pay
child support for our daughter, claiming she's not his child. He's filed
for a divorce." Cara noticed **MattIwas** didn't type a response while she
poured out her troubles. "That's my story. What do you think? Any suggestions for how I can find out who did this?" she typed.

"I'm so sorry this happened to you. <Sobbing> Life can be a bitch
at times. Where are you?" he responded.

Against her better judgment she typed, "Chicago. Where are
you?"

"Small world, isn't it? I'm in Chicago, too."

Cara didn't type a response. Immediately, she wished she had
told him she lived someplace like Alaska or Rhode Island. The fact that
they lived in the same city made her feel uncomfortable. Then she typed,

"Matt, are you still there?"

"Yeah, I'm here. Let's talk again tomorrow," he responded.

"Sure. In the meantime, good luck finding your family," she
typed.

Cara's thoughts about their chat bothered her. *Why didn't he say
more? Did he care about my problem? Oh boy, I told him too much too
soon.* But then she reasoned, *all he knows is that we both live in Chicago.
He doesn't know my name.*

Cara left the room and noticed **MattIwas** had signed offline.
Curious, she checked and learned he didn't have a profile.

Chapter 12

Cara dazzled over how beautiful Chicago was at this time of the year. Colorful perennials and young lush green trees lined the medians dividing the north and southbound traffic on King Drive and Stony Island Avenue and other major streets on the South Side. It was a city filled with tourists from all over the world who'd converged to see the celebrated attractions in Chicago. People covered miles of beaches along the shores of Lake Michigan. Not to mention, how love and romance seemed to fill the air.

But she had more important things on her mind.

On Thursday, she waited in the conference room for her orientation session. Clearly, an interior decorator had worked miracles. She glanced at the satiny parquet floors, partially covered with beautiful Persian carpet, and antique tables and lamps. Also appealing were live plants trailing from hand-painted pots. She had a flair for that sort of thing, having once considered studying interior design in college. Instead, she had chosen primary education and now she was glad that she did.

Minutes later, a young, attractive, nicely dressed lady of Hispanic origin, wearing a department ID badge walked into the room and greeted her.

"Hello. I'm Karen Torres. It's good to finally meet you."

"The pleasure is all mine, Ms. Torres," Cara responded with a smile and a handshake.

"Good. Then let's get started, shall we?"

Cara followed her to a small private room.

Within an hour, Cara had completed and signed a stack of forms and posed for her job I.D. badge. Later she reviewed her job description, work schedule, agency assignments, and protocol procedures. She was given several brochures, recent department memos, and the operational manual to take home.

"Excited?"

"Yes, and you've been a great help, Ms. Torres."

"Just doing my job. Is there anything else you'd like to ask me?"

"No, I don't believe so." Cara stood and smiled. "Well, thanks again. I'll see you on July 15." She waved good-bye.

Cara approached the elevator a few minutes later. The door opened and two men hurried off. The tall man with a thick moustache was Duncan Tate.

"Hi, Duncan." She greeted him warmly.

"Hello," he replied, returning her smile. She'd met Duncan right after she and Jennifer became friends. "Cara Fleming, right?"

"Yes, it's me. How are you?"

"I'm okay. Surprised to see you. What're doing here?"

"Would you believe I just got hired?"

"Good for you. Congratulations."

"Thanks," she replied and forced herself to look at the other man who seemed familiar. He had a face too cute for a man and his hair was slicked back on his head. The man looked off into the distance, distracted as if Cara was not even standing there. She shuddered, wondering if she was losing her touch. Duncan hadn't introduced him, so she smiled and quickly turned her attention back to Duncan.

"It was good seeing you. Tell Jennifer I'll call her."

Later as she fought the traffic on Michigan Avenue, somehow she didn't mind the lines of the bumper-to-bumper cars or the hundreds of pedestrians trying to cross Michigan Avenue. From Cara's research about Chicago, she remembered that at least a million people piled the downtown area, leaving work this time of day. She'd never been able to imagine it, but today she understood.

Her mind started to drift back to Duncan Tate and the guy whose image she couldn't shake. Frustrated that she couldn't remember where she'd seen him, she decided to concentrate on his eyes and mouth. Nothing, not a clue, popped into her mind. Maybe, there was something about his hair that was different from before. She'd always been able to put two and two together and get ten. *It'll come to me.*

An hour later she arrived home and saw Mrs. Walker watering the potted marigolds in the yard. They chatted a few minutes and then Cara got her mail and went inside to relax.

After a long stimulating shower, she ate leftover tuna salad, and a can of pineapple for dessert. Feeling grateful that she'd have nearly six hundred dollars once the bills were paid, she developed a new budget. Some of it would go to her parents to help with Ashley and the rest to her savings account.

Later, she signed on to AOL and checked her buddy screen. **MattIwas** did not appear in her buddy list. Scrolling through her e-mail messages, she was disappointed to find nothing from him.

———

Since Bradley had fallen asleep earlier than usual, Mary Lee decided to call Cara around seven o'clock that evening.

"Hi. How're things going with that young mother? Were you able to help her?" Mary Lee prodded.

"I'm happy to say that I was. In fact, that one was easy," she replied. "Would you believe, I'm helping someone over the Internet find his birth family? What's strange is, I don't know this person's identity." Suddenly Mary Lee thought about her older son who died in a tragic fire not long after he was kidnapped. She knew all too well how it felt to lose someone special. "Really? I'm impressed," she said hesitating for a moment. "I'm curious. What else did this person tell you?"

Cara reached for the printed sheets from her chats with **MattIwas.** "Okay, I'm referring to my notes. Abducted at the age of five...."

"   That's sad, to be taken away from your parents like that. "How old is he now?"

"Thirty-something...I can't be sure."

"Does he remember where he was when he was abducted?"

"Yes, according to him, that's one thing he's always remembered. He was with his mother one day. She stopped to get some gas. She left him in the car while she went inside the station to pay for the gas. A man and woman approached the car, claiming his mother had taken ill. He never saw his family again."

"Oh my goodness! What's this man's name?" Mary Lee asked anxiously.

"**MattIwas**," Cara said.

"What kind of name is that?"

"It's his AOL screen name," Cara replied. "On American Online, people can call themselves whatever, as long as the screen name is not already in use," Cara said.

Mary Lee coughed uncontrollably and her breathing seemed irregular.

"Are you okay, Mother Fleming?"

"Yes, I think so," she said, continuing to sound as though she wasn't.

Once Cara was sure her mother-in-law had the latest version of AOL, she told her how to create a screen name."

"Thanks for your help. I'm still new at this."

By the end of their talk, Cara felt strange about Mary Lee's intentions. *Does she think I'm lying about my online buddy? Or, is she playing amateur detective, thinking this guy might be my lover?*

———

No sooner than Mary Lee had hung up, she remembered the devastation, shame and guilt that she and Bradley felt when they had learned that their oldest son had died in a tragic house fire along with his abductors. Bradley had refused to take a lie-down-and-die attitude. Within a month after the abduction, he hired a black private investigator to locate Matthew. That effort failed. Feeling heartbroken, helpless and ultimately despondent, they sold their home in Greenwood, Mississippi and moved to Memphis. The worst part of it for Mary Lee was that Bradley made her promise to never tell anyone that they had an older son, including Mario. But no one felt more blame than did Mary Lee. After all, he was taken while in her care. *This man has got to be my son,* she thought.

Although she was grateful to have learned this intriguing information from Cara, she took the necessary steps to keep the secret from Cara. So, she created a new screen name, **Leewoman44**. Then, Mary Lee placed **MattIwas** on her Buddy List, and entered Family.com. Seconds later, she noticed he was online, too. This was her opportunity to find out what she needed to know about this man, so, she sent **MattIwas** an instant message under a new screen name.

———

MattIwas browsed around the main page for a few minutes. Just as he joined a chat room discussion, the instant message screen signal beeped. Naturally, he figured it was **Current Wife**, but as he peeked at the instant message, he saw the unfamiliar screen name.

"Hello," **Leewoman44** greeted him.

"Hello. Who are you?" **MattIwas** typed. He'd only chatted with **Current Wife**. Then he thought, *After my last chat with* **Current Wife**, *I believe I know her true identity. It can't be anyone but Cara Fleming."* Her words still rang in his head. *I've left my husband. Someone told my husband I was having an affair. It's possible he created this lie. I believe he's in love with another woman.* Out of curiosity, he decided to confirm it.

"Possibly someone you're looking for," **Leewoman44** responded.

"Oh, yeah," **MattIwas** typed. Still looking at the instant message screen, he thought **Leewoman44** could be an innocent bystander he missed seeing in the chat rooms. "Okay, Leewoman, what's up?" He typed.

"Hope you don't think I'm crazy. I'm looking for my son. His name was Matthew. It's been so long. Haven't seen him in thirty years. Losing him almost destroyed us."

"Hold on. I'll be right back." He stood up from the computer, paced the floor for a few minutes, poured a straight shot of gin, and returned to re-read what **Leewoman44** had typed. He thought he was dreaming. *How could this person know all about my past? What should I say? I need time to think.*

A minute later, he typed, "Your story is similar to mine. But first, I need to know a few things. Where do you live? How did you find me online? Are you willing to meet me?"

"Sure, I can do that. My name is Mary Lee Fleming. I need answers, too. Just think about it. If you must know, I got your name from someone you know as **Current Wife**. She's my daughter-in-law. I live with my husband, Bradley, in Memphis. When you're ready, e-mail me."

"I just might do that. I'll get back to you later, okay?" He typed. Alderman Bennett signed offline and his body rocked. Mixed feelings bombarded his heart, while insecurity about the future and his new life in Chicago thrust through his mind. Suddenly it hit him. *Current Wife is, without a doubt, Cara Fleming. Could it be that her mother-in-law is my real mother?*

Chapter 13

The next day the e-mail Mary Lee hoped for had arrived. *If you want to know if I'm your son, meet me in Chicago on Monday morning, nine-fifteen at the Hampton Inn. It's near Midway Airport. And please come alone.*

Mary Lee thought about how she would tell Bradley she needed to go to Chicago, alone. She had never traveled anywhere without Bradley, and somehow, she had to find a way to go to Chicago without him. *It's now or never,* she thought.

Bradley came home from work shortly after five o'clock and he seemed exhausted. He told Mary Lee that he'd had a rough day in the sun and that he needed to lie down for a few minutes. She brought him a glass of water and left him alone to relax before dinner was ready.

Forty minutes later, he woke up and came to dinner. His favorite meal was on the table: baked chicken, southern-style succotash, string beans, buttered homemade rolls, and iced tea. For dessert, she served fruit-laced Jell-O topped with fresh mint leaves. He seemed refreshed from his nap and his conversation centered mostly about his schedule for the next week, which included a meeting with the Memphis Businessmen's Association, one hundred and ten lawns to cut, and a landscape to build for two new homes that were being constructed.

After dinner, they finished their second glasses of iced tea. They sat in the wicker two-seater near several red and yellow rose bushes.

"Would you mind if I go to Chicago for a couple of days?"

"What're you up to now? When were you planning to leave?"

"Monday morning, early."

"That's two days away. What's the rush? Is it Mario?"

"Yes, and I'm concerned about him. What mother wouldn't be?"

"Did it ever occur to you that I would want to go, too? Wait until next weekend. I'll join you." She didn't respond. Bradley rattled on and on letting her know that he suspected she wasn't being truthful.

She folded her hands and started to worry. She knew that she had an obligation to be honest with Bradley. During their thirty-seven-year marriage, lying to him was a no-no. She trusted him and he trusted her.

"Mary Lee, what on earth is the matter with you?"   •

"Oh, you won't believe what has happened."

"What did Mario do now? Is he hurt?"

"No, it's not about that son."

A probing query came into his eyes. "We only have but one son."

Right away, she knew that Bradley couldn't mention Matthew's name, not even to her. *I've been punished long enough and need to be strong for a change.*

"What if I told you it's possible Matthew didn't die?"

Bradley turned abruptly to look at her. "I don't believe you said his name. You promised never to mention that name again. Didn't we suffer enough over losing him?" he sniffed, holding onto his chair.

"If I go to Chicago, I can verify whether or not he's our son. Don't you think I deserve to do that? After all, I lost him." She told him about Cara's involvement and how she'd talked with the man through e-mail and instant messages.

"Does Cara know this man?"

"No. Anyway, the man described exactly where and how he was abducted, whom he was with, and the age he was at the time. That's too much of a coincidence for me," she added.

"So Cara's been a regular busybody. That's probably how she ruined her marriage. Poor Mario."

"Why are you so down on our daughter-in-law? I've talked with her. What she had to say convinced me she was framed, Bradley. Anyway, she's a woman with strong convictions and she's nobody's pushover. Just watch. She's going to be an important leader someday."

"That'll be the day. She needs to get her own life in order before she attempts to lead others." His shoulders slumped. "Look, I'm so tired of this. First, it was your crusade for Cara. Now you're on our dead son's bandwagon. Who's it going to be next? Shouldn't it be the son who's alive and trying to move on with his life?" He gestured with his hands and hit the flowerpot on the table between them.

The words took a second to sink in. She had come this far and was not about to stop now. Without saying another word to Bradley, she stood and walked inside the house, leaving him high and dry.

Chapter 14

It was a humid Tuesday evening in July and by now, Cara felt somewhat content. She had a new job and worry about how she'd survive was gone with the wind. She'd arrived home later than usual, making sure she got to the post office before it closed in order to send money, clothing and toys to her daughter.

After she phoned her parents to check in on Ashley, she leaned back on the sofa and reflected about her first day on the job; flowers from the staff, refreshments, and a brief tour of the floor where her cubicle was located warmed her heart. Dexter Grady, her supervisor, seemed more than friendly, too much so in her opinion. His words still rang in her ear,

"Care to join me for lunch today?" with an almost seductive tone.

"Thanks, but not today, Mr. Grady," she'd told him as politely and as professionally as she could under the circumstances. "There's so much to read and learn. Perhaps another time?"

"Sure, I'll hold you to that. On that note, how about going with me to the Taste of Chicago?" When she shrugged her shoulders, he threw her a smile and quietly walked away.

Then she remembered her conversation with Shirley Carr, the thirty-seven-old West Side coordinator who worked in the next cubicle. The first thing out of Shirley's mouth was, "You're a fresh face around here. Count on me to help you through the rough spots." Cara really appreciated knowing she could count on someone. She got a brief history about office politics, games the workers played, whom to watch out for, and whom not to trust. Shirley had explained the pitfalls dealing with program directors and teachers and how to cover your behind.

Cara knew all too well what she meant, having just left a director's position. She'd always managed to work well with Human Services staff and had garnered a great reputation. As overwhelming as it seemed, she was eager and primed to perform beyond expectations.

Later that evening, she wrote a time management plan. Taking an hour for lunch at a restaurant was not in her plan. And, neither would she consider having lunch with Mr. Grady. A packed lunch from home to save money and time was more like it. Mondays and Fridays would be devoted to completing and filing reports and making minor schedule changes for the next week.

After outlining her time management plan, she signed onto AOL, hoping to join MattIwas in their private room. It had been four days since she had gotten a message from him. She found it odd that he didn't instant message her, as he always did immediately after she signed on.

After an hour of browsing Family.com and Ancestry.com for more resources, she deleted junk mail and checked her horoscope. She sensed that **MattIwas** no longer cared to chat with her. Perhaps, he was busy following through on her suggestions.

So, she wrote him a message. *Dear Matt: Are you okay? Where are you? I've located some information that might interest you. Please respond.*

The phone rang a little after nine o'clock. She almost didn't answer, but when the caller's name and number appeared on her machine, she decided to answer.

"Hello."

"Hi. This is Dexter."

"Hi, Mr. Grady," she replied.

"Hope it's okay that I called so late. Your line was busy," he explained. "By the way, everyone at the office calls me Dexter."

"I'll try to remember that. But, don't get mad if I forget occasionally."

Then Cara paused for a moment, waiting for him to say more before she would end the conversation.

———

Around midnight, Mario parked his car at the *Due Drop Inn* shortly after ten o'clock that same evening, thinking the walls in his new apartment had started to close in on him. Freddie Sanders was at his usual post, pacing from one end of the bar to the other, keeping his regulars happy.

Mario ordered a Bud Lite and let his mind drift to Cara and the divorce. His lawyer had informed him yesterday about her counter petition. She wanted monthly child support and one-half of Ashley's college education tuition to be given to Ashley when she turned eighteen. After he'd shamelessly swore to Cara that he wasn't Ashley's father, this was going to be a big problem for Mario and he knew it. *How am I going to fight a court order demanding child support payments?*

He just couldn't think about any of it for the moment. Suddenly, and with an irritated sigh, he bowed his head, closed his eyes and remembered that he hadn't found anyone to fulfill his sexual needs since Cara left him. Cara was the only woman who made him feel complete as a man. Too stubborn to admit it, he missed Cara. Yet, he knew he had no one else to blame but himself. As he drowned in sorrow, he let himself believe that she was gone forever from his life and his bed.

When Freddie, the bartender returned with Mario's beer, the two of them talked. Mario shared his fears about his marriage and his future. Freddie mostly listened and then he told Mario what he believed he needed to hear. "Nobody's perfect. At some point even the woman you love and adore is going to bring out that side of you. You lose control and act like a fool. Try not to beat yourself up about it." Freddie said.

Mario thanked Freddie but somehow the words of wisdom didn't do much to put out the fire that was burning out of control within him.

Minutes later, he drove home and while he cruised his car down Forty-seven Street, he devised a plan to locate Paula Coles, whom he hadn't seen since he ended their affair a few years ago. Was she still attractive? Would she want him again? Running his fingers around his glass, he decided that Memphis would be a great place to start.

The next day, Mario's plane landed at 9:50 a.m. An hour later, he'd checked into his room at the Comfort Inn East. Even the liquor he'd consumed last night hadn't dulled his body to a peaceful sleep. He needed to remain alert, so that he could think and certainly look his best. Quickly, he unpacked, took a long shower, and put on fresh clothes.

He searched the white pages in hope of finding Paula's number. He remembered that she was making plans to go to Italy after their affair ended, but he had his doubts.

Within two minutes he found two listings. The first number was disconnected. He tried the second one. Bingo! The lady's voice on the answering machine was familiar. His hands were shaking. "Paula," he hesitated, "this is your long-lost friend, Mario. I'm in town for the weekend. I'd love to see you. Staying at the Comfort Inn East on Poplar Avenue in room 614. Please call me."

He hung up the phone and hoped she would return his call. Ten minutes past lunchtime, he heard the phone ring.
"Hello?"
"Mario? Is that you?" Paula asked, in a silky voice.
"Yeah, it's me."
"I, I don't know what to say, except that …"
"It's good to hear your voice, too," he interrupted her. "I figured you'd be out of the country. What happened?"
"Well," she paused. "It didn't work out with Howard. We tried to make it work; seems I stayed away from him too long," she said.
"I'm sorry to hear that." His voice was low and purposefully seductive.

"Yeah, and now I'm back in Memphis starting all over again.

"That must've been rough on you."

"It was. Can we talk about something other than me and my ex-husband?"

"Sure," he said.

"Where're you and the wife living now? Heard you guys left here a year ago."

"Chicago."

"Really? How nice. You like it?"

"Yep. It's a cool place to live."

"Are you sure it's safe for you and me to get together? I don't want another mishap with your wife." She spoke in a broken whisper.

"Trust me; this time, it's safe."

"What does that mean?" Paula asked.

"I missed you. Can you come to the hotel and meet me today?" There was a clingy desperation in his voice.

"I'm on my way."

He went out and bought a bottle of her favorite wine, chilled it, and relaxed.

———

When Paula had arrived and parked her car, excitement bounced like tiny red-tipped sparks on her face. She ate like a bird and walked every day to maintain her sexy, five-seven, small framed, slim body. She applied a light coating of raspberry-flavor blush on her full lips and sprayed on a lightly scented fragrance, one that Mario always liked on her, in all the right places.

Minutes later, she walked up to the hotel like a woman who knew how to get where she wanted to go.

She tapped on his door once, and right away, Mario was in the doorway dressed in a Louis Vuitton V-neck beige silk shirt and tailored brown slacks. The gold chain around his neck added certain sexiness. He captured her heart all over again.

"Hello you," she said, smiling. She took three steps and was inside his room.

"Hi, Paula. It's good to see you again." Mario thought she looked better than before, more mature. But, it was her eyes that drew his attention. They were dark, intelligent and unflinching. Her tinted brown and blond streaked hair was cut in a short bob style that high-lighted the shape of her round face. *Still, as sexy as before!*

They held each other in a long embrace.

"Thanks for coming to see me," he whispered while still holding her. "I've missed you so much."

"Missed you too. I..." The simple sentence she'd started told him what he wanted to know. She still wanted him. She managed to pull away and sat on the love seat.

He filled two glasses with chilled wine and looked at her admiringly. "I need a friend." A grin flashed across his face.

"What led you back to me?"

"Cara and I are getting divorced," he said, sitting down without looking at her. He began by telling her the important things about his marriage, including the birth of Ashley and the reason they left Memphis. Finally, he got to the reason for their divorce. "She cheated on me," Mario stammered, unable to hold it any longer.

"I don't believe you."

"Believe me, it's true."

Paula folded her hands in disbelief. "Not the woman I met as your wife who preached to me about morality and exposed her open wounds to me in verbal terms you wouldn't believe," she blurted out, fumbling with her hands. "Mario," she said, eyeing him quizzically, "do you really want me in your life?"

"Yes. Why not?"

"What exactly does that mean? We ended our relationship just to save your marriage. It was difficult, but I did it," she said.

Holding her close, Mario continued. "All that's behind us now. All I know is that I need you in my life. Let's take it from here and see what happens."

She looked at him, and licked her lips. "Welcome back, Mario."

Chapter 15

Cara strolled down the church steps after service wearing a lavender summer dress and off white shoes.

Not far away, was Barbara Rhodes helping an elderly lady get into a CTA special transport van for seniors and those with special needs. She caught up with Barbara and shared her good news.

"I couldn't be happier for you. When did you start?" Barbara asked.

"Last week and it's been great. Thanks, for the tip."

"You're welcome. Remember, you put forth the effort. Congratulations."

Cara smiled. "True, but it was your call that led me there. I'll forever be grateful that God blessed me through you, Barbara."

Suddenly, Cara remembered the pastor's upcoming anniversary, a formal attire gala in early October.

"By the way, how're the gala ticket sales going?"

"Like hot cakes. We're expecting a huge turnout," Barbara replied, looking away momentarily. Barbara waved at Alderman Bennett.

"Let me know if there's anything I can do to help with the reception," Cara said.

"Just come and have fun. I've got everything under control," Barbara told her.

"All right. Enjoy your Sunday." Cara smiled and waved her good-bye.

———

After leaving church, dreadful of going right back to her lonely apartment, she decided to take a long drive on Lake Shore Drive and enjoy the beautiful scenery of Chicago's lakefront. She needed air to fill her lungs with the pungent scent of autumn, as she passed through the little dramas that took place in her life.

Ashley crossed her mind and Cara thought about the fun Ashley would have playing outdoors with her granddaddy. She remembered how it was when she was a little girl, throwing balls, playing hide-and-seek, taking neighborhood walks, and even playing board games at the kitchen table. He'd always let Cara win, letting her believe she was better than he was.

When Cara reached Forty-eighth and Lake Shore Drive, she glanced for a moment at the high rise she and Mario once lived in and couldn't suppress the memories of that night from haunting her again. She recalled leaping down two and three steps at a time, like a bat escaping hell. The memory was so vivid. *I can't let him catch me. What if I don't make it?*

It had all come back, only more profoundly than before. Her face was drenched in wetness and her heart palpitated. Suddenly, she realized that she was about to drive straight into the cement wall that protected the outer drive from the violent waves of Lake Michigan. She quickly steered her car to the left and luckily, she decelerated just enough to keep from hitting the vehicle in front of her. Her hands shook so badly that she had to pull over to the side of the road twice. Cars whizzed by her and she didn't see them.

Gathering her strength ten minutes later, she pulled back onto the Drive. She had started to feel at ease when she approached the Museum of Science and Industry, the largest museum in the world. It was then that she realized that somehow she had to launch a search for the culprit who framed her. But before that, she had to try and put that night far out of her mind or else she'd have an accident for sure.

She soon approached Soldier Field, home of the Chicago Bears, and several other tourist attractions… the Aquarium, Adler Planetarium, and Field Museum. It wasn't long before she had arrived in the heart of the city, known as the Loop, home to the financial district and tall skyscrapers. The Sears Tower was more than impressive. She glanced over at the lake. People were sailing off on their private yachts, while some lazily sprawled around on those still docked. She tried to visualize what life must be like for the people who could afford to own such majestic boats.

As she swerved around the curve past Randolph Street, she saw the tall magnificent structure to her right. *That's where Oprah Winfrey and other mega-rich people lived,* she thought. She continued to drive north to the North Avenue exit and then turned around to go back to the South Side, wondering how she would spend the rest of her Sunday.

It was almost three o'clock that afternoon when Cara walked inside her apartment. It was just as she had left it… cleaned, plants watered, and with sufficient light flowing from the windows. From the refrigerator she pulled out her dinner that she'd cooked the night before - baked chicken breasts, lima beans and cornbread. All there was left to do was toss a salad and cut a slice of watermelon for dessert.

Later, she booked a flight home for Thanksgiving, scheduled an appointment with her doctor and dentist, and set a date to treat Jennifer to lunch. She made a notation to check on Teresa Peyton. She planned her meals for the entire week.

Then she phoned her folks. Naomi answered.

"Hello."

"Mom, it's me. How you doing today? How's Ashley?"

"We're fine. How're things with you?"

Gleefully, she told Naomi about her trip home for Thanksgiving. Yet, it seemed like forever when she'd see her daughter again.

"I'll make the sweet potato pies," Cara said.

Naomi yelled out to Frank who was sitting in his big chair watching the Saints football game. "Cara is coming home. It'll be like old times."

He took the phone joyfully. "Hi, Baby girl. I'm glad you're coming home. Just so long as you leave Ashley here with us," he chuckled.

Cara loved it when her father called her that. It made her feel snug and tight like a cuddled teddy bear. "Oh, Daddy, you worry too much. I do want my daughter with me, but for a little while longer, she may stay with you and Mom."

Cara ended the call on a happy note thinking that her day had gone well.

Then the phone rang.

"Hello. Hello," she repeated. The caller slammed the phone without saying a word. Cara hung up annoyed. The anonymous calls had started to wear on her mind like an over wrung dishrag. She figured it was time to do something to retaliate.

She recorded a new voice mail announcement: *Hello, since you've decided to hide your name and your number, I won't answer this call. However, if you choose to leave your name, your number and the nature of your call, I'll get back to you as soon as I can. In case you're not an anonymous caller and I'm unable to view my Caller ID, I don't want to miss your call. So leave me a message. Thank you.*

Chapter 16

As a man trained to observe, Alderman Bennett recognized the woman who stepped inside the lobby at the Hampton Inn. She seemed overly friendly and warm, a memory he'd clung to over the years. Her eyes, facial shape and unblemished skin, colored like a pecan, were identical to his. Her hair was blended with gray and black hues and styled in a neatly cut Afro. She was overweight, but not by more than ten pounds. In an emerald laced, two-piece blue-jean suit, she looked smashing for a woman her age. It had all come back to him. She was still a good-looking woman, but aged like a good bottle of wine.

He was anxious and nervous as he eased toward her. "Hello. I'm Matthew. You must be my mother."

"Yes, it's me," she beamed, looking him over from head to toe. Her voice gave him a thrill deep in the pit of his stomach. Everything about her fit together, everything in his world was all right. There were no pieces misplaced, mismatched or mistaken. Tears streamed down his face and he couldn't imagine what the viewers walking in and out thought as he grabbed and hugged her.

Alderman Bennett gently pulled her from the middle of the lobby to the side and they embraced, holding each other tightly and unable to fight the tears.

After a few minutes, she pulled away slightly. "Thank you, Jesus," she said looking up momentarily. "You're really Matthew. You're alive. You're here in the flesh. There's so much I want to say, if I could only stop crying." She hugged him some more.

"It's okay, Mother. You know, we have every right to let it all out."

From her purse, she pulled out enough tissue to share with him and they both dried their faces.

"Let's go inside the restaurant. I'll order breakfast. We can talk all day if you want." He led the way pulling her carry-on luggage behind him.

The restaurant was half filled, mostly with people in between flights. He had chosen it on purpose because hardly anyone there would recognize him. Soft music played in the background. The polished floors, striped-papered walls, chandeliers beautifully spaced apart from the ceiling, and rows of live tropical plants staged a lovely scene. They were seated at a corner booth that offered a clear view of the sprawling traffic on Cicero Avenue.

Mary Lee looked away long enough to gather from her purse a few mementos from his past... his kindergarten class picture, a mini family photo album and his birth certificate. She'd managed to stash them in a private safe deposit box away from Bradley until now. He looked at each one and smiled.

"Fancy that! It's little o' me," he exclaimed, holding the picture in his hands. His face was rounder, as he showed a toothy grin.

"It was all I had left of you."

The waiter appeared with a pot of coffee and took their food order. They each ordered pancakes, scrambled eggs, sausage, juice, and coffee. Bennett poured their coffee. Mary Lee preferred two packs of Equal sugar and he poured his sugar from the glass container. He took a long sip of his coffee and looked at the pictures. "Do you mind if I hold onto these just until you're ready to leave?"

"All of it is yours to keep. I no longer need them, Son." She couldn't help but notice how well he looked. Except that he had Bradley's body shape and a receding hairline, he was the spitting image of her. She wondered what he was like otherwise. What type of work did he do? Was he married, single or divorced? Were there children? What was his life like? Still overwhelmed by the experience of seeing him, all she could think of at the moment was how she'd been robbed of the opportunity to raise and love her own child herself. She wanted to tell him how she felt about the people who took him away, but she didn't. That warm look in his eyes might disappear if she did. Mostly, she felt grateful that he had come through the ordeal seemingly all right.

"You've grown into such a fine looking man. Your dad would be so proud."

"How is he?"

"He's all right. He was skeptical as to whether you'd turn out to be our son."

"I'm sure. It bothered me that I didn't remember his name."

"You were so young. He won't hold that against you. What happened to you was not your doing."

"It was rough growing up with strangers. Although I never gave up hope that I'd find you someday, my knowledge of my past seemed to fade with time," Alderman Bennett said.

The waiter returned and placed their steaming food on the table. Afterward, Mary Lee and Matthew hurriedly covered the pancakes with maple syrup and ate in silence for a few moments. She wondered why Matthew asked her to e-mail him to a new screen name he had created. Why didn't he want Cara to know it? Obviously he had his reasons and she decided it was best to leave that one alone, too. Perhaps at another time they could talk more openly about everything that mattered.

"I can't wait to see your father's face when I tell him you're alive," she said, savoring small portions of pancakes and eggs.

"I can't wait to see him."

"Now that we're together again, I want to know all about you," Mary Lee said, before sipping her coffee.

Taking his time to draw in a deep breath, he was prepared to tell only what she really needed to know at this point. He checked his watch.

It was 10:30 a.m. He remembered that he had scheduled a few appoint-ments in the event that Mary Lee turned out to be a hoax. *Everything and everyone will have to wait until later,* he thought.

"Mother, I guess if there's anyone I can tell the truth to, it's you. How good are you at keeping secrets?"

"You're looking at someone who deserves an Oscar for having kept a lifelong secret."

"What on earth could that have been?"

"The secret was you. No one knew you existed except your father and me. Your father couldn't handle the publicity surrounding your abduction; nor could he handle losing you and knowing he'd never see you again. He swore me to secrecy. We moved away from where you were born and started a new life in Memphis. Mario, your brother, thinks he's our only son."

He looked at her, jaws slightly clenched, taking another long deep breath. "Wow. That's heavy. I remember, he was so tiny, lying in the crib. In a way, I guess I can understand my father's decision. But to never tell my brother about me? I... I want to know his reasoning."

"Your father is a wonderful, hardworking, courageous man who can't deal with the hurt and pain. His decisions are rash, and he's quick to make judgment. Mario is just like him. Losing you almost took your father off this earth. I think pushing the memory of you to the back of his mind was the only way he could survive and make something of him-self. He owns a lucrative landscape business and has taken good care of us."

In dazed exasperation, he hesitated with bewilderment. "It must've been awful for you to pretend all these years."
He opened the photo album, searching for another glimpse of the man he thought might be Mario. She stopped him before he turned to the next page. She pointed to the man wearing a graduation cap and gown.

"This is Mario? He resembles Dad a lot," thinking that he only had Cara's picture and nothing of his brother. He wondered what Mario looked like today.

"He's slightly taller than you, good-looking, loves sports, and he keeps himself in good shape. He and Cara have a little girl named

Ashley." Her pleasant smile quickly faded. "But now, his family has
been disrupted. His wife left him. He's angry most of the time."

A muscle flicked angrily at his jaw and he grew uneasy. He could
sense her pain. "I'm sorry to hear that."

"I know you are. You were going to tell me something earlier,
something you could only tell me."

"Yes, I remember. I go by a different name and a new identity.
Because of my shaky past, I'm Giles Bennett."

"Oh," she stammered. "Giles. How interesting. Is that the name
they gave you?"

"Yes. A woman and man named Loretta and Kirk Bennett raised
me. I hated living with them, but then I got used to it." He smiled bland-
ly. "That's not all, Mother. I wear the title, Alderman. You can't tell
anyone about me, except Dad."

"My God! So my big boy has a new name and he's a Chicago
politician. This will knock Bradley off his rocker. Matthew, I mean,
Giles. I'll keep your secret. But can you tell me why I should do that?"

"It's a long story; maybe someday, I'll tell you why."

After they finished eating they left the restaurant and walked to
the hotel entrance. Alderman Bennett reserved a suite at the Hampton
Inn for Mary Lee. He used his cellular to reschedule his appointments.
He would spend the rest of the day getting re-acquainted with his birth
mom, treating her to lunch and dinner. He would show his real mom
some of Chicago's illustrious attractions.

Breathing a sigh of relief, Alderman Bennett was happy and content, if only for the moment. The thing that had mattered the most to him
was finding his birth family. That was now something that he could
check off his to-do list. Since he had turned his life around to become a
good guy, he knew he would be risking everything he'd accomplished if
his secret were to be revealed, even to a brother that didn't know he existed.

Chapter 17

Rushing back to her cubicle from the ladies' room, Cara thought about the paperwork on her desk and knew that she had a lot to do before the day ended.

The phone rang. "Hello."

"Cara, it's me," Shirley replied. "I was about to leave the building. How's it going?"

"Really well. I think I'm going to like it here." Cara was glad to hear from a friendly soul.

"That's what I like to hear. Don't forget we have a staff meeting tomorrow."

"Thanks for the reminder. Our supervisor came by to tell me. He can be a real bull in the collar at times," Cara whispered.

"Don't let him hear you say that. But you're right." Shirley's voice lulled, and then she laughed. "Just don't step on his toes and you'll be all right. He's a perfectionist and you can't bitch about it. He drives himself even harder than he drives the rest of us."

"I appreciate the warning. Sounds like someone to stay away from," Cara said. Her reply lacked a ring of finality. She almost told Shirley that Dexter Grady had called to put the moves on her early that morning while she used the copier. But she had shrugged him off, seemingly without any repercussions. *I wonder if she knows about his other side,* she thought.

"That, my dear, is up to you. He's had some kind of chip on his shoulder for years," Shirley added. "And, now I've got to run. I'm off to visit two of my agencies on the West Side."

"Well, hope the rest of your day is a good one."

Halfway through the first report, Cara couldn't help but recall the encounter that she'd had with Dexter Grady.

"How was your weekend?" he asked. His rugged good looks and toughness reminded Cara of Richard Roundtree. His eyes would look at you and take hold, and then on the other hand, squeeze you for a moment and then drop you when you least expected it, as though life on the job were a game.

"Peaceful. I went to church Sunday. How about yours?"

He had told her that his weekend would've been better had she been with him. "Oh, pay me no mind. I guess I find you so damn attractive. What's a man supposed to do?" he said.

Cara remembered thinking, "You could leave me alone and let me do my job." Instead, she told him she would take what he'd said as a compliment and she walked back to her desk. He wouldn't give up. He followed along and asked if she had a few minutes. "A few, but then I must get those reports done for you." She told him.

She didn't find it difficult at all deciding if he was serious or joking. There was an edge of sarcasm to certain things he said, except for this time.

"So, how's the job so far?"

"Pretty good, actually. I plan to visit the agency on Forty-fifth Street tomorrow to review their operations."

"Oh, by the way, been meaning to ask you something."

"Really? What?" She sensed it wasn't about the job and started to feel uneasy around him.

"I've got this cocktail party tomorrow night. I'd love it if you could come with me," he announced, brushing against her arm. "It's a party for a police detective, Lester Miller."

A multitude of thoughts raced through her mind. *I won't turn this one down. Lester is someone I need to talk to. Maybe I can pick his brains. I have to believe that Lester will tell me why Mario was so sure that I'd cheated on him. It's a chance I'll take.*

"I hate to say…." she said, wondering what he must think of her now.

"I refuse to take no for an answer," Dexter interrupted.

"Why me? I'm sure you know a bunch of ladies you could take," Cara said jokingly, but cautiously. "It's not my style to mix business with pleasure, but this time.... All right, I'll make an exception." Her voice was uncompromising, yet oddly gentle.

He seemed pleased by her answer and he finally walked away.

Cara rushed to finish everything on her list for that day, thinking that she must be out of her mind to go out with a supervisor. She couldn't let that slip in judgment bother her now, especially with things going her way for a change.

———

Cara drove to work the next morning, dressed in a three-piece cherry suit just right for the office and yet stylish enough for the party. Her hair was styled perfectly in a rolled ball, and she wore a mild touch of makeup, and soft blush on her lips. She brought along matching heels, 14-carat gold matching earrings and necklace, a beaded crème purse, and toiletries.

As she turned to enter the outer drive, she noticed that the black late model car that had followed her since she left home was still behind her. *Am I being paranoid or what this time?*

She slowed enough to read the personalized license plate, *AGIA*, and to see that the driver had medium brown complexion, wore sunglasses, a suit, and a tie. *Who is he and why is following me?*

By the time she'd reached Michigan Avenue, the stalker suddenly disappeared.

A short while later, she parked her car and entered the building.

Quickly, she stepped inside her cubicle, hoping for a small amount of privacy.

Moments afterward, there he stood smiling.

"Good morning, Ms. Fleming. Did I see you come in earlier?"

"Hello, Mr. Grady. I'm not sure if you did or did not."

"You look very nice," he said.

Cara smiled, thinking he couldn't decide what he wanted to call her. "Thanks," she murmured while starting to read the memo on her desk.

"I don't know how I did it, but I'm glad I changed your mind."

She smiled. "What time shall we leave?"

"Six o'clock. I should let you get to work," Grady uttered.

"Good idea. I'll be ready."

Cara reviewed job procedures, department memos and typed reports. Happily, she finished her work before noon.

Then she thought about **MattIwas** and checked her e-mail on the office computer. To her surprise he had sent her a message. Opening it, she read, "I'm out of town for a few days, don't know when I'll return. I'll get back to you later. Hope life is treating you well. In the meantime, here's something to keep on your mind: There's hope when something has died. There's hope when you think you're down and out and have nowhere to turn. There's hope when you've been lied on and had to give up your happiness and peace of mind. Best regards, Matt."

After she'd read his message over and over again, she was pleased that at least he hadn't fallen off the face of the earth. He cared enough to give her inspiration. She was impressed.

While she ate her lunch at her desk, she thought some more about Matt. *Why did he stop sending me e-mails? I want to help him find his birth mother, but he doesn't seem to care anymore.*

The rest of the afternoon went perfectly. No interruptions from Grady and no phone calls. Before touching up her appearance, she checked on Jennifer. She let the phone ring more than enough, only to get no answer.

At exactly six o'clock, Dexter Grady was waiting on the first floor near the main entrance. Cara copped a friendlier-than-thou attitude for a few seconds, wondering what she'd talk about with Dexter. *I still can't believe I'm doing this. It's definitely the first and last time.*

Dexter stepped forward wearing a tailored dark blue suit and tie. "Well, hello again. Ready?"

"Hi. Ready as ever. I'll follow you there," Cara replied.

"It's better that you ride with me. I'll see to it that you get back to your car safely."

"Oh, I don't know. I think I'll just follow you."

"Okay," he said, shrugging his shoulders. "If you insist. It's only a few blocks away."

Dexter had deemed Cara an enigma. No matter how hard he tried, he couldn't figure her out. Why would a woman built like she was and with a face like hers pursue a career in education, of all things? She could have made a fortune modeling at a New York fashion agency.

A few minutes later, he pulled into the entranceway of the John Hancock parking deck, spiraling up and around several times until he found a parking space. Cara was right behind him. They parked and got out of their cars.

"Well, I see you made it without any problems," he cackled.

"Yep! It was a little scary at first."

Moments later, they boarded the elevator.

"Brace yourself. The ride to the ninety-sixth floor takes about three minutes."

"Oh. Sounds a little scary if you ask me." She felt the push upward, and watched the numbers increase on the display. She held her hands together tightly. Cara felt pain in her ears. It reminded her of the way her ears felt during takeoff on a flight.

They both walked inside the semi-quiet elegant *Signature Lounge.* Soft music played. Men dressed in police uniforms and women clad in dressy attire were busy chatting, strolling about, and enjoying themselves.

Right behind them came Renita Dates, an attractive yet more-than-casual friend of Dexter's. Her spoon-shaped body was clad in a blue suit. With her was a short, petite lady wearing a very stylish, sleeve-less black jumpsuit and heavily adorned with a sparkling gold necklace and earrings.

"I see you made it, Dexter," Renita greeted them.

"Hi," he replied. "Nice to see you. Meet Cara Fleming."

"Hello. It's nice to meet you," Cara said, in her usual friendly manner.

"Likewise," Renita replied. "Dexter and Cara, this is Keisha Hayes, wife of Commander Stanley Hayes from Area 2." Keisha and Stanley had been happily married for ten years. She was his stronghold, the woman behind a successful black man who had made it near the top on the Chicago police force. Stanley had been Lester's mentor and boss. He took Lester under his wings like a brother, guiding his career from a rookie cop to detective in less than six years. The cocktail party for Lester had been Stanley and Keisha's idea. Lester had been awarded a medal of honor for his investigative work on a high profile case. He ingeniously cracked a case involving the mysterious disappearance of a young girl, linking the crime to the perpetrator.

"Hi. It's nice to meet you and thanks for coming. We're expect-ing a nice turnout for Lester," Keisha said, gleefully.

"When is the guest of honor due to arrive?" Grady probed.

"Seven-thirty," Keisha replied, checking her watch.

"It's a surprise party, but you know how word can get around. We think he's aware," Renita said.

"What a lovely thing to do," Cara said.

Keisha looked at Dexter and Cara and said, "Hope you guys enjoy the party. There's plenty of food and the drinks are on the house."

Just as the two ladies started to walk away, Dexter glanced at Renita. "Check you later," he said, eying her guardedly. He knew he'd have some explaining to do later, but on the other hand, he relished the thought that this was payback on Renita, even though it hadn't been his original plan. For a year or so, Dexter and Renita, a two-year rookie cop assigned to domestic violence, had dated each other purely for sexual relief outside their respective marriages. It was understood that when in public, they would behave professionally, regardless.

While leading Cara to a window table, Dexter was forced to get his mission right. He recalled a phone conversation with Joe Michaels two days ago. "Grady?"

"Yeah, speaking. How can I help you?"

"I need some information about a new employee, Cara Fleming."

"What do you want to know about her?"

"I'll take whatever you can get."

"The dirty, low down, stuff you can't get on your own, being the clean guy you are. Right?"

"It's very important, Grady. I need it ASAP."

"In that case, I'll get right on it."

Since that day, Dexter Grady had to work fast to put his plan in action. Cara hadn't been an easy subject to know. Phone calls, constant attention to her on the job, lunch invitations, nothing seemed to work until now. Although he was glad that he'd found something that appealed to her, he wondered why she finally accepted an invitation from him.

Dexter threw Cara a coy smile as he got up to go to the bar.

A few minutes later, he returned to their table holding two glasses of white wine.

Dexter sipped his wine and watched her for a minute. "Are you having fun?"

"Yeah. I must admit, it feels good to get out of the house."

The wine had started to warm his insides and his spirits, but she'd seemed preoccupied.

"You wouldn't object to a question or two, would you?" he asked, and she turned to look directly in his eyes.

"Ask away."

"The word at the office is that you're the loner type. You keep to yourself."

Cara grinned. "It's true. I'm not there to socialize."

Initially they talked about the job, how she was getting along with the staff, and her prior experiences as a teacher in the South.

"I am curious about something. Are you married or single?

"For the moment, I'm separated from my husband."

"Too bad. How did he ever let you leave him?"

"Sorry, but I don't care to answer that one. How about you? What's your marital status?" Cara asked.

"I'm hitched. Been like that for fifteen years."

"I thought as much. It's good that this party isn't a date situation," she said.

"Why'd you say that?"

"I respect the sanctity of marriage. It's as simple as that."

Dexter smiled. *That being the case, why is she out with me tonight?* he wondered. The fact of the matter was that he thought he had her all figured out. Although, she appeared to be prim and proper, he figured she'd eventually come around.

"What if you met and fell in love with a married man? What would you do?" he asked.

"Stick to my guns."

"Ever heard the old saying that there's always a first time for everything?" he asked.

By now she was bordering on boredom. It's no wonder why she felt the need to put a stop to his interrogation. "Dexter, so that you'll know, I'm different. I loved my husband very much, was faithful to him from the day we met and fell in love. For some reason, I'm still faithful. How does that grab you?"

Shrugging his shoulders, he replied, "You're definitely not like most women. That's for sure. Seems to me your husband let a good woman get away."

"Thanks. I appreciate that."

"Do you have children?"

"A daughter. She's three, more like going on twenty-three."

Dexter excused himself and stepped away to chat with a few people.

At the same time, she got up and walked to the window. She looked at the vast expanse of blue water. She remembered that when she'd browsed the Internet, she'd noted important facts about Chicago's John Hancock building. It was a few floors from being the tallest building in Chicago, second only to the Sears Tower. It housed everything from ground floor shops and restaurants to corporate offices and residential apartments. As breathtaking as it was, her view from the ninety-sixth floor was that of a child gazing at a miniscule toy play arena. The people and the cars that moved on the street below seemed like tiny ants.

She started to think about Lester and remembered that before the split, Mario had never introduced her to him. He promised to do so at the annual Police Ball in December.

At 7:35 p.m. everyone stood and rendered applause, as the tall, lean and extremely handsome detective stepped into the lounge alone. Her heart tripped into overdrive. His true age hidden by his unblemished light-skinned face reminded her of someone famous. He wore a dark brown suit that radiated sex appeal.

Mario had surely played down Lester's looks, she thought.
Dexter Grady returned to their table. He'd rubbed Renita the wrong way. Unable to tell her the truth about why he was with Cara, he needed to regroup.
"Hi. I'm back. Missed me?"
She spoke to him, thinking, *No way, Jose.*
Then she focused her attention back on Lester. He strolled about the room, shaking hands with the guests. Then he stopped at Cara and Dexter's table.
"Dexter, my man, how's it going?" Lester asked.
"Hey, I can't complain. Congratulations on your award."
"Thanks," he said quickly, while glancing at Cara. "Hello," he

said, in a slightly deeper voice.

"Hello," she replied.

"Oh, excuse my manners," Dexter stammered. He quickly introduced them. For a moment, he noticed that Lester seemed to want to say more, but instead, he just nodded his head and excused himself to the next table.

Dexter took Cara's arm in a possessive manner.

"Would you care to dance?"

"I suppose it would be all right."

They danced, not too close, to "One Moment In Time" by Whitney Houston. But all Cara could think about was how she was going to get Lester alone, just for a few minutes. It was now or never.

When the song ended, Dexter left to get more wine and Cara returned to their table. Alone again, she started to feel awkward. By chance, she looked up seconds later. Lester had returned. Was it her imagination or did their eyes lock every time they looked at each other? For a moment, they only gazed at each other, both of them obviously thinking about something different.

"Ah! You're alone, finally," Lester said. "Mind if I ask you a personal question?"

"No, not at all," she replied, noticing the faint light that twinkled in the depths of his light brown eyes.

"I have a friend; his name is Mario. Are you...?"

"Yes, I'm the one, Detective Miller," she announced, feeling more at ease.

"Really?" he questioned while blushing. "Please, call me Lester. As they say, it's a small world at times." He folded his hands together.

"So, how're you doing?" He sat down across from her.

"I'm okay," she said and smiled. "Actually, the main reason I'm here with Mr. Grady, of all people, is because I need your help. Only I couldn't tell him that."

"Is that right?"

"He's my supervisor. For some reason, after several attempts to take me to lunch, he approached me yesterday about a cocktail party. He said it was a surprise party for you. Of course, I accepted his offer."

"Well, on that note, I'm glad we finally met. So, how can I help you?"

"It occurred to me," she said, moving around in her seat, "that as Mario's friend, you could possibly answer some questions for me."

As he studied Cara more intently, Lester realized that Cara was even more beautiful in person. With a gentleness that surprised even him, Lester merely touched her hand with confident, but careful fingers. He figured that for her to go to such lengths to meet him, it had to be important.

"I hate what happened to you guys and if there's anything I can do..." he said, gently but timely pulling away.

"I was hoping you'd say that," she said, politely.

"So, how're you doing otherwise?"

"Mostly okay now, but lately, I have reason to believe I'm being stalked."

"Really? What happened?"

After she explained her reasons, Lester pulled a business card from his jacket pocket. "Take this and call me soon. We'll talk." He took out another card and asked her to write her phone number and address on the reverse side.

"I don't know what to say," she said, feeling relieved. "You're a nice guy, just like Mario said you were."

He threw her a reassuring smile. Just then Dexter walked to the table and she got quiet.

"Hey man, take care of this lady," Lester said, without reservations. "She's precious cargo."

———

As Lester drove home from the party, he soon realized that Cara could be in danger. In any case, learning the truth about the Fleming marital situation had piqued his interest.

He walked inside his condo at 10:45 p.m. and called her.

"Hi. This is Lester."

"Well, hello," she said, sounding surprised.

"I noticed you and Grady left the party early. Did you get home okay?"

"Yes, it was his idea to leave, actually. It couldn't have come at a better time for me."

"Good. You got rid of him and you're home safe and sound. We need to talk about this stalking matter. The sooner the better."

"I agree. When did you have in mind?"

"How's tomorrow night, say seven o'clock at my apartment? I'll whip up a gourmet dinner and we'll talk then."

Without hesitation, she gingerly blurted, "Dinner? That isn't necessary. The most I'd hoped for was a chat over the phone or...."

"Or, what?" he gently interrupted her. "For my friend's wife, that just won't do."

"Okay, then dinner it is."

"Terrific. Looking at the address you gave me, I'm only a few blocks away from you. Is seven o'clock okay?"

"Really? How close are you?" she asked.

"7447 South Shore Drive."

How interesting, she thought, remembering that Joe Michaels lived in the same building. "I see. Okay. I'll be waiting."

At eleven o'clock, just when she was thinking about her dinner for the next night with Lester, her phone rang. It startled her. It was Jennifer and as much as Cara loved talking to her, she hated getting late calls. It turned out that Jennifer only wanted to find out about her date. Cara told her that it went well and that, to her surprise, she had met Mario's detective friend.

When Cara tried to get Jennifer to share things about her own situation, Jennifer merely said that things had gotten better between her and Duncan.

Chapter 18

Bradley had become emotionally traumatized since he learned that Matthew was alive. But in one sense, he was relieved and happy. The son he'd buried out of his mind and his heart was back. His son was a man with a new identity and a sense of purpose guiding him. Despite the misfortunes thrown his way, he had somehow become a powerful political figure in Chicago, of all places.

As Bradley sat on the patio he stared at the surroundings and tried to sort his feelings. He remembered that during the drive from the airport, Mary Lee had filled him in on the details. "Matthew has your strength and determination to succeed, but physically he's the spitting image of me, Bradley." Her words made him feel like his world was about to disintegrate all over again. Like the world he once knew after Matthew was kidnapped.

As Bradley moped around the house, he wondered how he would explain Matthew's emergence, especially to Mario? He cared what others would think, too. His reputation for truth and integrity, and for being a devoted husband and father, a church-going man, and a respected member of his community was about to crumble.

He'd also lost face with his wife, the woman who delivered the same son twice, *in birth and from death.* Even his command over her had weakened.

Around three o'clock on Monday afternoon, Mary Lee prepared lunch for them... tequila chicken wings, black-eyed peas, bacon risotto and rolls. She knew Bradley hadn't eaten anything all day.

"Come and eat, Bradley. You need to keep your strength up," she said, watching him relax in a chair on the patio.

Without a word, he got up, walked to the kitchen and sat in his favorite chair.

"What're we going to do about this?" Mary Lee asked.

"I'm all out of answers," he finally said, lifting a wing to his mouth.

"Do what I did. Go and see your son. Talk with him," she pleaded.

"You think Matthew would come to Memphis?"

"Just call him, Bradley. You might be surprised."

They ate the rest of the meal mostly in silence. Mary Lee noticed how quickly he cleaned his plate.

"Feeling better?"

"Yeah, somewhat." He got up and walked back to the patio.

She followed. "As I see it, you haven't committed any crime. My God, losing Matthew like we did was too much to handle back then. You did what you thought was best for us. I'm just as much to blame. Remember, I agreed to go along with the plan, keeping his existence a secret," she expounded.

"Now it's come back to haunt us," he added

"Isn't it time we tell the truth?" Mary Lee asked, looking at him intently. "Haven't we let guilt shadow our lives long enough? Explain why we did it and let the chips fall where they may."

"You're always right about such things. As my wife, you've always been the conscience for wisdom and for doing the right thing. You never wanted to keep him a secret, but you did, in honor of our vows. I'll always be grateful to you for that," he said.

Mary Lee put her arms around him and held him tightly. "I love you, too, Bradley. Everything is going to be all right," she whispered, remembering that he always showed her that he loved her, but had over the years found it difficult to say the words.

"You've always been there for me and you have suffered enough. Now I'm compelled to be honest with you, first," he said.

"Oh? About what?" Mary Lee sat looking at him afraid of what he'd say.

"Mario is seeing another woman. Her name is Paula Coles."

"No. Really? Did you meet her?"

"Yep," he replied softly. "And, there's something else. I acted like a fool with Cara over the telephone. I'm too ashamed to face her again. I can't believe I did that."

"None of this has been easy for you, has it? We'll get through this together, Lord willing," she offered.

Mary Lee had left their phone number with Matthew. She believed Matthew was afraid to make the first step. Just as she was about to go inside the house, she stopped and looked back at her husband.

"When you're ready, call your eldest son in Chicago. Talk to him before it's too late."

On those words, Bradley got up and walked inside the house and dialed Alderman Bennett's cellular, thinking *it's now or never*. There was no answer after four rings. Then Bradley heard Matthew's voice on the answering service, "This is Alderman Bennett, leave your name and number. I'll get back to you as soon as I can."

"Matthew, this is your father, Bradley Fleming. Call me back, Son."

———

By the time Alderman Bennett returned to his office late Tuesday, he'd decided not to contact Current Wife again. He counted on his mother keeping her word. All he cared about was seeing his father and getting to know him. Nothing else and no one else seemed to matter to him now.

Somehow, he felt he would meet Mario. Someday, they'd become friends. The problem was that he didn't know how to do that just yet. "I'd love him like a brother; only he wouldn't know I was his brother," he whispered softly behind closed doors.

Then he decided to check his voice mail messages. He had several. When he got to the one from Bradley, he stopped listening and dialed the number Mary Lee gave him.

"Hello, Fleming residence," the faint male voice answered.

"This…this is Matthew," Alderman Bennett said, trying to sound impressive.

"Oh, my God! My son, it's really you!" There was silence for a moment. Seems neither man could think of what to say next.

Finally Alderman Bennett spoke, "It's good to hear your voice, Dad."

"Likewise," Bradley coughed. "Matthew?"

"Yes, it's really me, Dad. How you doing?"

"Fine, now. I just wanted to say," Bradley panted, "this is the greatest thing to happen since man landed on the moon. I missed you, Matthew. My life was never the same after they took you away."

"I can't wait to finally see you again, Dad."

"Why don't you get on a plane and come home? Me and your mom will be glad to have you."

"Okay, I'll leave tomorrow morning," Alderman Bennett promised, expecting a response. When there was none, he wondered whether his father was overcome with emotions, or if he'd stepped away to call his mother to the phone. What he didn't know was that she had walked outside to water the flowers.

"Dad! Dad! Are you there?"

Chapter 19

Around five-thirty that afternoon, Cara unlocked her apartment door and was glad to be home. She thought that her day had gone exceedingly well, considering that Dexter didn't come to work. The rumor at the office was that he took a sick day. However, Cara suspected that he had probably taken the day off to be with Renita. Whatever the case, when he returned to the office, Cara was prepared to thank him for inviting her to the party and to make sure he understood it was the first and last time she'd go out with him.

After calling to see how Ashley was doing, she took a long, hot shower and dressed for her dinner engagement with Lester. Then she checked the kitchen calendar and noticed she had a hair appointment on Friday. There was also a notation to mail the electric and phone bills by the end of that week. On Saturday, she'd penciled in "have lunch with Jennifer."

She walked across the living room and pulled back the shade. Cara saw a shiny dark-blue sedan pull up. At the mirror, she quickly checked her appearance. She wore an off-white silk skirt and a deep pink embroidered blouse, an outfit that highlighted her figure. Her long dark brown hair had been brushed and swept out behind her in a healthy mane.

She had on low-heeled, off-white sandals that exposed her fresh pedicure.

She grabbed her purse and locked her door.

Lester got out of the car and opened the door for her.

"Hi," he said, throwing her an admiring smile. "You look nice."

"Thank you." She smiled the feline smile that was so perfect for her voice. She slid her body into the squeaky-clean, air-conditioned car.

When Lester got in and closed his door, he looked at her and smiled once more. She noticed that he was even more handsome than the night before. His warmth surrounded her as he reached over her to get a CD from the glove compartment. She caught a whiff of his cologne. *Wow, he smells good,* she thought.

"Shall we proceed?" Lester asked, giving her a warm smile.

"Yes. I can't wait to taste your cooking." She breathed it all in, feeling comfortable around him and she speculated as to what kind of person he really was. For starters, he seemed like a normal guy who had normal feelings and one who cared about others. He appeared to possess a gentle spirit, uncommon for a man, and he spoke with kind words while smiling often. Also, he seemed to give full attention to what would please her, making sure she felt safe and at ease around him. So far, so *good,* she thought.

Lester's building was a skyscraper with twenty floors or more. The building security guard seemed to eye them as they walked through the lobby to the elevators. Walking down the hallway on the eighteenth floor, she felt as if she were in an office tower or hotel. He turned the lights on and held the door opened, letting her enter ahead of him.

"Here we are. Make yourself comfortable. I'll get the wine," he said and hurried off to the kitchen.

Cara noticed the buff colored trousers and a black Pierre Cardin shirt that he wore. She sat and gazed around his tastefully decorated living room. Everything, especially the papered walls in soft earth tones, the vertical blinds and the off-white carpet, impressed her.

He returned holding two decorative glasses of white wine.

"Hope you like it," he said, handing one of the glasses to Cara. They sat facing other æ Cara on the couch, Lester in an armchair to the side.

She took a couple of sips. "Umm, I like it." She gazed at the surroundings again. She admired the blooming peace lily in the corner of the room. "Your apartment looks really fashionable. Did you have help decorating it?"

"No. It was a matter of putting what I liked with what worked well together."

"Well, you've done a terrific job for an amateur."

"Thanks," he said, smiling again.

"What's for dinner?" Cara decided to speak.

"Steak, double-baked potato, and veggies of course."

"Hmmm! Sounds terrific."

"Good. Now while I get dinner together, make yourself at home. I have a pretty decent CD collection. Why don't you play some music for us," he suggested.

"Sure. I think I can do that."

He left the room and she put the wine glass down on the black and gold coaster and stepped to the music center. She chose a Lionel Hampton CD. The system at first seemed a bit complicated. She scanned the features... a six-disk CD Player, with Dolby and Pro-Logic settings.

Soon, smells of onions and garlic wafted from the kitchen. As if on cue, she looked toward the kitchen and saw Lester looking at her, holding his wine glass. She wondered how long he'd been standing there. Somehow she had to focus and remember their reason for being together. It wasn't because she was lonely or because he was lonely. The reason was to pick his brains, Cara reminded herself. He knew more than she did about the reasons for her marital mess.

She located the play button on the CD player and adjusted the volume. Once more, she glanced toward the kitchen door and noticed Lester watching her.

"Lionel was a good choice. Is jazz a favorite of yours?"

"Yes, it is. Is it for you, too?" she asked.

"Oh, sure. Jazz and R&B are my favorites. Care to join me while I finish the steaks?"

Cara settled at the dining room table and admired the table centerpiece... flaming candles in brass holders, over a soft metallic gray tablecloth.

"How do you like your steak?"

"Well done," she answered with slight hesitation. She recalled the last time she ordered a steak that way it came back burnt.

While watching Lester skillfully handle the steaks, she wondered why Mario never talked much about Lester. *Was the detective dating someone? Was he ever married? Did he have children?* A few minutes later, he plated the meal and delivered it to the table. Then he took the salad bowls from the refrigerator and placed them on the table, poured more wine and sat down across from her.

Before taking a taste of her food, she quickly bowed her head and blessed the meal.

Afterward, Lester opened his eyes and lifted his wine glass in a toast.

"Cheers!"

She sipped her wine and cut a small piece of her steak. He doused his steak with A-1 sauce, sprinkled some salt and cut a portion into cubes.

"Wow, you're quite a chef."

"I'm glad you like it," he said.

"According to Mario, you're fantastic in the kitchen." She smiled and left it at that. The mere mention of Mario's name seemed to reopen wounds that were still too deep. After a brief moment of silence, she did talk openly with him about other things during the meal.

Twenty minutes later, he wiped his mouth. "The guest bath is down the hall. Make yourself at home. Oh, feel free to check out the place; do whatever ladies do while I clean up," Lester chuckled.

"Thanks."

Inside the bathroom, Cara noticed the round wicker basket that sat in the middle of the aqua ceramic covered vanity. Colorful towels, an unopened toothbrush, breath mints and cologne spray were neatly arranged. She had to smile at the tidiness.

She stepped silently toward his bedroom. It was furnished in much the same way as the rest of the apartment, with pearl white walls and muted gold-carpeted floors. The oversized master bedroom had a king-size bed, a matching nightstand and an armoire. The floor length windows revealed a full view of Lake Michigan. The light from the evening sunset spilled straight over blue water and through the floor-to-ceiling windows, tinting the room with gold and orange colors on one side of the room. The walls showcased professionally done landscapes.

A few minutes later Cara entered the kitchen. Lester was putting the last item into the dishwasher. He washed his hands, while keeping his gaze on her. He thought about what he knew about her. Cara had always been a major topic of conversation between he and Mario. Vivid images of her had taken shape in his mind, highlighting her beauty inside and out. Now, he figured he knew why his friend hadn't wanted his lovely wife exposed to other men. But now, he'd decided he wouldn't let that bother him. If nothing else, he would get to know Cara and let her interrogate him.

"Did you find everything okay?"

"Yes, I did. The view is simply breathtaking. It must be nice," she said.

"It's my haven away from the world of robbers, murders and drug dealers."

She smiled, walked back to the living room, and sat down.

Lester soon joined her and sat in the chair. He realized that Cara was remarkably able at tossing the conversational ball. They talked about everything but Mario, until he could stand it no longer.

"Not that you want to know, but I saw Mario on the courts two weeks ago," he said with his detective face on.

"Really? How is he?" she asked, feeling as if the air in her balloon had been released.

"Okay, I suppose. I never beat him at tennis," he joked.

"That's your friend, always the competitor." Cara exhaled a couple of deep breaths and looked away for a few moments. "In case you don't already know, we haven't spoken a word to each other since we parted."

Lester arched his eyebrows mischievously. "You miss him?"
She gathered her thoughts. "There're times I can't help it. But then that's expected, don't you think?"

"He wouldn't admit it, but I know he misses you, too. Perhaps he couldn't bring himself to tell me that. He was heartbroken the night that we talked."

"Well, so was I, Lester. Does anyone ever stop to think how this thing affected me? Honestly, I've been to hell and back a million times over."

He studied her for a moment and then he touched her hand gently. "I know this has been rough on you. You can talk to me. Sometimes, the temptation to pass judgment is just that. However, you can trust me."

Cara's temperament cooled down a bit. "I'm innocent. Someone framed me!" she exclaimed.

"Did he tell you what the caller said?"

"Nothing that explained why he felt the evidence was so convincing. Can you imagine that? I asked how he could believe an anonymous caller. His crazy answer was, and I quote, 'Based on what he said, I know he wasn't lying.'"

"I don't mean to upset you, but do you have a peculiar birthmark anywhere on your body?" Lester asked.

"Unfortunately, I do. Why?"

"The caller described it in detail. He also said the two of you had plans to get married. Oh, yeah, there were also photos of you and this guy," he said, watching her reaction. "Mario didn't mention that either?"

"Pictures? He told me absolutely nothing. I wouldn't confess to a lie, not even to save the marriage. So, he got mad again and ordered me to leave our home."

"No, he didn't! What was he thinking?"

"If I knew, I'd tell you that, too."

"Well, I thought running after you with a gun was a stupid thing to do and I told him so."

"When did he talk to you?" she asked.

"Two days later. We met at the Due Drop Inn. I suggested that Mario work things out with you. I thought he would take my advice."

"Want to know the truth? He was hell-bent on believing I was guilty."

"I see what you mean."

"Lately, I've started to doubt whether the anonymous call was real. Maybe Mario needed a reason to end our marriage. As I see it, no one other than he, my parents, and my doctor know about the birthmark," she added.

Lester shook his head. "So the guy ordered you to leave? Wow. I'm so sorry."

Suddenly she was driven to tell him more. "Three weeks later I moved out." She finished her wine. "To top it all off, he's disowned our three-year-old daughter."

He stared in complete surprise. "Why?"

She raised her eyes to find him watching her. "Oh, Lester," she blushed awkwardly, "it's too embarrassing to repeat."

"I'm a professional prodder. Don't feel like you have to tell me if you don't want to."

Then she got quiet and seemed to be miles away. It gave Lester cause to wonder whether there was another man in her life.

"Are you dating anyone?"

"No. I'm still a married woman."

"I'm impressed," Lester said. He stood up, smiling with satisfaction, thinking that she was a good woman just as he'd imagined. "I'll be back; hold that thought," he added, easing his way to the bathroom.

A few minutes later, he returned. "For purely selfish reasons, I'm glad it's taken this long to meet you Cara."

She wanted to smile at that, but in her state of mind, the memory and the pain controlled her actions. "Would you believe he's already filed for a divorce?"

"Really?" Lester said.

He got up and sat beside her. He wanted to put his arms around her, to comfort her, but it would have taken some major adjustment. Instead, he took her hand in his and held it for a few minutes.

"For what it's worth, I believe you. Charge it to my gut instinct, but know that I do."

"You sure?" Cara asked.

"Yes, and that's my final answer about this matter."

"Thanks. Now why do I want to believe you?" she replied.

"Humph, blame it on your instincts. You've got some good ones. So, what's this about someone stalking you?"

She told him everything. "I got the license plate number. Can you find out who the car is registered to?"

"You bet. First thing tomorrow, I'll take care of it."

"Dinner was just superb and I've enjoyed our talk," she said checking her watch.

On that note, Lester escorted her out of the apartment and locked the door.

Ten minutes later he parked and walked Cara to her apartment door. They stood there for a moment.

"I hope we can get together again. I could use a good friend, too," he said, staring at her.

"That would be great, Lester. It might be nice to have a male friend."

"Cool. I'll call you tomorrow, okay?"

"Sure. Good night and thanks for everything," she said graciously.

Cara turned the key to open the door and walked into her apartment. She decided to check her Caller ID. Two unknown calls and one from her parents registered on the display. She had to laugh, wondering what the unknown caller must've thought listening to her tough words.

Thinking it uncommon for her mother to phone after nine o'clock at night, she returned the call.

"Hello," Naomi answered.

"Mom, I just came home from a dinner outing. Is everything okay?"

"Mario's father had a heart attack two days ago. He's in the intensive care unit at Memorial Baptist."

Chapter 20

Somehow it was times like these that encouraged loving, spiritual thoughts. Although Bradley's maltreatment toward Cara broke her heart, it was not the time to feel uncaring. Her thoughts filtered back to that night. *You've ruined his life. I promise you that I'll see to it that you lose custody of my granddaughter. You are unfit to raise that child.* She prayed for her ailing father-in-law.

Just before she left work, Lester called. He told her that the license plate belonged to Alderman Giles Bennett.

"Are you serious? Why do you suppose he'd want to follow me?"

"Cara, is there something you haven't told me?"

She brought him up to speed about the accident and how'd she learned Joe Michaels' relationship to Alderman Bennett. "My girlfriend's husband has worked with him on some projects."

"Can I come to your place this evening? We need to talk some more."

"Yes, of course. I can whip up something quick to eat."

"Great, but since this is last minute, don't put yourself out for me," he said, pausing. "I'm not a fussy guy, okay?"

At 6:45 p.m., he rang her doorbell and she welcomed him inside.

"You have a neat and charming place," he said.

"Thanks."

She filled him in on the strange details of how she landed her new job.

"What a story. Seems to me, you have an anonymous benefactor. Course, that sort of thing is commonplace here." His brows were set in a straight line. "What's the church member's name?"

"Barbara Rhodes. She's the administrative assistant to the pastor."

"What church do you belong to?" Lester asked, trying to suppress emotion from showing on his face at the mention of Barbara's name. "Turner Chapel A.M.E. Church. Why?"

"Oh, just asking." A warning voice whispered in his head. The thought of having to question Barbara left his face clouded with uneasiness. *She's the last person I need to face, especially in such a delicate matter as this,* he thought. "The pieces all seem to fit."

"Can you explain what you mean by that?" Cara asked, hesitating.

"That all indications point to Alderman Bennett. That he probably helped you get the job. That he's been keeping tabs on your whereabouts. Need I say more?"

She returned his frank and admiring look with a smile. "As strange as it seems, you could be right. If it's true, I want to know why," Cara replied.

"So do I. Politicians don't do favors without expecting something in return. But guess what? As far as they're concerned, you're in the dark...in the shadow of someone's brilliance."

They exchanged a subtle look of amusement.

Cara brought up the accident again...

"I don't like the sound of that," he replied.

"I wouldn't have given it a second thought if Jennifer hadn't told me that Michaels was a top member on Bennett's staff. Oh, I just remembered something else," she said excitedly. "He lives in your building." "Michaels?"

"Yes. He was kind enough to write down all of his contact information on the back of his business card.

"I'm grateful for his stupidity." Lester promised to make her safety his number one priority.

He lifted her chin and managed to pierce her uneasiness. "We're going to get to the bottom of this mess," he said firmly.

"You're a good friend, Lester."

"So are you and thanks for the meal," he said, as he cleared their plates from the table.

As they tidied the kitchen, Cara started to think some more about the alderman. *If Alderman Bennett is the culprit, what's his motive?*

Lester broke her train of thought and got her to talk about her supervisor. "You said some things that night at my party that left me puzzled. Be careful around him. He can make trouble for you."

———

The next morning, Lester pulled out of the garage at eight o'clock and stared through the car windows at the gray clouds hanging low over the South Side. It looked like it would rain.

Later, he bought coffee and a doughnut at McDonalds. He parked and called Barbara on his cellular. After three rings he got her voice mail. He left her a message to call him at his office.

Lost in his thoughts about Cara, he continued on in the morning rush hour traffic on Stony Island Avenue. He couldn't shake the romantic attractions he felt for her. She was, without question, the most extraordinary woman he'd ever met. No woman had reached inside him and captivated his attention the way Cara had. Certainly he'd met women as beautiful as she was. He'd dated and made love to women who were just as intelligent and articulate. Yet, none of them came close to rousing the things that Cara had stirred up inside him. Without a doubt, he cared about his friendship with Mario, but not to the point of denying himself a close friendship with someone he was undeniably attracted to.

Thirty minutes later at the office, a knock at the door revived him from his thoughts.

"Come in," he said, rising to close the windows. Outside, it had begun to rain again. Thunder rumbled and Lester saw flashes of late summer lightning through the window.

Carl Jerome, an average-looking guy with a goatee and hair shaved closed to his head, entered Lester's office. He was twenty-nine and a third-year uniform officer. Although he was single and never married, he had a three-year-old son by the woman he was living with. Because of his dedication to protecting women against crime, Lester chose Jerome to coordinate the surveillance team.

"Good morning, Detective Miller. Got a minute?"

"Sure. Come on in and pull up a seat."

Officer Jerome sat down. "We're ready to get this show on the road," he said, handing Lester the schedule.

Lester read the plan... officer names, dates and times.

Officer Jerome leaned back in his chair. "As you can see, five of the boys decided to pitch in and help out with a few off-duty hours, including the weekend. Some can do more than others. They'll keep in contact using their cellular phones as the shifts change. I'm the point man to contact if there's a problem. They'll keep a detailed diary of where the subject goes, dates and times."

Lester supplied Jerome with Cara's name, address, phone numbers and a complete physical description of Cara and the car she drove.

"Occasionally, she has to travel to the South Side on job assignments. She rarely goes anywhere in the evening and weekends, except to make personal errands on Saturday. She goes to church on Sunday. She'll keep me posted if and when her schedule changes."

"Okay, I believe I got it all down," the officer said, closing his note pad.

"I can't thank you enough," Lester said, standing up and beaming with satisfaction.

"Hey, we stick together, don't we?"

"You got that right." Lester further emphasized that they pay close attention to anyone who seemed to be following her. "Get the license plate and a description of the person, if possible. Call me when you have something to report. Doesn't matter what it is or how late the hour. Oh, and make sure she stays safe," Lester said.

"Will do. Now if you'll excuse me, I'll get busy."

As soon as the officer left, Lester reviewed his notes about a murder case concerning black prostitutes who'd been strangled in the Wentworth area. As he jotted down additional notes, the shrill sound of the phone interrupted him. He started to feel a bit uneasy, thinking it was Barbara. Nevertheless, he was still comfortable with her decision to end their relationship a month ago.

"Detective Miller speaking."

"Hi. This is Barbara. I'm returning your call."

"Hello. How are you?"

"I'm doing fine. What can I do for you?"

"I have reason to believe you're in a position to help me." He was courteous and yet patronizing.

"For the life of me, I don't have a clue how I can do that, but ask anyway."

"Remember Cara Fleming?"

She muttered hastily. "Yes. Someone asked me to tell her about a city job."

"And let me guess," he replied solemnly. "They wanted to be anonymous, huh?"

"How did you know that?" Barbara asked.

"It would take too long to explain. What I can tell you is that I need to know who the person is. It involves Cara's safety."

"How so?"

"I think someone is stalking her."

"I see," she replied. "Is she in any trouble?"

"No," Lester replied.

"Is she still with her husband?"

"They're separated," he answered, trying hard to remain cordial. "From what she's told me, it's not due to any fault of her own."

"How did you get involved, Lester?"

"She came to me for help and I agreed. I understand she's a member of your church. Won't you do this for her, if not for me?"

She cleared her throat. "All right. A guy named Joe Michaels came to see me. His boss, Alderman Bennett was just doing a good deed to help a fellow citizen of the community. I didn't give it much thought. It's common knowledge that Bennett helps people, with no strings attached. He's a member of our church. He seems like a good guy. We look out for our church members."

"Yeah, I know. You did a good thing helping Cara. I honestly believe that without this new job, she wouldn't survive on her own."

"It's nice that you care. Does she know you're talking to me about this?" Barbara asked.

"No," he said, clearing his throat. "Oh, by the way, the transaction between you and Michaels is strictly off the record."

"I'm counting on it. Trouble from a politician is the last thing I need."

"Thanks. I owe you one," Lester said.

After hanging up the phone, he locked his door to think and to reflect some more about Cara. He didn't know where it all would end with her. If anything, he was going to determine Bennett's interest in her.

Chapter 21

On Saturday, Cara called her folks in Memphis and discovered that her father was off on his twice-a-month fishing trip with a neighbor, while Naomi stayed home with Ashley. When Naomi put Ashley on the phone, Cara was delighted to hear how many new words her daughter had learned. Before ending the phone call, Cara and her mother talked about Bradley's condition, which had not changed.

Looking ahead, Cara figured that she might be going home sooner than Thanksgiving, if her father-in-law passed. The thought of a funeral made her cringe. She decided to get on her computer, which usually put her in good spirits. As she checked her e-mail, suddenly she thought, *MattIwas should've returned from his trip. What's with that guy? For some reason, I can't let go that easy.* Checking her watch, she turned off the computer, locked the windows, and grabbed her purse. She locked the door and walked out of her apartment at 11:30 a.m.

She got in her car as though she didn't have a worry in the world and pulled off, looking through the rearview mirror. A few seconds later, she noticed a white vehicle pull out behind her. Her cellular rang and she answered.

"Ms. Fleming, this is Officer Jerome. I'll be your watch guard for the next eight hours."

"Good morning, Officer. Thanks for letting me know that. I'm going to the *Wok-n-Roll* restaurant in Hyde Park to meet a girlfriend."

"How nice. I'll go along, too, just for the ride," he said, jokingly.

Around noontime, Cara and Jennifer surprisingly arrived at the restaurant entrance at the same time.

"Hi, girlfriend," Cara said, giving her a hug.

"Hey, Cara. It's good to see you. How are you?" There was a slight gentleness in her voice.

"I'm doing okay, and you?"

"Wish I could say the same," Jennifer replied.

Then they walked inside. Other than a few people arriving to pick up orders, the restaurant was empty and quiet. They walked to the counter and Jennifer ordered an egg roll, shrimp-fried rice, and sweet-and-sour chicken. Cara opted for an egg roll, a small beef-fried rice, and a small chicken bok choy.

They sat down at a window table. It was a lovely sunny day. People strolled along the sidewalk; cars passed by on the busy street. Jennifer's face was set, mouth clamped and eyes fixed as she sat down. She seemed far away in thought, as the sunlight streamed through the windows.

"How're things at home?" Cara asked.

Jennifer turned to face Cara. "With what, me and Duncan?"

"Yeah. What else?"

"We live under the same roof, but sleep in separate bedrooms and we come and go as we please. Most of the time we're cold and distant toward each other," Jennifer answered.

Ten minutes later, their order was ready. They returned to sit down at their table.

"Are you sure you're happy with the way things are between you and Duncan?" Cara asked, taking out the egg roll.

"I don't know. I'm not leaving him if that's what you're thinking. Before I do that, I'll do something else."

"What's that?" Cara asked.

"Would you believe, have an affair, too? I got needs, too. It's the only thing I can think to do."

"Are you serious?" Cara questioned, sipping on her diet Coke. "As long as Duncan doesn't catch you, because it could be a reason for him to divorce you. Think about it. You'd defeat your purpose of staying with him."

"Why the hell would he care? Based on what I know, he'd welcome it. I just want to get even and at the same time, get on with my life," she replied, in a quick, firm voice. "But, I'll be damned if I'm going to walk away and lose what I've worked hard for all these years." Cara grinned. "You don't fear catching a sexually transmitted disease, or worst, AIDS?"

"That's why they make condoms. Yesterday I checked out a shop in the Loop called *Bedroom Stuff.* I've always been embarrassed by dirty bookstores and sex shops. This place is different though. You won't believe how relaxed you feel when you walk in."

"Interesting. Did you buy anything?"

"No, just looked around," Jennifer replied. "I guess I needed something to do that day. On my way out of the place, a guy hanging around the discreet entrance told me he was waiting for his girlfriend, like I needed to know. But guess what he said after that?"

"What?" Cara inquired with a snicker.

"He said there ought to be a tasteful place next door for guys. That it's not just women who find porno stores disgusting."

Then Jennifer hesitated for a moment longer, not sure if she could say the words aloud. But then she couldn't hold it any longer. "Maybe I ought to go back and get me a few play toys, including a plastic man to make it totally real. The only thing I'll get then is Plastic AIDS."

Cara laughed hard. "I suppose your fantasies can be as good as reality. Of course, I've never heard anyone say something so private, so downright funny."

After they'd finished joking around, she confided in Cara about her growing alcohol problem and how it was about to threaten her job. A few days ago, another teacher found Jennifer napping during lunchtime. A half-empty vodka bottle was partially concealed inside her purse. The teacher obviously pretended not to see the bottle and didn't say anything, except to nudge Jennifer awake and tell her the bell had sounded.

Stunned, Cara said, "I hope you'll forgive me. But I need to throw out some food for thought. You can let the words go in one ear and come straight out the other, but please hear me out," she pleaded with an air of tenderness.

Jennifer exhaled and put her fork on the plate, but not at all eager to listen.

"A woman, just like a man, has the right to be happy. You need to find courage to be strong and determined. Consider all your options before you decide to stay in a marriage that could ultimately destroy your health."

Jennifer turned away at times, hands clenched stiffly at her sides. Cara knew it was time to change the subject. "I've got something to unload. Mario told me, and I quote, 'I want your ass out of here.' So there it is, I said it. Sorry I kept that from you."

"So that's what happened?" Jennifer finally spoke. "To be honest, I thought you left him in a moment of rage."

"Not quite," Cara said, politely.

"But a grave injustice was done to you and I'm still mad as hell about it."

"True, but I'm not going to let it erode me into oblivion," she boasted. "Where there's a will, there's a way. I believe that with all my heart and soul."

"I hear you, Preacher Woman." Jennifer straightened her shoulders and cleared her throat. "Anything else?"

"Yeah. Feel up to coming to church with me next Sunday?" Cara asked.

"Oh, boy. I'm too messed up to go there."

"Okay, now let me tell you some things that I learned from my mother. You don't have to be a saint free of sin to go to church? Life is all about living and learning. It's the best place I know to learn God's Word to help guide you along the way."

"I hear you," Jennifer mumbled. Then she paused for a moment before saying, "I don't know. Maybe I feel that way because I have a problem with hypocrites, the pretenders and the want-to-be Christians."

Cara nodded and smiled. "Okay. Think about this one. Each of us has to answer to God someday. You're responsible for saving your own soul, just like everyone else. If it makes you feel any better, I admit I'm no saint either. It's okay to fall by the wayside sometimes. What's important is that we get up and try again."

Chapter 22

Mary Lee had kept a constant vigil by Bradley's bedside. Fearful that she'd lose her husband, she cried often. Flashbacks of Alderman Bennett flying to Memphis to be by Bradley's side the day before flurried her mind. He'd hoped his father would regain consciousness. It was a hush-hush trip and he wore plain-looking clothing, sunglasses and a white bibbed cap. She had introduced him to the nursing staff as a friend of the family from Mississippi.

She remembered asking him, "Won't you please change your mind about meeting Mario? He'd never forgive us if he should learn the truth," Mary Lee had whispered, unable to decide what to call him.

"That's a chance I have to take. You're a champion when it comes to keeping a lid on things. If you don't, I won't. The chance of Mario finding out are a zillion to one," he whispered back, at the same time watching Bradley. "I believe that the past is the past and that's that! Considering everything that I've done to start a new life as a respectable citizen, revealing that secret could ruin it all. It's one secret that will have to stay buried forever."

Somehow, that didn't make any sense to Mary Lee. Cooling her temper, she could only hope her son would change his mind.

Before he left Bradley's side, Mary Lee remembered that Bennett hugged Bradley and kissed his father's cheek. She always carried a disposable camera in her purse. As Bradley slept, she took a snapshot of them cheek to cheek.

The secret was more than she could handle. Matthew had turned out to be like Bradley and Mario, stubborn. She couldn't help but wonder what was wrong with her Fleming men and their pride.

Lester's secret investigation into Bennett's life revealed a clean record, not even a traffic ticket. He was single with no claims against him for child support.

Using his police connections, Lester found Bennett's social security number. Through the Internet, he performed a credit and criminal background check. He found nothing alarming, except that Bennett had earned wages using a Detroit address dating back only to 1993. What did the guy do before then? It was as if he didn't exist before then.

He decided there had to be more and he wasn't going to stop until he found it. He called a detective friend in Detroit to get him everything they had on a Giles Bennett.

By 12:30 p.m. on Monday, a four-page report came across his office fax. Three people with the name Giles Bennett were located. One was incarcerated in Michigan State Penitentiary, another was deceased, and the third one had served two years for prostitution and was released four years ago.

Lester called his detective friend back and asked for all the information they had on the third Giles Bennett. Within two hours he got the results, a phone listing for Loretta Bennett.

Immediately, he dialed the number.

"Hello. My name is Lester Miller. I'm calling from Chicago. May I speak to Mrs. Loretta Bennett?"

"This is Mrs. Bennett. How may I help you?"

"I'm calling about someone very important to you."

"Just who might that be?"

Lester sensed her hesitancy. "It's about your son, Giles. I was wondering if you'd agree to talk with me. I can fly to Detroit tomorrow morning. Just name the place and time."

"How is he? I haven't seen Giles since he was fifteen."

"He's doing quite well."

"Thank God," she said. Then she told Lester where to meet her.
"Thanks, ma'am. I'll see you tomorrow around noon."

———

Dexter Grady took a call from Joe Michaels at the office. He gave
Michaels a glorified report about Cara Fleming and it seemed to satisfy
Michaels. Further information on Cara was no longer needed. Dexter
was left wondering about Michaels' interest in Cara.

He decided to push his luck with her. Before she clocked out that
day, he fell in step with her as she walked to the water fountain. She
clutched a stack of papers in her hand.
   "Hi. I've got two tickets to see Gladys Knight and Deniece
Williams in concert this Sunday. Do me the honor and come with me,
please." he asked, jubilantly.
   There was a long pause as she studied him. She had been rehears-
ing the words in her head all afternoon, just in case he approached her.
"Mr. Grady, I hate to be rude, but I simply won't go out with you again.
Perhaps at another time or another place in my life, it wouldn't be a prob-
lem."
   "I see," he sighed deeply. "It's Lester Miller, isn't it?"
   She noticed that his smile had completely vanished. "Detective
Miller and my husband are good friends. I needed his help with some-
thing you couldn't begin to understand. That's all there is to it," she said.

Cara waited for a staff member to pass by before it was safe to
continue. "But then, why should I have to explain that to you?" She
spaced the words evenly.
   "Just wondering, 'cause women somehow fall for that guy right
off the bat. Actually, I envy him," he said, with a smirk that set her teeth
on edge. He leered at her for a few moments. "Ms. Fleming, believe it
or not, you're so transparent. Even Ray Charles can see that," he
remarked, as he walked away.

   Whatever. I just hope this is the end of you.

Chapter 23

Right before Lester boarded his flight to Detroit, he pushed the number one on his cellular phone to speed dial Cara. After she told him that Dexter Grady asked her out on another date, he was glad she'd turned him down and warned her to be careful what she did and said around her supervisor. Cara seemed pleased he was going to meet the alderman's mother and wished him a safe trip.

An hour later, Lester took a taxi from Detroit's International Airport to Bennigans on Brush Street. Inside, he walked past several booths filled with people and approached a middle-age lady sitting alone. She wore a red blazer and black skirt. Although she wore too much makeup, she looked ordinary as she stared blankly through the window

"Mrs. Bennett?"

"Yes, and you are?"

"Lester Miller. How do you do?" He held his hand out for a handshake. "Thanks for seeing me like this."

"Please. Sit down," she said in a polite voice. A waiter arrived and took his order for a cup of coffee.

"Is he in trouble again? What is it you want to know about my boy?"

"Whatever you can tell me, ma'am," Lester assured her. "In fact, he is doing just fine." She seemed relieved and calmed down.

"Giles was once a good kid turned bad. He ran away from home when he was fifteen. To this day he has never called us. After he turned eighteen, we learned that he was arrested and served time for his crimes."

"Would you like to see what he looks like now?" Lester asked, while pulling out a newspaper clipping.

"Sure."

She scanned the picture that showed three men standing at a groundbreaking ceremony. Her eyes filled with tears, as she read the short article. "This is Giles," she said, pointing at the second man from the right. "I can't believe he's a Chicago alderman," she beamed. "I never would've dreamed it."

"I can see you're proud of him."

"At least something good came out of it."

"Care to explain that?"

"It's a long story, Mr. Miller. All I care to say is poor Giles had a rough time growing up. It's a wonder he's alive today. I suppose it's okay to talk about it now that my husband is gone. God rest his soul."

"I'm sorry to hear that. When did he pass on?"

"Two years ago. He had colon cancer."

"Giles and his old man, did they get along?"

"Right. He beat the boy a lot; sometimes he went too far. All I could do was try to comfort him afterward. Guess as time went on, Giles just got tired of the beatings. I couldn't stop Kirk. I didn't dare to," she admitted while holding her head down.

"If it helps any, your husband reminds me of someone, my step-father. I guess now I know how my mother must've felt. The sad thing is that the child repeats the same cycle of abuse with his children. Even today, the problem is widespread and there seems to be no end to it. Men and women abusing children, wife abuse, you name it. The subject has received national attention."

"It's just awful if you ask me. What has all this got to do with your coming here to talk to me?"

"For some reason, your son is stalking a lady friend of mine. Someone mysteriously framed her as an adulteress. She left her husband.

Then out of the blue and using his political power, your son got her a job with the city making almost twice what she was making before. Recently he's been following her around the city."

"You sure he's the one who framed this woman?

"That's my problem. The dots don't connect."

"I don't see how I can help you. Whoever this woman is, I wouldn't know her from Adam or Eve."

"Cara Fleming is her name. She's from Memphis, Tennessee. She and her husband moved to Chicago a year ago." He noticed her facial expression change.

She pulled a photo of Alderman Bennett from her purse and passed it to Lester. "This is what he looked like when I last saw him. Have you met my son?"

"Not personally. Mind if I ask where your son was born?"

"Detroit," she blurted out nervously.

"What about his relatives, namely, brothers or sisters, cousins? Perhaps they can help me."

"He's an only child. My dead brother had a son, but he was killed in the Desert Storm war."

"What's your son's birth date?"

"March 10, 1963."

Lester calculated that he was thirty-eight. He figured he had something concrete to work with. "Now that you know where he is, do you want to see him again?"

"Yes, but only if he wants to see me. If he were to walk through the door right this minute, I'd welcome him with open arms."

"That's good to know," Lester said.

"I pray Giles is not involved in this young woman's troubles."

Lester grinned and leaned back in his seat. "If you do decide to contact your son, don't mention our meeting." He gave her one of his business cards. "You see, the alderman isn't aware that I know these things about him. It might make him nervous."

Quickly she glanced at the card and exhaled. "You're with the Chicago police? What's really going on here, Detective?"

"Just a routine check to make sure the alderman is not in any trouble. Honestly, the Chicago public thinks he's a good politician."

"That's a relief."

"So, as I said, if you can think of anything that would connect him to the Fleming name, call me. This might be your last chance to help him."

He laid a fifty-dollar bill on the table. "This should more than take care of our tab, and thanks. You've been more help than you realize."

———

Less than thirty minutes later Lester arrived at the main police headquarters. He would run a complete search on Kirk and Loretta Bennett. It was clear to him that Mrs. Bennett was hiding something. He had doubts about the alderman's birthday. It was worth it to prove his suspicions right. At best, he could secure a copy of the birth certificate.

An hour later, the results came back. From the three-page report, Lester read:

Kirk Bennett and Loretta Bennett - owned a black cosmetic retail store and a women's hair salon in Meridian, MS for fifteen years. Both were sold in 1961 for $300,000 <end of field>; no dependents <end of field> Own a home in Detroit, MI since 1969. <End of field>; Kirk, deceased 1997, arrested for spousal abuse 1970, charges dropped; <End of field>; Loretta, living, unemployed homemaker, SS recipient. <End of record>

Finally, he looked at the last page hoping that the alderman's birthday would be confirmed. The words stood out like a blinking neon sign: "Search results for male, Giles Bennett Detroit, MI born on March 10, 1963. *No results found.*

"Damn, that can't be," Lester whispered. He asked his police buddy to search police records for Meridian, MS.

Less than thirty minutes later, Lester leaned back in his chair, hands folded behind his head. He studied the second report. "Search results for male, Giles Bennett, Meridian, MS. *Found (1) record: Giles L. Bennett, born February 23, 1963 to Kirk and Loretta Bennett, subject died on November 18, 1967, Cause of death, third degree burns, child abuse.*

What the hell is going on here? Lester thought.

———

Bradley passed away at 3:45 p.m. that afternoon. Mary Lee felt as if her whole world had come tumbling down around her. After the body was removed, she managed to pull herself together and drive home. Sitting in her living room an hour later, she called Mario. Understandably upset, he promised to come home right away. Scarcely able to do anything else, she rested on the sofa flat on her back and cried some more. Suddenly she thought about her son who preferred the name Giles Bennett to his given name. Then she called him.

"Hello, Giles. How're you doing?"

"Okay," Alderman Bennett said. "I was thinking about my father before you called. How is he, by the way?"

"He's gone. Your father just passed," she said.

"Oh, no!" There was a long silence. "I'm so sorry," he said frantically. In a choked voice, he continued, "Are you okay, Mother?"

"I'm holding up okay for now."

"I wish I could be there with you," he said.

"I know. Don't suppose you'll come for the funeral?"

"No, I can't. E-mail me the arrangements. I promise to call you later that evening."

"Is that all? Please son, we...I can't lose you again."

"You won't." He paused for a moment. "I just realized you didn't call me Matthew."

"I'm playing it your way, only because you asked."

"Thanks for understanding. But it doesn't mean I'm not proud to be a Fleming or that I don't love you, Daddy, or my brother."

"Good. I needed to hear that. But you know, a mother's love is like a rubber band, stretchable as far as possible until it snaps," she whimpered.

Then she called to tell Naomi and Frank the news. Both were sad and expressed their condolences. "My friend, I'm here for you, no matter what you need. Just call me, okay?"

"I will. When this is all over, I need to have a private talk with you," Mary Lee said.

After she hung up, she took the family Bible and walked to the kitchen. It was where she sensed Bradley's presence the most. She spoke to his spirit. *I'm alone now. I've got two sons living as strangers in Chicago. I can't live with the way things are, not by myself. Oh, Bradley, you've been my life partner for so many years. What am I going to do without you?*

———

Lester arrived in Chicago around 5:45 p.m. He showered and changed into a pair of jeans, a black silk shirt and grabbed a cold beer from the refrigerator. Sitting on the sofa, he opened his beat-up attaché case and pulled out the manila folder labeled Alderman Bennett. He read his notes and printouts from the massive computer search. Three things stuck out in his mind as puzzling. Other than having had a criminal conviction, working as a car salesman for four years, and having no record of his birth, Bennett didn't have much of a past. According to the Bureau of Vital Statistics in Mississippi, Giles Bennett died when he was almost two years old. More than likely, the father was responsible. So who is this guy? Where did he come from? How did he come into this family? Lester soon realized that he was dealing with a man who had a blemished past, not to mention an illegitimate one.

Of course, the conviction record would've posed problems for him getting elected and somehow no one cared enough to do a thorough check into his background.

However, a deeper question was nagging at Lester. *Could it be that Bennett wanted Cara for himself? Frame, ruin, rescue, and claim would make sense. Nothing else seemed to jive up to this point.*

At seven o'clock the phone rang, interrupting his thoughts.
"Hi. This is Cecil."
"Hey. What you got for me?" Lester asked.
"It required some digging, but I found out how Ms. Fleming got hired. My boss, Alderman Tucker, twisted some arms. Just between you and me, I believe he did that as a favor for his friend, Alderman Bennett."

"Is that right? Okay, thanks, Cecil. I owe you one. Maybe I'll see you on the courts this weekend."

"I'll be there. Hate to cut this short. I got another stop before I go home."

"Sure. You've been a big help."

Hanging up the phone, Lester realized that Bennett had good reason to maintain his anonymity. He finished the beer, checked his watch, and saw that it was fifteen minutes to six. He needed another excuse to see Cara and decided to ask her to dinner. *Surely, she'd want to know what he had learned in Detroit,* he thought.

He dialed her number and let the phone ring three times. Then he heard her soft faint voice say, "Hi, Lester."

"Hello, are you okay? Sounds like you got a cold or something."

"I'm fine. It's Bradley Fleming. He died today." She let out a sigh.

"Gee, I'm sorry. How did you learn about it?"

"My mother. They're all torn up over it. Bradley was a good friend to my family."

He thought about Mario and how much he loved his father. It had been over a month since he hit a few balls on the court with Mario. Several attempts to reach him by phone just to see how he was doing had been unsuccessful. Lester had taken that to mean his buddy had hit pay dirt and found a new love.

"How was your trip?" Cara asked.

"Glad you asked. Feel up to grabbing a bite to eat?"

"Sure. It'll be good to get out for a change. I'll meet you there."

"I can come by to get you."

"Someone could be watching me. For both our protection, we shouldn't be seen leaving the apartment together again, at least until my divorce is final."

"Right. Okay, meet me at the *Medici* on Fifty-seventh around seven o'clock."

An hour later, Lester waited at a table facing the main entrance. The place buzzed with voices of semi-casually dressed men and women dining out for the evening. The high ceilings and cheerful Italian décor gave the place a posh setting, though the atmosphere could at times get a bit loud for in-depth conversations. Spacious but packed, in the heart of the diverse Hyde Park area, the restaurant was wildly popular with University of Chicago students. The food ran the gamut from American to Italian to Mexican, with hearty breakfasts that seemed to ease the effects of a hard night of partying.

Lester noticed Cara as soon as she entered. He gestured to her to move in his direction. She looked lovely in a solid gold blazer and black fitted skirt.

"Hi. Aren't you a sight for sore eyes," he said and hugged her casually.

"Hi, Lester. I needed that." They both sat down.

"It's good to see you." She tossed her head and gave a gentle tug at her sleeve.

Momentarily, a friendly, slender waitress appeared, poured some sparkling water into each glass, took their orders and pranced off.

"Are you going to attend the funeral?" he asked, lifting the menu from the table.

"Yes, of course. I'm taking a flight to Memphis on Friday," she replied, anxious to hear about his trip.

"Loretta Bennett was as mysterious as her son."

"Meaning?"

"She lied about his birth date and where he was born." He opened the folder, pulled out the reports on Bennett and asked her to read them.

When she finished, the salads arrived. "I don't know about you, but I'm starving," Lester said, digging into his salad. "I hear you have the mind of a Sherlock Holmes. What do you think?"

"I don't know." She quickly scanned through the documents again. "According to this, Kirk and Loretta's four-year-old biological son died due to child abuse. His name was Giles. "Oh my goodness!" she said, reading further. "Then came another child, around the same age and with the same name. He's the Giles Bennett we know."

"It's puzzling, to say the least," Lester said. "You want to know what I believe? Alderman Bennett is interested in you. All the signs are there. Since you left Mario, he's made it possible for you to make more money. He followed you around the city and he was probably behind the strange phone calls."

She didn't want to go there just yet. She tasted some of her salad while thinking about Loretta Bennett. "The more I think about it, Loretta Bennett definitely lied to you. It's as if the second Giles Bennett appeared out of thin air."

"Right," Lester said.

"Oh, and by the way, the alderman is wasting his time. I want nothing to do with him."

"Glad to hear that. Some women are attracted to powerful men who can offer them security. Maybe he figures you're one of them. He laid the foundation, and now it's payback time. When he makes his move, you'll know. And, I'll be watching."

"I feel better already. I don't need any more battles to fight. Alderman Bennett won't win this one," Cara declared with confidence.

Chapter 24

Early the next morning, Jennifer overheard a conversation between Duncan and his friend Cecil.

"Man, I need to talk to you about something in confidence. Promise you won't tell a soul?" Cecil begged.

"Sure. Go ahead," Duncan replied.

"Remember the lady we saw at Human Services?"

"Sure. She's Jennifer's best friend."

Cecil explained his involvement with framing Cara. "I told her husband that she and I were having an affair. At the time, none of it made any sense."

"I think we should talk privately. Jennifer's other habit is listening to my phone conversations," Duncan said.

"Say no more. Meet me at Gladys' Restaurant."

Thirty minutes later, the door slammed shut and Duncan pulled his car out of the driveway.

Jennifer hurriedly phoned Cara.

"Good morning. You got a few minutes?" Jennifer asked, in a voice that was fragile and unsteady.

"Yeah, what's up?"

"I got something important to tell you," she said. "Hope you're sitting down."

"I am. Go on," Cara said eagerly.

"I know who framed you..."

"Oh, my God, I remember now!"

Mario had played tennis that day and she went alone to a church member's wedding. Cecil Hawkins was the guy with the pretty face and curly hair. He led her to believe she could get a modeling job, easily. They took pictures together and some of her alone. Cara considered the matter fun and frolic and pushed the thought out of her mind.

"Cecil was the guy I saw with Duncan. His hair is different now," Cara said, realizing that she finally had the proof to vindicate herself.

"Oh, okay. I'm glad I thought to call you," Jennifer said.

"Can you tell me more about this man?"

"You don't want to know. They're all crooks."

"Why? Do you know something I don't?"

"Trust me. Someone got him to pull it off," Jennifer assured her.

———

The sun was shining brightly on the pavement when Duncan arrived at the restaurant. Cecil was seated at a table near the window. The breakfast crowd was buzzing with conversation and smells of sausage and coffee permeated the air.

"Hey," Cecil said, glancing up from the menu. "What took you so long?"

Duncan sat down. "Man, there was a major accident on the southbound Ryan. What're you having?"

"The usual." The waitress came and took their orders and placed a large pot of coffee on the table.

For a moment Cecil stared into space, sipping his coffee.

"I hate that I'm involved."

"You're sure it's the same woman?" Duncan asked.

Cecil leaned forward, "Yeah, I'm sure."

The food arrived. Two plates with the same order... biscuits, sausage and eggs. Duncan sprinkled salt and spread ketchup on his eggs.

"What else did you tell her husband?" Duncan asked.

"That she had a birthmark on her butt that looked like a strawberry."

"You got to be kidding."

"No, I wish I were. I had to convince her husband that I was her lover. Anyway, I dropped off a package with the pictures at the security desk of their apartment. I gave him details about where she worked and the time she got to work and left each day."

"Why didn't you tell me you recognized Cara?"

"Guess I wanted to forget. A guy I play tennis with sometimes, asked me to find out who sponsored Cara Fleming's job."

Suddenly Duncan shook his head and laughed.

"Don't laugh," Cecil's voice was delicate. "I did what I was told."

"I don't believe this. Thanks to your shenanigans, they're separated."

"Hey, don't blame me if her husband was crazy enough to let things get that far," Cecil continued to spill his guts. "A month ago, Joe Michaels asked me to follow her around."

"This is getting crazier by the minute. I'm concerned that Mario can finger you as the caller. Can he?"

"Dammed if I know," Cecil said and pointed to his head. "Now you know why I changed my hair. Anyway, Mario has probably trashed the pictures by now."

"You don't suspect anything criminal going on, do you?" Duncan asked.

"I don't know. Doing what I did couldn't have been as innocent as Michaels made it sound, but if something criminal went down, I'm screwed."

———

Lester had worked late at his office, preparing a testimony for a double murder case. Exhausted, he piled the papers in a folder, turned out the lights and clocked out. Later, he bought a whopper meal from Burger King.

Arriving home at ten o'clock that evening, he checked the mail first. He noticed a mysterious letter postmarked in Detroit. It was mysterious because it was missing several important details... a return address, date, and the sender's name. His heart escalated like an airplane thrusting forward on a runway. After he opened it, the words typed on a sheet of ruled paper shocked him.

I hope this helps the young woman you spoke of. I've got cancer. I need to clear my conscience. The man in the photo is not our biological child. We took him and raised him as our own. My late husband did it to please me. Because of our situation, it was easier than adoption. We had sold our business and were headed North to start over. During a three-day stop in a small Mississippi town, I saw a woman at the mall. She had a small boy I believed could pass for our own child. They had a young infant, too. But, we took the older child. Anyway, my husband used the woman's license plate to trace her name and address. The next day we followed the mother until she stopped at a gas station. She left him in the car. While she was paying for her gas, we seized the moment and told the boy his mother was ill. We convinced the boy we would take care of him until the ambulance came for her. We fled with him and never looked back. I loved the boy as my very own. In his own crazy way, my husband loved him, too. That's why at first the boy didn't run away. He often cried for his real parents. He ran away from us when he turned fifteen. Try not to be too hard on him. He's a good man. I just know it.

Floundering in shock, Lester flopped his body back on the sofa, staring at the letter. *Wow! Thank you for small miracles*, he thought. Tossing Cara's name out during the conversation with Mrs. Bennett did the trick. The pieces of the puzzle were coming together, but there were still too many loose ends.

Chapter 25

The next day, Cara arrived in Memphis. It was the middle of August and the weather was a perfect sunny 80 degrees. During her flight, she reflected on her departure from O'Hare. Lester had insisted on driving her to the airport and she had let him. He focused mostly on her and not their secret investigation this time. She sensed that he wanted to come with her.

Somehow thoughts of Lester disappeared when she saw Frank, Naomi and Ashley. She greeted them with long embraces and tears to spare. Frank ushered them into his seven-year-old Chevrolet and drove to the Slaters' home where it took Naomi less than fifteen minutes to put a home-cooked meal on the table. Afterward, they relaxed in the living room and continued their reunion. Holding Ashley close to her, Cara talked about the job, her apartment, Mrs. Walker and how glad she was to have Jennifer for a friend.

Ashley added a little spice to the conversation when it was her time to get a few words out before bedtime. "Mommy, buy me a 'puter for Christmas, please, please... I want to be like you."

"In that case, yes. Santa will put a computer under the tree," Cara said, barely able to control herself. *Like mother, like daughter,* she thought, laughing some more. She gave Ashley a bath and put her to bed.

Later, when Cara said good night to her parents, she tiptoed into her bedroom, pulled back the covers and positioned herself close to her daughter.

"Hi, Mommy. I fooled you. I wasn't sleep," Ashley said, startling Cara. "I love you mommy. Glad you came back home." she said, arms wrapped around her mother.

"I love you too, Honey."

"Can I bring my friend Tee-Tee over to play tomorrow?"

"Sure. I can't wait to meet her. Go to sleep now." Cara continued to rock her quietly while humming Ashley's favorite lullaby, *Rock-a-bye, Baby.*

"So glad we've got each other," Cara whispered, watching Ashley fall asleep. She was grateful to have a beautiful child who loved her no matter what. She wondered how long she could continue to let her stay hundreds of miles from her. It wasn't long before her thoughts turned to Mario and how she would react seeing him at the funeral. The only thing to do was to be kind, sympathetic and as friendly as possible.

———

The Slater family had arrived at the church, dressed in black and looking somber. Flowers encircled the casket. Soft music played while droves of people filled the church.

Alderman Bennett sat a few rows from the back of the sanctuary, disguised as an older gentleman with gray hair and a beard. He wore dark tinted sunglasses and a black suit. He watched Cara walk past holding hands with a little girl. He figured the toddler was his niece.

He opened the obituary again. Bradley's oldest survivor was omitted. *My name should be there too,* he thought.

Less than two hours later, the pallbearers moved the casket down the aisle and the family followed. Alderman Bennett realized that Mario looked more like their father than he did. As he gazed at his family, he wished he could reach out and touch his brother. He wanted to share the grief; yell and scream out loud for his dead father. He wanted what he had missed for thirty years. He yearned for the family he wasn't allowed to know, the history, and the family traditions he had not been a part of, simply because his identity had been staked on false information. He wanted what Mario had been given while growing up... love, support, and family togetherness. The strangers he grew up calling his parents were like a distant memory to him. He wanted to unravel his fake appearance and announce that he was alive and well. But he couldn't because someone knew too much... too much for his own good.

Abruptly, he recalled that day in his office nine months ago when an acquaintance from his past called.

"Hi. Remember me?" Paula asked.

"Vaguely. It's been quite awhile. Refresh my memory. How do I know you?" Alderman Bennett asked.

"We met when you lived with my sister, Odessa Grant."

He paused to think. "Oh, yeah. How are you?"

"Good. I recognized you on a WGN news clip recently," she said. "How does it feel to be a Chicago alderman?"

"To tell you the truth, it feels good. Why?"

Then she asked him to do the unthinkable.

At that moment, he had to set aside thoughts of Paula and what she forced him to do. For now, his dead father carried more weight and sadness. If only he'd had the chance to grow up with his father, get to know and learn from him. Besides being a good, hardworking husband and father, he started to wonder what the real Bradley was like and the price he paid to become a successful businessman. Alderman Bennett knew all too well how he had to sacrifice some of his principles to get elected and still maintain a good-guy image. He wished he could talk to his father even for a few moments. The thing he was sure about was he couldn't let the past rob him of the joy and sense of pride he now has a Chicago alderman. *I must protect this hideous secret at all cost,* he thought.

Once the family had proceeded down the aisle, he joined the crowd exiting the church. Moments later, he saw Paula. She stood outside alone ogling the family. She looked slightly older. He thought she'd taken good care of herself, but then that's what the Grant sisters did.

Only he couldn't remember if she worked the trade like Odessa.

At the gravesite Alderman Bennett's mind was riddled with more sadness and guilt. He stood in the back of the large crowd and listened as everyone sang *Jesus Keep Me Near The Cross*.

Hesitantly, he walked to his rented car. Tears flowed down his face as he heard the words, "Ashes to ashes, dust to dust." He thought, *I lost him years ago and I've lost him all over again. Unlike every great tradition, my father had to die before I could understand how much I miss him and what he means to me. The only way I will know my father is to try to understand the world he left behind. But given my past and the new life I've created, I could never be anything but an outsider.*

Meanwhile, Mario watched Cara talking to his mother while he was reunited with Ashley and Naomi. As soon as Cara was alone, he walked up to her.

"Hi. Thanks for coming."

"Hello," she responded, wavering for a moment. "I'm so sorry about Bradley. How're you holding up?"

"Okay, I suppose. I still can't believe he's gone."

"Neither can I. I'm sure he's in a better place now."

"How've you been?" he asked.

"Oh, okay. How about you?"

"The same," Mario replied, fumbling with his tie. "I've got to go. Thanks again for coming."

She turned away to walk toward her family and noticed Paula Coles talking with another woman. Cara felt as violated and betrayed as she had after their encounter a year ago. She couldn't believe Paula had come from Italy to attend Bradley's funeral. *Did she leave her husband? Where was she living? Did she know that Mario was about to be a free man?* All at once, she was swept with anger and loneliness so fierce that she couldn't bear to stand there any longer.

Paula looked at Cara and waved with a smirk on her face.

Cara waved back. She swung her purse over her shoulder, trying her best to shake the unpleasant thoughts. She walked along with Frank, Naomi and Ashley to the car.
She was the last one to get inside and while not wanting to, she overheard Ashley whisper to Naomi, "Why didn't my mommy and daddy sit together in church, Grandma?"

Hearing that and remembering her brief interlude with Mario outside the church made her realize how alone she felt. She had imagined she would feel relieved, free to feel unattached from Mario. Instead, she felt abandoned and at risk for more heartbreak.

No one spoke a word while Frank drove, until Naomi asked Cara, "How did your conversation go with Mario?"
"Okay, I guess."
"Have you heard from your l-a-w-y-e-r?" Naomi winked at Cara.
"What's that Grandma?" Ashley blurted out.

Cara had to smile. Frank remained quiet and listened. She sensed that Naomi wanted to hear more about the divorce proceedings, but she lacked the energy to talk about the matter.
The short ride back to her parents' home was mostly quiet. Shortly after they got out and went inside, Frank changed and got busy raking leaves from a neighbor's backyard. Naomi went grocery shopping.

Cara took Ashley on a shopping spree at the mall, buying presents for all of them. She even bumped into a few old teacher buddies. She waved, and they exchanged meaningless friendly chat. Following a light snack on McDonald's burgers, she played with Ashley in the park.
Cara returned home at 4:35 p.m. with several new outfits for Ashley and gifts for her parents. Then she watched Ashley play with her friend, Tee-Tee.

Around eight that evening, Naomi prepared dinner.... fried catfish, homemade rolls, meatless spaghetti, tossed salad, and ice cream for dessert.

At the table, all heads were bowed and hands held while Frank offered the blessing. "Thou are great. Thou are good. We thank thee for this food, our daily bread, Lord. And, we thank you for bringing Cara home safe to us. Amen."

During the meal, Cara thought, *I really miss being here... the easy laid-back lifestyle, fresh air, and especially the food. But, I don't miss the lack of privacy.*

After they'd finished, Frank and Ashley went into the living room to watch a rerun of Good Times. Cara helped Naomi clean the kitchen and she later presented them with the gifts. Opening them, they didn't whoop and send the wrapping paper flying the way they used to in the old days. Her parents took their time, preserving the lilac and lavender paper and the gigantic ribbons.

Frank pulled out the green robe and matching slippers. His face expressed sheer delight. "Baby girl, how did you know this was what I needed? Thanks," he said, giving her a hug.

Naomi seemed more than overjoyed as she sat looking at all nine pieces of a new cookware set. "Out goes the set I've had for the past six years. I'll cook breakfast in these tomorrow," she said, laughing and hugging Cara.

Cara spent some quiet time with Ashley. When her daughter was in bed, she joined her parents in the living room. Frank mentioned to Cara that teacher salaries had improved in Memphis and that she should consider returning home to live.

An hour later, she went to bed, but had a hard time falling asleep.

So she read a bestseller about a perfect, faithful wife and mother who'd discovered that her husband had cheated on her. She couldn't help but relive some of her own experiences from Mario's affair and how she'd reacted when she learned the truth. The heroine in the novel had been jilted and left alone, but in the end, she found true love and happiness with another man.

Cara considered the story in contrast to her own life. She had a second chance with Mario after his affair. Yet, only a year later, it blew up in her face over a blatant lie. She knew how she was framed. Once she pieces together, then she could move on with her life.

Finally, she thought about Bradley and was glad she'd forgiven him. *It's good to say what needs to be said and mend fences while you're still breathing. When you're gone, it's all over. Nothing can be said or done then,* she thought.

The next morning, Naomi yelled, "Get up, sleepy heads! Breakfast is just about ready." Cara had been awake a few minutes before she heard her mother's voice. She had sneaked in and out of the shower and was almost dressed. She happily washed Ashley's face and watched as she brushed her baby teeth.

Later at the table, they all sat down to sausage, pancakes, hot syrup, and scrambled eggs cooked to perfection. Cara cut Ashley's pancakes and generously poured pure maple syrup. They ate in silence for a few minutes.

"I don't wanna go to Chicago," Ashley said, laying her fork on the table. "Mommy, when you coming back home to live?"
She glanced at Frank and then at Naomi, her eyes searching for an explanation. Then she watched the playful emotions on Ashley's face. She knew then that she had to give some serious thought to her plan. Cara just smiled and scooped the rest of her eggs into her mouth.

After clearing her throat, "That's a good question, Ash," she stated while again eyeing her parents. Feeling helpless to do anything about it now, she had been moved by her daughter's comments. "I'll think about it, Darling."

"Good answer," Frank spoke, swallowing a big gulp of his coffee. Naomi shrugged her shoulders and looked at Cara. "Those are your daughter's feelings, not mine!"

"Yes, but keep what Ashley said in mind," Frank said.

When breakfast was over, Cara finished packing and Frank put her small carry-on in the car.

They arrived at the airport an hour later and with time to spare. They talked some more. Cara had always agonized over leaving them, and it wasn't any easier this time, especially with Ashley begging her to stay. Frank brought the camera for picture taking. He took several photos of his Slater women.

An hour later, Cara got up to take her place in the boarding line. Naomi embraced her tightly and said, "I love you and I'm so proud of you. Whatever you decide will be okay with me."

"Love you too, Mom. Thanks. You're the best. I'll call you." She felt a clutch in her heart as the words stuck. Yet, she had to put on a good face for her mom.

Then she picked up Ashley, kissed her and held her close for as long as she could. Feeling lucky to have her, too, Cara told her how much she was going to miss her. She seemed so adjusted living with her grandparents. Cara started to think about the day she'd upset her parents.

Waving them good-bye, she thought, *I'm bringing my daughter to live with me in Chicago sooner than you think, Daddy.*

Chapter 26

Suspended in a cocoon between her past and her future, the airplane was a special place to be alone amid total strangers to think. Cara felt like she was being propelled into a metamorphosis that she wasn't prepared for. As the plane soared high over Memphis, her heart tugged painfully as she looked down to the rapidly shrinking places. *It once meant everything to me. Growing up as a child, getting my education, my marriage and the birth of Ashley. Memphis will always hold a special place in my heart. But now it seems as though I'm sliding from one fantasy into another.*

An hour and forty-five minutes later, she breathed excitement. The vast Chicago skyline! Towering skyscrapers, the endless flow of water, and millions of homes and buildings were breathtaking. She exhaled a sigh of relief and whispered to herself, "This is home to me now. I'm still in control of my destiny. I've got to make the best of it, whatever that means."

Safe on the ground, she used her cellular to notify her parents of her safe arrival. Then she rushed through the connecting tunnel and saw Lester. She lit up inside. They looked into each other's eyes and all was right with the world.

She took a step toward him. "Hi."

Lester hugged her. "I'm glad you're back."

"Good to be back. Seems we're forever hugging and welcoming each other back from somewhere."

"Yeah, it does." They pulled apart slowly and shortly afterward, made their way through busy O'Hare on the escalator and up to the next level to board the people-mover train to the remote parking lot. The temperature roared in the low nineties and it looked as if it might rain.

They chatted back and forth during the five-minute ride. He took her baggage and they piled into his car. From there they went to the checkout booth where he paid the parking fee. In no time he was driving full speed on the Kennedy Expressway.

Feeling sure of herself more than ever around Lester, she took the lead.

"I know how I was framed."

"Well don't keep me guessing," he said excitedly. "How did you find that out?"

"There just wasn't time to tell you before I left." She said it before she thought about her promise to Jennifer. "Can you keep my source anonymous?"

"Of course," he said, voice resigned, wondering how many more times he would have to make such a promise.

"It was Jennifer who told me. She overheard a phone conversation between Duncan and a guy named Cecil." She gave Lester the same recount of the story Jennifer had given her.

"What the hell?" Lester nearly choked on his words.

"You know him?" Cara questioned, staring at him.

Lester let out a long, audible breath. "Yep, I do."

Lester and Cecil enjoyed an occasional drink when their paths crossed after a game of tennis. "As a favor to me, he checked around at Human Services. It seems Alderman Tucker got you hired as a favor to Bennett."

"Holy cow. You're kidding! So, that's why I got hired so quickly." She turned her head away and pushed her hair off her clammy forehead.

"There's more. Loretta Bennett sent me an anonymous letter confessing how she and her husband kidnapped the alderman from his mother."

"It's starting to come together, don't you think?" Cara mused.

Lester felt his head swirl around like a kid would feel on a fast moving merry-go-round. He knew he'd stepped into a messy situation that had begun to reek with more intrigue by the minute.

"This situation is definitely getting interesting. So, how did things go for you in Memphis?"

"The best part of going home was seeing my child and my parents. However, the funeral was sad and short and the same can be said about being around Mario."

Lester smiled and shot a quick look at Cara. "I left Mario a voice mail, but he never returned my call. I figured he'd already left for Memphis. So, how is my old buddy?"

"I could tell that losing his father was really rough for him, but he's holding up okay. He talked to me for a hot minute after the burial. Thanked me for being there. Then he was off to attend to his mother."

"Have you noticed that I don't mention his name anymore," Lester asked.

"Yes, I have. Why?"

"Mario has put some distance between us. I haven't not seen him on the courts in over a month."

"You want to know what I think?" Cara blurted. "I believe he's seeing his old flame, Paula Coles. For some reason, she's returned from Europe and she was at the funeral."

Just as she said those words, like a tremor that started in her head and moved through her body, it came to her. *Could it be possible?* She closed her eyes, deciding to think about Paula later.

"Talk about being bold! Did you see them together?" Lester asked.

"No. Perhaps this time around, they're being careful."

Lester picked up speed, veered into the right lane and merged cautiously onto southbound Lake Shore Drive.

Thirty minutes later, he approached her street and drove on.

"Where're you taking me?"

"Don't worry. I'll get you home. But first there's something I want you to see."

Soon Lester parked his car in the ground level deck.

"I won't be long," he said, getting out to go inside.

While she waited, Cara thought about Lester's subtle advances. *Should I give in or tell him to get lost?*

Cara was so lost in her thought that when Lester opened the door, he startled her.

"Here it is," he said putting the opened envelope in her hands. While he drove, she read the letter over twice.

Five minutes later, he parked in front of her apartment.

"Do you have a few minutes?" she asked.

"Sure I do," Lester said.

"Come with me. I have something to show you, too." He grabbed her bag and followed her up the steps.

Once inside her apartment, Cara pulled open the blinds and turned on the air conditioner.

"Help yourself to something cold to drink." Then she walked to the computer room and grabbed the chat room file.

Lester looked inside the refrigerator and saw that she had bottled water, orange and cranberry juice, skim milk, and a half bottle of wine to choose from. He chose the water and returned to the living room holding the bottle. Still alone, he turned the radio on to station FM95.

Cara returned with the folder labeled **MattIwas** and sat down beside him on the sofa. She watched him read the printed sheets. Then she told him about her online adventures and how she came to meet the anonymous character online.

When she finished bringing him up to speed, she asked, "What you want to bet this screen name belongs to none other than Alderman Bennett?"

Lester leaned back on the sofa. "I don't know. That's a long shot, Cara."

"Take another look at the one where I told him I lived in Chicago.

For a while I was puzzled as to why he stopped communicating with me online. Foolishly, I told him where I lived and about being set up. Who knows? Perhaps it scared him off. Why else would he fear keeping in touch with me? Think about it. His screen name is **MattIwas** and his license plate reads, *AGIA*. It has to represent *AldermanGilesIAm*. What do you think now?"

"I see what you mean," Lester said, looking at her intently.

"Now read what he had to say two weeks after I told him my story." Cara had carefully highlighted Matt's words of encouragement.

"Cara," he interrupted, lowering his head before her, "when I meet a master, I bow." He stood and lowered his head again and smiled.

"Stop kidding me. If only I could figure out the rest."

"No, you're good. I can see how important it is to you to learn the truth."

"Absolutely, and it has nothing to do with getting Mario back. I want to prove my innocence, clear my name and bring order to my life once and for all. I can't move forward unless that happens."

Cara quickly got up and went to her bedroom. She returned seconds later carrying the engraved briefcase she'd bought while shopping at the mall.

"This is a little something for you from the South," she said, handing it to him.

"You shouldn't have," he said, noticing the engraved initials, D.L.M. "It's just what I needed. Thanks."

"You're welcome. You've been too kind and I thank you," she said. She went to the kitchen for a glass of water.

A few minutes later, Lester followed her. She turned and there he stood a few feet away, eyes brimming with tenderness and passion.

"We make a great team. And, I'll help you through this ordeal. He paused and walked close to her. "Cara, I...I'm falling in love with you. I guess I just wanted you to know that."

"Really?" Cara offered a smile, feeling as if she should say something.

"Did I shock you?"

"No," she smiled sweetly.

"That's an honest answer, one that I'd expect from you. I didn't want to scare you off or anything. I just wanted to tell you how I felt."

"I see," Cara hesitated, with her brow dimpled. She walked past him to the living room, not willing to say more.

"Cara, wait!" He caught up with her and took hold of her arm. She refused to look at him and he wondered if he had said too much too soon. "I'm sorry. I guess I couldn't help myself."

Before she could open her mouth to respond, he took her into his arms. She was powerless to resist him. His mouth searched for hers, and she didn't turn her head. She opened her mouth to him and he kissed her long, slowly and deep.

"Lester," she murmured while breathing heavily, with a giddy sense of pleasure. "What about your friendship with Mario?"

"Should I care about that now?"

Although she was surprised to hear his answer, she wasn't quite ready to embark on another relationship. She'd learned the hard way to take things slowly when it came to matters of the heart.

"I'm afraid, and although the past is the past, I need you to be patient with me."

He looked stricken. "For you, I can do that. I've got nothing but time."

Lester seemed reluctant to let go, but he gradually pulled himself away, and she walked him to the door.

He turned to face her. "I would like nothing better than to spend next weekend showing you the city. Please say you'll let me."

"Sounds exciting," she said. "I'd like that."

"Great! Now, as much as I hate to, I'd better leave while I can. I'll call you later."

"I'm not going anywhere."

He blew her a kiss on his way out. A few minutes later, before he got in his car, he glanced up toward her living room window. She waved and he waved back at her.

She couldn't believe what had just happened. Revived to a legitimate state of deep caring, passion and romance for another man, she felt as though he'd left a burning mark on her. *Everything I thought I knew has changed me into something different today, and it isn't necessarily a bad thing,* she thought.

———

Cara put her thoughts about Lester in the left corner of her mind. She considered important matters left on her plate... *the adultery allegation and the divorce hearing.* Did the lawyer persuade the judge to grant a court date? Although Jennifer told her about Cecil, it was the bit about her birthmark that bothered her the most. No one other than Mario, her parents, and her doctor knew about the odd marking on her rear end. Her problem was figuring how Bennett could have known about it.

She searched her memory further about why Bennett would've gone to such trouble. *According to Lester's theory, Bennett wants me for himself. But, not once has Bennett made a move on me. Why would someone with his public ranking, notwithstanding his shady past, go to such lengths and risk his political career? Where's the motive?*

Thinking long and hard got Cara nowhere. She had a mountain of circumstantial evidence, proof that he'd done these things, but no motive. Her head was spinning like she was sitting on a roller coaster at Great America, moving up and down and all around in a one-dimensional sphere.

She opened the folder and she laid out every document she had saved from computer printouts, including e-mail, instant messages, private room chats, Lester's police investigation, and Loretta Bennett's anonymous confession letter.

She let her eyes focus closely on the opening words of Loretta's letter: *I hope this helps the young woman you spoke of. I've got cancer and I need to clear my conscience.*

It was enough to cause Cara to want to know more. Moving her fingers through Lester's notes, she found Loretta's phone number and address.

Chapter 27

On Monday, Cara's Southwest Airline flight had landed in Detroit. She took a taxi from the airport to Loretta Bennett's home. After standing outside the dimly lit two-story brick house for at least a minute, she quickly eased her way up the steps. She rang the doorbell once. A tall middle-age lady dressed in a yellow robe gradually opened the door. She had a sour expression on her face.

"Yes? May I help you?"

"I hope so. Are you Mrs. Bennett?"

"Yes. Who are you?"

"I'm Cara Fleming. May I have a few minutes of your time?"

"I wasn't expecting you, Ms. Fleming. What is this about?"

"It's about me. My innocence. My future. I think that you can help me connect a few dots."

"Well, you people don't give up, do you? Come on in. I'll give you a few minutes. I'm usually in bed around nine every night."

The living room was amply decorated, somewhat appealing, lit only by a brass floor lamp and minus a flow of cooled air.

"Thanks, Mrs. Bennett. I won't take much of your time. My flight back to Chicago leaves at ten o'clock tonight."

Cara sat down in a tall leather chair near the lamp facing Mrs. Bennett. She embraced her mission with dynamic vitality. She explained how she met a character named **MattIwas**. Mrs. Bennett crossed her legs and moved her body forward in her chair. Cara figured she'd made it to first base and was encouraged.

"It's not his real name, just a screen name. Everyone who uses the Internet has one. It protects your privacy."

"Please, go on."

"Okay," Cara eagerly replied. "The man and I were in the same chat room. The conversation was about adoptions and children lost from their biological families. I told him why I was there and somehow I guess he thought I might be able to help him. We became online buddies. We sent e-mail messages and chatted often in a private room. One day he told me what happened to him thirty years ago. So, when Detective Miller showed me your letter, I couldn't believe the similarity of the two situations."

"What exactly are you trying to say?"

Cara pulled out a copy of a chat room printout and the letter she sent to Lester. "Please read both sheets and then tell me what you think."

When Mrs. Bennett had finished, she was momentarily speechless. "I had hoped my writing that letter to your detective friend would be the end of this. I see it wasn't," she said. Then she stared at Cara and paused a few moments. "I hear you have a young daughter?"

"That's correct."

"Then you know what it's like for a mother to want to protect her child. It's true, I didn't give birth to Giles. Right or wrong, I considered him my child. Our own son died. We gave the new son his name, *Giles*."

"If it makes you feel better about this, Giles has a good reputation, a good heart, and he's doing well for himself in Chicago. You'd be proud."

"Really? What has he done to make you believe that?"

"Besides everything he does for the people in his ward, he made sure I found a prestigious job with the city. Without it, I wouldn't be able to make it alone. And he did it anonymously. He hasn't asked for anything in return. More interesting than that, we're total strangers."

"I'm glad he helped you. Women have a hard time as it is in this world."

There was a long silence. "All I want to do is prove my innocence. You're the only person who can help me. You wouldn't be hurting your son. I won't let that happen," Cara promised.

"How can you sit there and say that? Once the truth comes out, somebody is bound to be hurt."

"You'll have to trust me. In your letter, you stated you needed to clear your conscience. Well, I need to clear my name. Please, won't you help me?"

Cara fumbled around in her large handbag and found a business card. "Please, take my card. Call me anytime."

"Well what is it you want to know?" Mrs. Bennett asked, turning to look at the clock on the wall.

"I believe Giles's last name was once Fleming," Cara said, leaning forward. "I base my theory on what you said in the letter. Where did the family live? Do you remember his parents' name?"

"Bradley and Mary Lee," she uttered, without blinking. "At the time, they lived in Greenwood, Mississippi."

Cara looked at her in surprise. A soft gasp escaped her. "Is Giles his real name?"

"No, it was Matthew. My husband thought it best to change it. Kirk Bennett hated leaving loose ends."

Cara felt like an atomic bomb had exploded inside her. She felt weak at first and then clammy. Finally, with confidence she thought, *MattIwas, I got you now!*

"You know anything about these people, Ms. Fleming?"

"Yes, as a matter of fact I do. I am married to the younger brother, Mario."

———

Cara spent the fifty-five-minute flight time back to Chicago in a state of disbelief. She got what she hadn't expected, an earth-shattering bombshell. She now held the truth in the palm of her hands. What she hadn't expected was that it would change the lives of the Fleming family forever, including her own.

Sipping on bottled water, she wondered about Alderman Bennett's motive for ruining her marriage. *Revenge is the likely choice. He felt cheated out of a life that was rightfully his. Maybe he blamed the entire family for his misfortune in life. Why else would he have wreaked havoc on his own brother?*

Suddenly she remembered the strange way Mary Lee asked for her buddy's screen name. In her mind, it explained why **MattIwas** ended their cyberspace relationship. Cara also speculated that Mary Lee probably reunited with her other son and he knew Bradley had died. She wondered if the alderman attended his father's funeral? Perhaps, he came and was carefully disguised.

The plane landed on time and she boarded the half-crowded shuttle bus. In parking lot F, she located her car and she checked to see if anyone had followed her. She quickly got in and drove off, stopping to pay the parking fee.

As Cara turned left on Cicero Avenue, she detected someone following her. The man stayed with her as she turned onto the Stevenson Expressway. She wondered if it could be one of Lester's watchmen. Weeks had passed since he'd stopped the round-the-clock surveillance. Maybe he lied. "Doesn't he trust me?" she asked out loud. She sped up and changed lanes quickly. Looking up in her rearview mirror, she noticed that whoever was following her was gone.

Calming her nerves, she called Jennifer on her cellular.

"Hello, Cara. Where are you, Girlfriend?" Jennifer asked, before Cara could speak.

"Hi, I finally caught you at home," Cara replied.

"Whatever do you mean?" Jennifer replied, laughing louder than usual. "Where are you? I tried reaching you at your apartment a few times, but you didn't answer," she said, laughing.

"Ah, ha, I fooled you, didn't I?" Cara explained that she was using the cell phone to cut household expenses. "Anyway, I've been trying to reach you since I got back from Memphis. How are you doing?"

"I'm all right. How was your trip?"

"Oh, everything went well. The funeral was sad. Mostly I enjoyed being with my family. I took my daughter shopping. She's so amazing. Don't be surprised to see her living with me one day soon."

"Knowing you, I can believe that. What're you doing with yourself these days?" Jennifer asked.

"Busy doing the usual. But I'm managing to get on with my life. How's your situation at home?"

"Glad you asked. Duncan is acting really weird. Lately, I'm getting strange feelings about my safety."

"Uh, oh!" Cara knew all too well how such thoughts could wear on your mind. "Let's get together and talk. Something interesting is happening to me. I need to talk about it.

"All you got to say is where. Lord knows I need an excuse to get out of here," Jennifer said.

Cara suggested that they grab a burger after work the next day. Protecting her alibi for using the cellular, she told Jennifer she was going to take a bath and go to bed.

When Cara reached the King Drive exit she couldn't really determine if she was being followed or not. Whoever it was, Cara knew she was playing in the major leagues for sure. There was no turning back.

Once Cara parked in front of her building, she quickly went inside and locked the door. The first thing she did was to check her Caller ID. There were only three calls, two from Lester, and just as she suspected, a call from Jennifer. She called Jennifer back.

"Hi. I saw that you called. You wouldn't by any chance be checking up on me, would you?"

Jennifer explained that she had remembered her doctor's appointment tomorrow at five o'clock. They decided to meet at seven instead.

After Cara hung up she frantically dialed Lester's number. Checking the apartment over, she waited for him to answer.

"I called you earlier. Where were you?" Lester questioned.

"Hi. I'm all right. But, you won't believe where I've been."

"Well? Don't make me wait." There was a long pause. "Come on, you can tell me. By the way, your line is safe. I had it checked today as a precaution," he stated.

"Detroit." It was then that she realized he took watching over her seriously.

"You didn't! Why didn't you tell me? I would've gone with you."

"I'm sorry. There wasn't time to discuss it with you. Besides, I had a hunch that the name Fleming meant something to Loretta Bennett. Guess what? My hunch paid off."

"Fascinating. How did you get her to talk?"

"I was very direct and to the point. I showed her the information. From there, one thing led to another. She told me everything. She admitted to stealing Giles from Bradley and Mary Fleming. Can you believe his real name is Matthew Fleming?"

"Get out of here! Mario's brother?"

"Yes, they're brothers," she replied, sounding upbeat for a change.

"What led you to probe in that direction?"

"They never claimed him as a dependent on their tax returns. I figured they took him illegally."

He paused, taking a deep breath. "Yes it's all making sense now. Wow, you're turning into a regular Nancy Drew."

At that moment, she remembered Lester's two phone calls. "Was there a reason why you called this evening?"

"Yes. You know too much. I've seen too many cases where the guilty party decides to silence the one who knows too much. This one screams danger, Cara."

"Should I be shaking in my boots?" Cara joked.

"I'm serious, Cara. At the risk of repeating myself, you know too much."

Lester asked her to give him a minute or so to think of a plan. "For starters, don't talk about this matter with anyone, including Jennifer or your parents, especially using your home phone. Use your cell phone. Tomorrow, your line may not be safe to use."

Chapter 28

Mario took off during his lunch hour to get the paternity test results. He planned to surprise Mary Lee with the news later. Before he entered the main lobby at Jackson Park Hospital, he put out his unfinished cigarette in the large cement ashtray.

A little after twelve o'clock, he entered the reception area and introduced himself to the cheery faced, middle-aged lady who greeted him. He was on time for a change and she told him the doctor was waiting. He crept into the small, bright and neatly furnished room and sat down in one of the chairs facing the doctor's desk. He rubbed his head nervously and moved around in the chair more than once.

"Good afternoon, Mr. Fleming. Calm down or you might go into cardiac arrest." Dr. Onzette was a gentle giant with sparsely gray hair and mustache. He had aged well and his mild-mannered personality garnered a huge clientele.

"I didn't sleep well last night, Doc. Just buried my father a few days ago. My nerves are just about shot," he said as he slouched down in the chair.

"Oh, I'm sorry to hear that. I can understand what it must be like for you, but try to take it easy." The doctor offered Mario a glass of water. "You should try it sometimes. It's a good remedy for settling the nerves, when there's nothing else to grab."

Mario thanked him and got up to help himself to a cup of sparkling water from the corner dispenser. He gulped it all down faster than he'd ever drunk a can of beer.

"So, am I going to live or die?" Mario asked, sitting down again.

"According to the results of your annual physical, you'll live. Do you have any health concerns I don't know about?"

"No, absolutely not. I feel fine."

"Good. Then the only recommendation I have is for you to lighten up on the smoking. Better yet, stop."

"I'll try. As you know, old habits are hard to break."

Dr. Onzette shook his head and closed Mario's medical folder. Then he opened the file labeled M. Fleming's Paternity Test. "Now, about the paternity test. We've carefully examined both yours and the child's blood tests. There's a 99.9% probability that you are the child's biological father. In fact, she has your blood type."

"I am?" Mario settled back in his chair, his eyes gleaming like a shiny volcanic rock.

"Absolutely. There's no question in my mind. I hope this is good news for you."

Mario felt like a fool, but at the same time, he was relieved to know the truth. He shook hands with his doctor, thanked him and quietly walked out of the office thinking how he'd wasted precious time as far as Ashley was concerned. He knew he had no one to blame but himself.

As he scurried out of the hospital, his thoughts drifted to Cara. He knew that he still loved her, but couldn't bring himself to admit it. The hardest thing he had to do for now was to admit he was wrong for questioning whether he was Ashley's father.

He returned to work just in time for his 1:30 p.m. volleyball class. Thinking that today was a new beginning, the first thing he had to do was to pay child support, including delinquent payments. Although he was happy about the confirmation that Ashley was his child, a sense of sadness gripped him. He figured Paula was the one to help him heal his wounded heart, since his marriage to the woman once thought to be his lifelong love was about to end.

———

Mary Lee sipped coffee while she sat at the kitchen table reading over Bradley's will. As his sole beneficiary, she had money and plenty of it. Her worth was estimated in cash, savings accounts, stocks and bonds, a large insurance policy and the landscape business, to be worth more than $800,000. It was in her plan to honor Bradley's wishes and give Mario the landscape business valued at more than $200,000.

"But now," as she thought further, "there's Matthew to consider. Mario must be told he has an older brother."

Needing to talk to Naomi alone, she called and invited her friend to dinner. Then she defrosted two steaks, scrubbed two white potatoes, took out a pack of store-bought dinner rolls, and made iced tea to refrigerate for later. She planned to serve a tossed salad and steamed vegetables to finish the meal. She would broil the steaks in the oven once Naomi got there.

At exactly 6:05 p.m., Mary Lee put the finishing touches on the table setting and the doorbell sounded. She greeted Naomi who was standing on the porch holding a gift bag. Mary Lee smiled and thanked her. After both ladies embraced in a long friendly hug they relaxed on the sofa.

"It's just a little something I've put together for you," Naomi said, as she watched Mary Lee pull out the purple-laced bound photo album. It contained pictures Frank took over the years from when Cara and Mario first met, their first date, graduations, the wedding, reception, birth of Ashley, their first house, parties, picnics, and other family gatherings.

"This is so amazing. I had no idea you saved all of this. Oh, and there's the one I took with Bradley at Ashley's first birthday party. This isn't the only set of pictures you have is it?"

"No, don't be silly. You know Frank. Taking pictures is one of his hobbies. He always gets doubles. Anyway, we thought you'd appreciate the memories."

"I do," Mary Lee replied. "I'm so grateful to you and Frank.

Those were the good old days, weren't they?"

"Yes. A lot has changed since then, and we're always going to be a family. We won't let nothing change that, my friend," Naomi said. Mary Lee felt a warm glow radiate through her and then she jumped to her feet and checked the food. She returned a few minutes later and sat down on the sofa.

"It smells good. Whatcha cooking?"

"Your favorite, filet mignon." Mary Lee leaned back and closed her eyes briefly.

"I can't wait." Naomi sat erect. "Now, what was it you wanted to tell me?"

For a moment Mary Lee thought wistfully of Matthew and his cautious advice not to tell anyone about his connection to the Fleming family. *If only Bradley had been brave enough to tell the truth years ago, this wouldn't be so difficult now*, Mary Lee thought.

"I..." she began slowly. "I've been keeping a dreadful secret from everyone."

"Oh dear, what is it?" Naomi reached and grabbed her by the hand.
When Mary Lee had finished, Naomi knew everything. "Oh my God," Naomi gasped with her hand folded around Mary Lee. "Tell me about Matthew."

"I might as well... He's a Chicago alderman and his name is not Matthew anymore."

"You're kidding me, right?" Naomi interrupted. "Did Mathew come to the funeral?"

"No, I'm sorry to say."

By then, dinner was ready. Naomi took her seat while Mary Lee served the food.

"I see," Naomi replied, before blessing the food. "Couldn't he have come anyway? Who in Memphis would've recognized him? By the way, how is Mario?"

"He's okay. It's like he's gone off into his private world these days. How's Cara?"

"She seems to be doing all right. Frank and I both worry about her, how she's faring by herself and all. Now that she's making a good salary, I suspect she's planning to snatch our granddaughter to live with her."

"Snatch?" Mary Lee asked. Her eyes turned dark and insolent. "Please don't use that word."

"Oh, I'm sorry. I can certainly understand your reasons."

Following the meal, Naomi helped Mary Lee clean the kitchen.

Later in a quiet moment in the living room, Mary Lee mentioned about the money Bradley left. She had enough to help both sons. She worried that Mario would blow his inheritance and she feared Matthew would refuse his.

"I won't forget Ashley. She will go to college without money worries. Keep that to yourself, okay?"

"Gee, that's awfully nice of you."

Naomi started to suspect that her best friend was beginning to use her newfound power. Money! The root of evil, she thought. More importantly she got the message loud and clear. Keep her mouth shut and Ashley would be taken care of. She hated being used like that.

"Aren't you worried Mario will learn the truth?"

"Yes, but I'm also tired of keeping secrets. It's hard for me to sleep at night. Oh, there's something else you should know."

"What's that?"

"It was Cara who accidentally discovered Matthew in a computer chat room. According to Cara, they talked mostly about adopted and lost children trying to find their birth parents. Cara gave him advice to help him to find his parents. She told me things about this man that didn't seem coincidental. I faked a reason why I wanted his screen name. She gave it to me and the rest is history. Can you believe it?"

"Good gracious a life!" Naomi shouted. "Does Cara know who **MattIwas** really is?"

"No. Matthew stopped sending her e-mails. So much has happened since I talked to Cara… discovering my son is alive, Bradley's death, and the funeral ... Maybe I'm afraid she'll ask the wrong questions."

"Knowing my daughter, she's good for that."

"I'm glad I got this off my chest," Mary Lee said.

"Well, I hate to eat and run, but I need to get home and tuck Ashley in bed. She likes a bedtime story before going to sleep."

Naomi hugged Mary Lee good-bye. She drove home with a lot on her mind. She understood Mary Lee's dilemma, but it had become increasingly troubling knowing the truth.

She wondered why Cara hadn't mentioned the bits and pieces she'd come to know. There were no secrets between them, or were there? She thought about Cara sitting at the computer talking to strangers in chat rooms. *What's going to come of my child? Because of a few people living their lives in anonymity and harboring stupid secrets, my daughter's character has been defamed. Now, she's headed for a divorce.*

Chapter 29

Cara and Jennifer met after work at Fuddruckers in Calumet City, a south suburb of Chicago. Standing in line to place their orders, Cara couldn't avoid noticing Jennifer's appearance. Her face was puffy even with makeup heavily applied. Unfortunately, her perfume didn't shield the stench of vodka.

"So, what's up?" Cara smiled humbly and squeezed Jennifer's hands. "What's got you so afraid of living in your own home?"

"He's trying to get rid of me."

"I'm really starting to worry about you."

"I'm worried about me, too. All I seem to do lately is think the worst about everything. I'm not sure if I should stay there any longer. So much has happened in the past few weeks; you wouldn't believe any of it if I told you."

"Has he threatened or hit you?" Before Jennifer could respond, Cara stepped up and ordered a quarter pound cheeseburger platter, fries and soda. She instructed the cashier to put both orders on her tab. Seconds later, Jennifer placed her order. Cara selected a cozy window table for them.

Jennifer arrived at the table two minutes later and sat down. Among other emotions was a deep sense of shame on her face. "To answer your question, Duncan hasn't hit me…yet. I don't know; maybe I'm being paranoid or something. More and more, he's acting cold and testy. And I give him back the same," she said.

"What do you think is going on with him? Has he always acted this way toward you?"

"No, not like this. I think at one time I was an asset to himæ-someone he obviously valued as a companion, an occasional lover, and someone to help pay the bills to keep us in comfort. Suddenly, I've become a liability to him."

"Do you honestly believe he would harm you in any way? Is he having an affair?"

"Yes, to both. Only, I can't talk about the affair. Duncan purchased two 45-magnums, two automatic rifles, and several small revolvers. He keeps one in his car, unconcealed. I never liked guns and dared not say anything to him about it. Actually, he has more guns than he has shoes."

"My goodness. I couldn't even picture Duncan with a gun."

"He's become categorically mean and miserable to be around. One day he kicked our dog, Bagels in the head because the poor mutt peed all over the house. Two days ago, I broke down and cried over Duncan's decision to have him put to sleep. I convinced him to take the dog to the humane society."

"Jennifer, you can't work things out with a crazy man. It seems that men are protecting their pocketbooks more than ever before. It's that 'it's cheaper to her' mentality. Of course in your case, minus children and child support issues, you have marital property. Surely, you can get half of everything. What I want to know is what happened to make you believe he wants to harm you?"

Jennifer explained how she'd taken a carton of orange juice out of the refrigerator. She was going to take the juice upstairs and fill it with vodka. When she discovered it had been opened, she noticed he stopped eating his breakfast and that he turned his head, slightly watching her. She poured some of the orange juice into a glass. It didn't look quite right and she decided to empty both containers down the drain. Duncan shook his head in disappointment that she didn't drink it.

"It's a feeling I can't explain," Jennifer said.

"I don't like it that you have to live like that," Cara said, as tears filled her eyes. "What if he decides to create false accusations about you? Considering what happened to me, anything is possible."

Sadness was written all over Jennifer's face.

Just then, Cara's name was announced over the intercom. They

picked up their orders and walked around the buffet, selecting salad vegetables and toppings for their burgers. Stopping at the beverage machine,
they both chose diet sodas and returned to the table.

"I'm sorry if I overstepped my boundaries."

"Cara, you're my girl. Apologies aren't necessary," Jennifer said.
"You can say whatever you want. In the end it's up to me, right?"

"Then come and live with me until you can find a place to stay."
Jennifer leaned her elbow on the table and rested her chin in her hand.
"Where would I sleep? There's a lot in the house that belongs to me and
if I bring it all...."

"For you, I'd make room. Soon Ashley will come here. The
three of us can live under the same roof until we can both do better."

"Thanks. I'll think about it. Now, I want to hear your exciting
news."

"Oh, nothing is so exciting that it can't wait for a while," Cara
replied, with an adventurous toss of her head. She wished she could tell
Jennifer about Detective Miller and all the rest. Instead, she decided to
heed Lester's warning: *Don't talk about this matter with anyone, including Jennifer or your parents.*

They left the restaurant an hour later and Cara walked Jennifer to
her car and hugged her tightly. "I'm counting on you to be good to yourself. I'll call you everyday."

She had started to feel close, like a sister, to Jennifer. In blood,
sorrow and strength, she was committed to being there for Jennifer. Cara
thought, *Jennifer needs to see herself as the solution and not the problem. Forget what she might lose by way of assets, and consider that living a healthy, happy life is far more valuable. Women do it all the time.
They leave and start all over again, only to discover the tradeoffs are
worth it.*

It took Cara less than thirty minutes to return to the city. She
stopped and picked up toiletries, pantyhose, and Centrum vitamins before
driving home.

At her apartment, she got the mail, went inside and locked the door, still thinking about Jennifer. Four calls registered on the Caller ID and there were several from unknown numbers. Checking her voice mail, there was no indication that anyone had left messages. She felt as though the nightmare was starting all over again and that the voice message hadn't stopped the unknown calls.

After she undressed and changed into an oversized T-shirt, she looked through the mail and saw a letter-sized envelope with a surprising return address: Mario Fleming, 5340 South Blackstone.

She unfolded the letter and was astounded by a check from him totaling $2,100. She put the check aside and quickly scanned through the words: *Dear Cara, Ashley is my daughter. I'm sorry I doubted that and for how I've behaved toward her. Enclosed is the child support money I owe you. Court ordered or not, the payments will continue.*
Mario

———

Today, when Mario opened his apartment door, he felt as though he had redeemed himself. He was certified as Ashley's father, had reclaimed a friend from his past, and had more money in his bank account than he'd ever expected. Yet, he knew Paula or any other woman could never replace Cara.

"Damn!" What the hell is wrong with me? Just when our marriage was getting back on track, why did this have to happen to us? We were so happy and I'd put aside the notion of sleeping around with another woman forever. Cara seemed happy with her work and she loved keeping the apartment clean and attractive and she was always attentive to me," he mumbled to himself. He even remembered the guilt he felt during his affair with Paula and how hewould walk around the house in Cara's presence humming and practically prancing to the tune *Me and Mrs. Jones*.

Mario removed his clothes and stepped inside the shower. No sooner than the water started to wet his back, he snapped out of his depression thinking that with a conscience free of the deadbeat-dad stigma, he had to find peace with the way things were with Cara. He started singing *I Believe I Can Fly*.

Afterward, he sawed his body dry with the large blue towel with the embroidered initial "M" and thought about Lester and how long it had been since they hit a few balls. Lester had never been serious competition for Mario on the tennis court. Breaking a two-month long silence, he decided to call Lester.

"Lester, my man. How's it going?"

"Can't complain. How're you and the family holding up?"

Mario assured Lester that he and his mother were doing well and he thanked Lester for the sympathy card. "I told my mother about you."

"Good. How're you doing?"

Mario told Lester that he was seeing an old flame from Memphis and that he was finally caught up with his child support payments to Cara.

"What made you change your mind?"

"Why you say that?" Mario asked.

"Correct me if I'm wrong, but I seem to remember you talked about it before."

"Probably." Mario lied. He never mentioned Ashley and his paternity concerns to Lester.

"Hey, Man, I'm glad that matter is settled," Lester said.

"Enough about my problems. Feel up to hitting a few balls tomorrow morning?"

"Sorry, but I can't. I'm helping someone work through a difficult situation. Maybe, another time."

What's up Lester? What is it you aren't saying? Mario thought.

Chapter 30

Five o'clock marked the end of the working day for most people, but plainly not for Cara. Earl Dunlap had requested a meeting to discuss her less-than-satisfactory performance evaluation.

"I don't understand. This evaluation is not correct, Mr. Dunlap," she said, holding the form. He didn't appear to believe her and she was poised to handle whatever he had to say. Right away she knew she had to put up or shut up.

"Are you questioning your supervisor's conclusion?" he asked.

"No, not a question, but a protest! This report is wrong and it doesn't represent the truth about my work."

"Why is that, Ms. Fleming? It's hard not to believe someone with Dexter Grady's service record," he said, shrugging his shoulders to hide his confusion.

"Mr. Dunlap, I didn't mix business with pleasure. I was here to do a job and not to socialize with him or anyone else on the job. It just goes against my grain to mix the two."

"Can you prove your case?"

"I most certainly can."

"Good! Bring me the proof. I'll hold off signing the report."

"Thanks. I appreciate that."

She politely excused herself from his office and copied information from her files æ coordinator reports, memos, names, and phone numbers of her contacts at community agencies. She gathered attendance records from meetings and dates and times when Grady asked her out to lunch. She remembered that he called her several times at home and decided she'd bring her Caller ID. Grady's phone number was stored in memory. She piled her papers extending a foot high, into her brief bag and clocked out at six o'clock.

Just as she was about to pull out of the parking lot, her cellular rang. It was Lester.

"Hi, Doll face."

"Hi."

"Are you okay? You sound troubled about something," Lester inquired.

"Perturbed is more like it." She told him about her meeting with Mr. Dunlap.

That damn Grady, he thought. "It doesn't sound good. Can I come over? We can talk about it."

"Sure. Come around seven-thirty." She pushed the off button, without even saying good-bye.

The drive home took longer than expected and when she arrived, it was 7:05 P.M. She showered, changed, and paced back and forth while thinking about her situation.

Lester arrived on time and after they reviewed her defense plan, she began to feel hopeful. Then she mentioned the letter and the money Mario sent her.

"Yeah, I know. I talked to Mario yesterday."

"Really? What do you suppose changed his mind?" Cara asked.

"Beats me. We didn't talk long. He suggested we get together on the court. Seems he can't wait to whip me again. I turned him down; told him I was helping out a friend with a problem. That's the other reason I needed to see you. I've thought about what I said to him. I think I goofed."

"Really? Why?"

"It occurred to me that he had never talked to me about his daughter's paternity."

"Oh, no! If you're right, he will wonder how you knew and will start to get ideas."

"Let's hope not. Lately, it's hard to keep a straight head, especially around you."

She smiled. "Mario had a lot to drink that night. Maybe he won't remember what he did or didn't tell you."

Looking into Cara's eyes, Lester figured that for the sake of both of them it was best to stay away from Mario.

"I want you to think about your happiness," Lester said. "Put aside all the unpleasantness around us. You deserve to be happy for a change." He kissed her on the hand.

"Amen to that," she said, smiling.

"To keep you that way, I've got a plan," he said. The last stop on our date this weekend is a cruise on Lake Michigan. You shouldn't return to your apartment. Bring an overnight bag to my condo around two o'clock tomorrow. I'll arrange guest parking in the underground garage. You can stay in my guest room," he said.

"Really? Can I think about it?" Cara asked.

———

The next day, Lester turned off the stereo, thinking it was time to make a decision. He could either work to get his life in order or return to his old ways. He almost laughed when he realized there wasn't any choice at all. He'd already made his choice. He'd chosen Cara over a life of running around with different women. She would never fit into his old life. But he could fit perfectly into her life and he was glad she'd agreed to spend the night at his condo following their date. His spirits lifted suddenly when Cara walked out of the guest room.

"You look stunning," he said, admiringly.

"Thanks, and you've never looked more handsome."

"Are you ready for a night on the town?"

"Yes, I believe so," Cara responded and grabbed her purse.

A few minutes later, Lester escorted her to his car.

Dinner was at *One Sixtyblue* restaurant in downtown Chicago. Michael Jordan's involvement helped it become a people-watcher's paradise. Famous athletes often frequented the elegant eatery converted from a pickle factory. The architectural design, the black painted glass walls, thick black columns and wavy ceiling fixtures that looked like hard-candy ribbons, were rather masculine. But the warm indirect lighting and elegant table settings softened the blow.

Cara seemed wonderfully surprised at the charm that oozed from the understatedly lavish room. They both dined on a seared salmon fillet crusted with asparagus, expensive wine, and chocolate bars with mango sauce. The service had been impeccable so far. Their server was polite and friendly, and the food was prepared with a flair for presentation.

"Do you come here often?" Cara asked.

"Actually, no. A police buddy brought his girlfriend here for Sweetest Day. He gave it rave reviews. I figured it was a place fit for you."

"It's the best I've ever been to."

"There's more to see and do before this evening is over." He sipped some more wine.

She asked him about his childhood and was surprised when he didn't evade the question or pass it off with a joke.

"What do you want most out of life?" Cara asked.

"Mostly love, happiness and a sense of security. I've always wanted someone I could like as well as love. And following my mom's advice, I want someone with whom I can agree and disagree without becoming disagreeable."

Hands wrapped around her glass, she asked, "From all of the above, which is more important?"

"Let me put it this way, I don't want someone I can live with. I'm looking for someone I can't live without." He laughed.

She returned the laugh with a smile, and finished her salmon. "I have wondered about two things, your astrological sign and your marital history.

"I'm a Pisces, and you?" Lester asked.

"Scorpio. I've read that on a scale of one to ten a match between us rates, eight for comfort, nine for communication, and seven for chemistry."

"Is that right? I'm not up on astrology, but I'm glad we're a perfect match."

At exactly 7:45 Lester ushered Cara out of the restaurant. He took her to Grant Park. Amid a starry sky and an unseasonable 71 degrees in early October, they walked from Michigan Avenue to Columbus Drive. Lester told her it was where Chicago's major events were held...concerts, parades, fairs, carnivals, and festivals like the Taste of Chicago in July, and Venetian Night in October.

A Denzel Washington movie at Navy Pier was next.

Around midnight, Lester whisked her onto the Spirit of Chicago for a moonlight cruise on Lake Michigan. The three-deck ship accommodated up to six hundred passengers. Featured were narrated sightseeing of Chicago's skyline, live music, cocktails galore and all-you-can-eat buffets or seated dinners prepared by executive chefs.

Off in a world of their own, they danced, sipped wine and behaved like newlyweds on the Fiesta Deck among the large crowd.

After the ship docked, Lester took her home with him. It was 2:30 in the morning when they walked inside. Lester secluded himself in the master suite to shower. Cara showered in the guest bath, changed, and walked to her room. Just as she was about to enter, Lester appeared in the hallway. He was wrapped in a long robe. He took her breath away momentarily.

"I'm sorry if I frightened you." His gaze was as soft as a caress and she felt her pulse beat in her throat.

"Don't be silly," she said, still smiling. "I should get to bed if I'm going to make it to church in the morning."

The smoldering flame she saw in his eyes radiated a vitality that drew her to him like a magnet. His large hands slipped through her arms, bringing her closer.

"I thought a good-night kiss might be in order."

As though the words released her, she flung herself against him and was suddenly lifted into the cradle of his arms. His mouth covered hers hungrily, sending new spirals of ecstasy through her.

She could see pain in his eyes, but intense passion came from his lips. He kissed her again, followed by a series of slow, shivery kisses.

Then he whispered in her ear, "I want you so much it hurts."

"No, we shouldn't," she said, fighting the urge to push herself away, to get inside and close the door behind her.

"I know I promised I wouldn't do this," he murmured as his grip tightened while his attitude became more serious. "I just want to love you, that's all."

It surprised her that this time she had no desire to back out of his embrace.

Lester gently lifted her body into his arms and carried her inside the guest room ...

After what seemed like hours, Lester had made her a satisfied woman, unable to move at her own will. Settling back to enjoy the feel of his arms around her, she was happy. At that moment she didn't seem to care that she went against her morals and slept with a man who was not her husband.

She would let tomorrow take care of the shame and the self-disgust.

Chapter 31

"Good morning,"Lester said.

"Tell me it was all a dream." She felt ashamed. She was still a married woman. How could she? She wondered silently.

"Oh, but it wasn't. Last night, I made you mine. This morning, I make you breakfast," he stated passionately, wrapping his arms around her like a warm blanket. "Do you realize how beautiful you look when you wake up?"

"No, I haven't noticed."

"Because of you, my luck has changed."

"What do you mean?" she asked.

"Just that you're the type of woman who possesses everything a man needs and wants. Together, we can take on the world."

"Sure, tell me anything. Seriously, as good as it was, and as much as I needed it, this won't happen again," she said, shifting her body to look at the ceiling. "I'd like to shower and change. Then I'll devour whatever you dish up for breakfast." She watched him get up and throw on his robe. "I was thinking you might consider going to church with me today."

Turning to face her, "For you, anything. We can take off after we eat." He bent down and kissed her. Finally he pulled himself away staring deeply into her eyes.

She waited until she was alone to lie there, in only the soft, lingering glow of pleasure and reflection. The fact that he was Mario's friend didn't matter either. As good or as bad as it was to give in to Lester, she couldn't think of anything or anyone else at the moment. The rest of the day would be theirs together.

After she showered and dressed, she entered the kitchen and welcomed the smell of onions, green peppers and coffee. He delivered two plates to the table, each with a ham omelette and toast. He then poured them a tall glass of orange juice and filled two black mugs with steaming hot coffee. He waited until she blessed the food and they plowed into their meal.

"How is it?" he asked.

Her smile broadened in approval. "Better than any I've ever eaten. The eggs and seasoning are a perfect blend. I could get used to this."

"Good. I love spoiling you."

Exactly at ten o'clock they were dressed for church. Cara had on a two-piece Liz Claiborn, red jacket and coordinating long fitted skirt, taupe bag and matching shoes.

Ten minutes later Lester drove away from his South Shore Drive condo. Unexpectedly after he passed Paxton Avenue, he caught a glimpse of Mario's car, which appeared to be trailing a block behind them.

Instantly, he thought, *I don't need this. What's with this guy? Whatever happened to moving on with his life?* Without alarming Cara, he wondered when and where had the pursuit begun. A likely confrontation with her soon-to-be-ex worried him.

———

The next day at work Cara fought to keep self-control as she speculated what Dunlap had decided about her evaluation. She had turned everything in on Friday. Dunlap assured her he would speak to Grady. And, surely, she'd learn her fate before the day was over.

She completed two site visits, mingling with teachers and the children. When the day ended, there wasn't a word from Dunlap. "Perhaps tomorrow," she thought as she clocked out.

The phone rang just as she arrived home around six that evening. She answered, and it was her lawyer.

"Cara, I've got some bad news. Mario has thrown a monkey wrench in your divorce settlement. He's claiming you're unfit to raise your daughter. He wants custody."

Her breath quickened and her cheeks became warm. The words made her feel weak and sinful. She wanted to toss them back into Mario's lap and scream that he was without honor too.

Instead she asked the lawyer, "Why? Can he do that?"

"Prolong the divorce? Yes. Are you sure you've told me everything about your situation?" Garnell asked.

"Mario hasn't talked to me since his father's funeral. I haven't a clue."

"Fortunately, she masked the tremor in her voice. Then she mentioned Mario's letter and lump sum child support payment. "I'm sorry. Should I have called you?"

"Right. I can't help you appropriately if you hold back," Garnell demanded.

"Oh boy, it never ends, does it?"

"Don't jump the gun just yet," he said. "Let me find out what's going on. I'll get back to you as soon as I have something to report."

She plopped down on the sofa, thinking that a peaceful split was now out of the question.

———

Two days later Cara stepped onto the elevator trying to feel hopeful. As the crowd began to thin, little knots formed in her stomach. Half worried and half optimistic, she refused to consider her fate.

When the last two people got off ahead of her, she held her head up, fidgeting nervously with the strap on her briefcase and walking toward her cubicle. She couldn't help but pass Dexter Grady's office. As usual his door was open.

"Ms. Fleming?" he called out to her.

She stopped slowly to walk back to his office door. "Good morning, Mr. Grady." He waved for her to come inside.

"Can I have a word with you?"

"Sure," she replied, and walked inside and sat down.

"It seems that my behavior and actions have been inappropriate. I've corrected your evaluation. The new version should be on your desk. It was foolish to rush to judgment." By now, a cold sweat coated his forehead. Will you accept my apology?"

"If you are as sincere as you sound, I'm sure I can do that," she said, feeling as if a huge weight had been lifted from her shoulders.

"Thank you. I really mean that."

"You're welcome," she said, relieved, but wondering if her luck would hold out in the likelihood of another mishap.

"If that's all, I'll get to work now," she said, lingering a moment. He walked her to the door, shook her hand and wished her good luck.

Later, at her desk, she opened the brown envelope and found the revised evaluation report signed by Grady. It reflected her performance much more accurately. All that was left to do was for her to sign it. She did exactly that and delivered it back to Grady's office.

———

It was lunchtime and it couldn't have come fast enough for Lester. It was his day off and he surprised Cara on her job. In secret, Dexter Grady would have had hell to pay if she hadn't gotten the correct evaluation.

Lester found his way to her office with a little help from the receptionist. She stood staring out of the window, looking at the bordering skyscrapers. She had just finished typing reports due that day and had stepped a few feet from her desk to think. And, she lacked an appetite to eat her lunch.

He eased up behind her without so much as a sound. "Hi, Ms. Fleming."

"Hello. I know that voice anywhere," she replied softly and turned around to face him.

"I had to stop by and see you in action," Lester said.

"Well, it's good to see you," she whispered. She motioned for them to return to her desk and they sat down.

"So, how did it go with your evaluation?"

She showed him her official evaluation report. He read it and was pleased. "Congratulations! You won. I'm happy for you," he said, laying the envelope on her desk. Then he looked her over seductively. "I love you."

She pulled back and sat up straight in her chair when she heard her coworker's voice in the next cubicle. "Shh, don't say that," she whispered, taking a deep breath. Then she wrote on a sheet of paper, "You won't believe what Mario has done now."

Chapter 32

Mario took Paula out for lunch at a popular soul food restaurant. She was glad the paternity issue was settled. She urged Mario to go and see Ashley. More than anything, she wanted Mario to pop the question. But with the exception of occasionally mentioning the future, he avoided the M-word at all costs. "I believe last night's lovemaking did the trick, darling."

"Good. I love it when you're completely satisfied," he replied as he licked his lips seductively.

Paula continued to stare at him. Two years had done him nothing but favors; he was more handsome than ever. His body was perfectly chiseled and his washboard abs showed nicely through his yellow ribbed sweater. He seemed to be even more attractive than when they first met. He stared back at her with knowing dark brown eyes, full, sensual lips and a smile that would melt a stronger woman than her. He was definitely sexy and he knew how to work it. She'd taught him well and he gave unbelievable pleasure - enough to blow her off this planet when she climaxed. How lucky can one woman get? This time she decided to put all of her eggs in his basket. She had no plans of letting him go.

Mario started to tell her about his friend, Lester. "I'm not quite sure what's with the guy these days."

"Really? Tell me about him."

"Well, besides being my favorite tennis partner, he's a cop, married and divorced at least two times. At least, that's what I heard. Now, he's playing in dangerous territory."

A momentary look of discomfort crossed her face. Thinking she knew what he meant by that, she said, "I read somewhere that if the first marriage does not succeed, people will say that you were young and didn't know what you were doing. A second time around, they say that you're entitled to make a mistake. The third time, people start to wonder what's wrong with you," she replied.

"Is that right?" Mario asked.

———

Cara walked into her kitchen and tossed through her mind the belief that Mario was playing games with her. "You won't win this one, Mario," she said aloud. Deciding to skip dinner, she walked to the bedroom, got undressed and snapped a plastic hanger in two pieces trying to hang her blouse. "How dare he try to take Ashley from me!" she yelled.

She plopped down on the bed. A few minutes later, she realized that Jennifer hadn't returned her last two phone calls. Cara hoped it was because she had come to her senses and left Duncan. Cara worried about her.

At 6:35 p.m. she dialed Jennifer's number, letting it ring eight times. She waited fifteen minutes and dialed it again. This time she left a frantic message, "Jennifer, call me. It's important."

She tossed and turned for a few moments filled with worry. Right or wrong, she'd decided to go and see Jennifer the next day. Then the phone rang. She didn't look to see who was calling, figuring it was Jennifer.

"Hello," she said, letting it ring only one time.

"Ump", she heard the deep male voice blurt out. Then she heard a dial tone.

Fifteen minutes later the phone rang again. With her back turned to the phone on the nightstand, she was almost asleep and barely heard it.

"Hello," she snapped.

"Hi. It's me. Did I do something wrong?"

"I apologize, Lester. No, it's the hang-up calls and everything else on my mind."

"That's understandable. Have you eaten?"

"No, I wasn't hungry after I got home." She sensed he wanted to tell her something, but for her, she just needed to be close to him, to have him sit and hold her and make it all go away, if only for one night. But she would only admit that to herself.

"Great! Expect me around seven-thirty."

"See you when you get here." She took a long, steamy shower. Within fifteen minutes she dressed in a pair of perfectly fitting jeans and a red top. Being what many called a neat freak, Cara quickly inspected the apartment. The furniture was dust free; the kitchen floor tile was shiny; the carpet and rugs had been vacuumed; and her laundry was neatly arranged in the drawers or closet.

Lester arrived nearly on time at 7:39. He walked in holding a steaming hot pizza.

"Hi. Thought you might like something easy and Italian tonight?"

"Thanks." She politely took the pizza. "If it's okay with you, I'll put it in the oven."

"Exactly what I had in mind." He had to smile at her words, while reading something altogether different from them.

When she returned to the living room, Lester was sitting, leaned back with his head resting on the top of the sofa, both hands tucked comfortably behind his head. She sat down a few feet from him with her legs crossed Indian-style.

"What's on your mind?" she asked.

"Seems I've caused a problem for you. Mario knows about us. I would bet my life he followed us Sunday."

"What? Why would he care? From what I heard, he's hooked up with Paula again," she retorted.

"I wish I knew why, Cara. I just felt you should know."

"Well, that would explain why he wants custody of Ashley."

Hearing the words, Lester started to worry. *What if Cara decides to cool it between us until after her divorce? I can't imagine not being around her, not ever. A man in Mario's situation could be motivated out of revenge or jealousy,* he thought.

"I guess I underestimated the guy," Lester said.

———

Cara arrived at work the next day trying hard to deal with too many uncertainties and unanswered questions. She knew that before she could move her friendship forward with Lester, she had to resolve her larger problem. She would do better to listen to her inner voice.

Soon after she'd checked her phone messages and department memos, she used her cellular to call her lawyer. Waiting to learn something new about her case had become unbearable.

"Mr. Garnell, this is Cara Fleming. How are you?"

"Oh, there you are. I'm fine. I just left a message at your home number. We've got a court date. The bad news is the divorce settlement papers aren't signed. And, we know why."

Knowing exactly what he was referring to she asked, "What happens now?"

Chapter 33

While Cara sat at her desk, she took a call from Lester. He explained his involvement with a new murder case. A young black woman had been found dead at her home this morning from an apparent overdose.

"Are you sitting down?"

"Yes. Why?"

"Where did you tell me Jennifer lived?" he asked.

"In Pill Hill, why? Oh, my God, you aren't going to tell me it's Jennifer you found?"

"I'm afraid so, Cara. The first officer on the scene found her note. I have it. I'm so sorry."

There was a long pause and as Cara struggled to fight back the tears, she managed to ask Lester if she could call him back. When she pulled herself together she asked Grady for permission to leave and told him why.

Thirty minutes later, Cara drove away from her downtown office headed to Jennifer's house. Although the body had been removed, she needed to get another glimpse of the house, to be close to her again.

She parked three blocks down on Jennifer's street and she told herself to be strong as she got out of her car. She walked up to a point where she saw the yellow police tape.

A scene still busy ... police personnel going in and out of the house, several squad cars blocking the street, and several onlookers standing and talking to each other. Cara stood outside the line in a state of disbelief. Too angry to react, she looked up at the sky thinking Jennifer had to be up there and out of her misery. All she could think about was that Jennifer was dead and Duncan was alive and free to do what he wanted now.

Moments later, she saw something that made her take a deep breath. A man resembling Duncan walked out of the house with two officers. Immediately she wanted to scream out at him, but didn't. He looked worn and haggard. He stood along with the officers on the circular walkway, talking for a few minutes. She wondered what he had told them. More importantly, where was he when it happened? Had he spent the night away again?

The officers took turns shaking Duncan's hand, patting him on the shoulder before they walked to the cars. She felt another surge of anger, turned around and began to walk back to her car.

Just then her cellular rang. It was Lester.

"I was worried. Are you all right?"

"I'm okay." She gave him a full-blown report. "I'm just sick about this," she cried, feeling cold and angry.

"You and Jennifer were close. I can only imagine how you must feel."

"Yes. And I feel like I failed her." Fresh tears welled in her eyes.

"Come on, now. Whatever was troubling her, you didn't cause her to do this."

"True, but still, I wish I could've done more."

"I'm sad that you're sad. Listen, you're not alone; I'm your friend, too. And this friend loves you."

"Thanks. Our friendship is important to me," Cara replied.

"I've got to work later than usual this evening. I'll check on you later," he said.

"I understand."

She decided to go back to work.

When she arrived home later that day she walked inside her apartment feeling only marginally better. Even though Jennifer's situation was one that justified her state of unhappiness, it certainly had been totally unnecessary for her to end her life. Cara hoped that Lester would show her Jennifer's note. Perhaps, reading it would bring clarity and closure.

Exhausted, Cara dropped her body to the couch and fell asleep. When she woke up she felt the urge to call Naomi and tell her the sad news.

"My friend Jennifer was found dead today.

"Good Lord!"

"She was the only girlfriend I had here. She was in a very unhealthy, unhappy marriage. According to Jennifer, her husband was mean and extremely critical. If you ask me, it was a sign that he wanted a divorce."

"Why couldn't she have left him and started over like you?"

"I don't know. I practically begged her to do that."

"Don't beat yourself up too much, okay? Just pray that you find strength and wisdom out of it. There's something to be learned from every situation."

"I will, Mom."

They talked for a while and she felt a sense of relief rather than the sadness and the void she would feel for a long time to come. She felt it was time to change the subject and talk about her situation. She hoped it wouldn't cause Naomi to worry.

"If my lawyer can work a miracle, I'll be divorced soon," Cara said.

"Oh, yeah. Is Mario giving you problems?"

"Of course. First he started paying child support. No sooner than he did that, he told his lawyer I wasn't fit to raise Ashley. I've got to fight to keep my daughter, Mom."

"No way can he do that!" Naomi screamed. She paused for a moment. "Wait a minute. What payments? Why didn't you tell me?"

"I'm sorry. I meant to. So much is going on," Cara explained and told Naomi about the college fund she had set up for Ashley. "There's more I haven't told you," Cara blurted, before she'd thought clearly about how best to tell Naomi what she'd been up to. "I met a stranger over the Internet. It turned out that he's Mario's brother. More importantly, he's the kingpin behind me being framed."

"Have you mentioned this to anyone else?" Naomi asked.

It suddenly struck Cara that her mother's reaction was not what she'd expected. It was almost as if she knew about the Fleming secret, possibly more. Or was it her imagination? For a moment, Cara couldn't figure her mother out. She quickly disregarded the thoughts and told her mother the entire story.

"Well, my brave daughter, you have been busy. I can't believe you actually took off to Detroit to meet this woman. What was she like?"

"Aloof, nervous and yet poised. At best, she doesn't want the alderman's career destroyed."

"I bet. At least you got her to tell you the truth."

"But what good does it do me? *The man who ruined my marriage is my brother-in-law.* What I want to know now is, why did he do it?"

"Think carefully. Were you able to determine if the alderman knew he was Mario's brother before the whole frame-up situation?"

"No. I'd be surprised if he did."

Naomi let it all click around in her brain. Cara knew too much, way too much. To keep her safe meant keeping quiet about the Fleming secret. But, in doing so, her daughter could lose custody of Ashley.

"This could get sticky for you, Cara. If things don't go as you plan, are you prepared to live without your daughter?"

"No, I'm not and neither are you, Mom. No matter what, I'm going to fight these charges with all I got. I won't lose her."

Naomi hated reneging on a promise, especially the one she had made to Mary Lee and yet she knew what she had to do. But first, she'd try something on her own.

"I'll talk to Mary Lee. I'm sure we can work something out."

"Why would she want to, Mom?"

Chapter 34

Cara put two tickets to the pastor's ball in her purse. Initially she'd planned to go with Jennifer. But that was before she met Lester. Jennifer was gone and now the time just didn't seem right to be seen with Lester in public. As a gesture of good faith, she stopped by the church before she went home. She would ask Barbara to donate the tickets to someone who couldn't afford them.

When she entered the main lobby she noticed Barbara coming out of the mailroom.

"Hello, Cara. I'm surprised to see you."

"Hi. It's you I'm here to see," Cara said.

Since the strange looks Barbara had thrown when Cara was sitting next to Lester at church a week ago, the chill between them had escalated.

"I won't be attending the pastor's ball. It's such a shame to let the tickets go to waste." She passed the envelope containing two tickets to Barbara. "Please, give them away to whomever you desire."

"Sure. Thanks. It's been quite a while since we talked. How're things going for you?" Barbara asked.

Cara detected a thawing in her tone. Instantly, and for some yet undetermined reason, she felt vulnerable. "Things are going okay for me. And you?"

"Oh, I'm hanging in there and doing it my way," Barbara said. "It's not everyday I get to see you except on Sunday. Can I have a word with you?"

"Sure, but I only have a few minutes," Cara said, gesturing to the empty two-seater to the right of the security station.

Both ladies pranced over and sat down. Cara looked at Barbara with a calculating expression, waiting for her to take the lead.

"There's something bothering me. I can't think of anyone I know whom I can ask this question," Barbara's body slumped forward as she flipped the thin stack of mail in her hand.

Out of sheer habit, Cara crossed her legs and folded her arms around her.

Barbara exhaled a deep breath and continued, "I'm a single woman who's been roped around as far as men are concerned. I'm the wiser because of it. The problem I have is how do you tell a friend that the man she's involved with has a sketchy track record without hurting her feelings? If it were you, what would you do?"

"Don't tell her what she should know about this guy," Cara snapped, letting the words leap from her mouth. "She wouldn't want to hear it. Maybe, you could slip her an article about doing background checks. She could check him over before she commits her heart, if not her body."

"You're so wise for your age."

Cara smiled smoothly, betraying nothing of her annoyance. She knew exactly where Barbara was coming from. "Was that it?" Cara asked.

"Yes. On second thought, I could use a good friend to go places with," Barbara said, nudging her shoulder toward Cara.

Playing the devil's advocate, Cara figured Barbara knew Lester and worst of all, they were once lovers. *If they weren't once involved, why the need for a forewarning?* Cara thought.

Cara remained composed and checked her watch.

"Yeah, maybe we can do lunch," Cara said half-heartedly with a forced smile. "I really have to get home. See you Sunday."

————

Alderman Bennett relaxed in his ward office at six o'clock that evening, relieved to know his political career in Chicago was out of harm's way. He had one more goal to achieve – to build an ordinary friendship with Mario. His problem was finding a way to do that without revealing they were brothers.

It didn't take much to let his imagination conjure up a likely scenario. *At a small gathering of politicians and community folk, he meets Mario. They find time to chat and get acquainted. He learns of Mario's interest in tennis. He decides to take lessons and is soon ready to hit the ball well enough to play with Mario. Later they become more than sports buddies. Their friendship grows to a point where they're close enough to be brothers...* Bennett had it planned to the last detail.

The sound of the phone ringing interrupted his peaceful fantasy. Next, he heard his mother's uncontrolled voice.

"Matthew, uh, I mean Giles, we got to talk."

"Hi, Mother. How are you?"

"Cara's mother knows you're my son. After your father died, I had to talk to someone I knew I could trust. I'm sorry, the secret wore me down."

"Oh, no. Did something happen? Has her mom talked to anyone?"

"I don't believe she'd do that without telling me, but she could. I don't want to chance it any more than you do. Instead, she's asked for a favor."

"What is it that she wants from you?" Alderman Bennett asked.

"I've got to get Mario to stop his fight for custody of Ashley."

"Do you get the feeling she knows more?"

"Yes, but it didn't come from my mouth. Naomi says Cara can prove she was set up to look like she cheated on Mario. Don't ask me how, 'cause she didn't give me details."

Alderman Bennett didn't like the sound of that. In secret, he feared a bigger problem. One he wasn't about to tell his mother about. But still, he realized there could be a fatal flaw in his plan. His connection to the frame-up and what he'd done to help Cara may no longer be tightly wrapped.

"Well, give the lady what she wants."

"You're right. I'll talk to Mario."

Mary Lee had given Mario $100,000. She figured the money would keep him under her control.

"But, what if it doesn't work?

"I'll have to pull some political strings. Don't worry, Mario won't know anything about it." Alderman Bennett figured he could sway the judge to rule against Mario, if it should become necessary. She promised to work on Mario and report back to him right away.

"I love you, Mother. Call me once you have news. Good or bad."

Alderman Bennett hung up and sat in his chair to think about his next move. Thoughts about how Cara could've discovered the truth flashed across his mind. Clearly, the loopholes had been sealed. No way would anyone from his ward or Alderman Tucker's ward talk about this matter!

"Could it be that Cara is bluffing?" he wondered aloud.

Chapter 35

On Wednesday Mario left the Chicago Hilton after an all day athletic conference. He arrived at the *Due Drop Inn* at exactly five o'clock. He looked dazzling and successful in a three-piece camel colored suit– the first thing he had bought with his newfound wealth. He loved buying nice clothes, almost as much as Cara did.

After ordering a beer, he concentrated on his future. Part of it was anticipating Paula's arrival in Chicago that weekend. She was packed and ready to leave Memphis. She quit her substitute teacher job, settled her debts, and located a one-bedroom apartment at Seventy-first and Cornell.

Suddenly his cellular rang and he recognized it was Mary Lee calling.

"Hello, Mama."

"Mario, I need to warn you about something. It's about your divorce. Naomi told me Cara has proof that she never cheated on you. She's threatening to give this information to her lawyer and use it at the divorce hearing. There's more, but I can't tell you about it just now. So you'll have to trust me."

"I don't believe this. And, why can't you tell me the rest?"

Mary Lee wanted to say something like, "Have I ever lied to you before?" But she didn't because that very statement could come back to haunt her someday. "Mario, do this one thing for me, please."

"What? You want me to drop the charges and let Ashley go?"

"Yes, that's it. It's not like you won't have visitation rights. She'll always be your daughter."

"What is it that Cara knows?"

"I can't tell you. Naomi told me as much as she felt she could without hurting Cara's case. You can understand that, can't you?"

"I suppose. I need a little time to think about this, okay?"

———

Lester had telephoned Cara at her office, primed to tell her the truth about his past, but couldn't. Nobody was ever entirely honest about himself when they met another person, right? It took time to build a relationship and for some reason, mere mention of the word relationship didn't bother Lester nearly as much as it usually did. In fact, he freely told Cara that he loved her.

Meanwhile, Cara was at Brookins Funeral Home on Ashland Avenue viewing Jennifer's body. The body was elegantly garbed in a white nylon, long-sleeve laced gown. Her hand was perfectly positioned to hold a small black Bible. She looked as though she was sleeping peacefully, without worry or misery. Cara stood close, peering down into the brown shiny vault for a long time, letting heavy drops of moisture fall down her face. Quietly, the words parted her lips with questions that would never be answered. *Why Jennifer? Did I not do everything I should have to save you? Was there something you didn't tell me? Did Duncan do this to you? I need to make some sense out of this, Jennifer... for me, if not for you. I'm so sorry. I miss you. I pray your soul is taken in heaven. Rest in peace, my friend.*

A few minutes later, Cara walked out, unaware of her tear stained face, looking over the crowd of folks seated in the chapel. She noticed Duncan sat holding his head down and never looked up.

Still rattled by Jennifer's death, Cara drove fairly slowly on the Ryan Expressway headed straight to her job. She remembered the conversation she'd had with the woman caller before she left for the viewing that morning:

Hi. Can I speak to Lester?

Sorry, Lester doesn't live here.

Is this his girlfriend? the woman asked, sounding genuine and yet calm. Cara remembered thinking, Now what?

I'm a friend. Who are you? Cara asked.

His wife, the woman said. He didn't tell you he was married?

No, Cara said in a dull and troubled voice, thinking it had to be someone playing a joke.

"He usually doesn't tell people. Not even his friends."

What's your name? Cara had figured it was time to get some answers.

Brenda. He married me three years ago. I walked out on him because living with him was impossible. He became angry and filed for the divorce. Since then, we've been wrangling back and forth between our lawyers over petty stuff.

Cara asked her why she was still married to him.

He wants me to pay his legal fees and give up my share of the condo.

Is that right?

There's more you need to know. The reason I'm telling you all of this is because my mother persuaded me to warn you, hoping to spare another woman the same suffering.

Cara's feelings for Lester were now damaged. The man who'd satisfied her beyond her wildest dreams. Strangely, she was addicted to him.

Of course, she had only Mario for comparison. Needless to say, by now, Cara's heart had been torn apart once again. She could feel the sensations dwindling down to her stomach and didn't want to hear another word from this woman.

Well, Brenda, I suppose I should thank you. In truth, she felt ill and light-headed.

You're welcome. Women nowadays have to look out for each other, you know.

Yeah, don't remind me, she said thinking back to Jennifer and how she'd probably failed her.

Cara remembered hanging up the phone, feeling partly grateful and yet angrier than hurt. *This woman has burst my bubble and the sound can only be heard from within,* she thought.

After arriving at her desk, she sat down holding a heart already broken by Mario and now, thanks to Lester, her soul crumbled in a thousand pieces like sunflower seeds in a jar without air. Somehow she managed to let her mind drift back to the work stacked on her desk. She could never remember letting anything interfere with her work. She clutched the blue pen in her hand and struggled to finish one more report before she clocked out on time.

Forty minutes later, she pulled up in front of her apartment. Interestingly, she noticed Lester sitting inside his car parked in full view of her living room window. As she approached the entrance to her building, he quickly got out of his car and called out her name.

"Cara, hope you don't mind me stopping by. Can I come in and talk?" His voice faded, losing its masculine edge.

At the sound of his voice, she lifted her head. "Hi, Lester. Sure, you might as well."

She glanced at the parked cars and then stopped to think, "Oh, what's the use? Mario is probably somewhere licking his chops thinking he's got me cornered." Plainly, she was just tired of the rat race. At this point she didn't care if he was in one of the cars hoping to catch her. Lester followed her inside and sat down on the sofa next to her. His face looked tired and his eyes ravaged.

"You okay?" he asked.

But Cara diverted his gaze and nodded. Because of him, Jennifer, and everything else she had to deal with, she found enough strength not to shed a tear. She was tired of crying. Encumbered with emotions piled higher than the Sears Tower and the lack of sleep, she was exhausted and tense.

"I can't believe you couldn't tell me you're still legally married." She bit her lip until it throbbed like her pulse.

"What?" Suddenly his eyes grew wild. "How did you find out?" His voice was like an echo from an empty tomb.

"You say that as though I shouldn't have found out. Lester, I slept with you. For me, that's serious business."

She wanted to bring up Barbara Rhodes and force the truth from him about their relationship. Obviously Barbara had put Brenda up to calling her, she figured. *Maybe I should thank her, too. However, I'm not in the mood to thank anybody for breaking my heart,* she thought.

After staring at her for a moment, he gently pulled her closer and said, "Yes, you do have a right to know. Part of my reluctance was because I couldn't risk losing you. Knowing how you are about dating married men, I just couldn't. Think about it. Would you have let things get this far between us if I'd told you?"

Pulling away slightly, she narrowed her eyes at him, suspicious of his ability to read her mind. Nevertheless, she supposed there was still far too much left unsettled between them to let it go just yet. Lester had come to mean a lot to her and she figured she could someday forgive him and possibly reconsider the relationship. But now isn't the time to think about that, she thought.

Instead, she asked, "Why don't you tell me now? I want to hear all about this marriage you left hanging out there."

Lester explained, "She was materialistic. Later, I discovered Brenda was financially insecure and was after what I had. She stayed in the streets, leaving me to fend for myself. When she walked out on me, I realized I didn't really love her after all."

Cara remained silent and pressed her hand over her face thinking that his life was a mess like hers. Had Brenda been totally truthful? Even so, how could she continue the relationship with Lester while he was still married?

"It seems we're both in the same boat, paddling our way to face a judge. Considering our situations, it's best you and I don't see each other until we're free to do so."

A glazed look of despair began to spread over his face. "Okay, I hear you. Just don't give up on me. Please! I'll make it right," he begged.When she didn't respond, he asked, "Did you hear what I said?"

This time she just nodded. She was confused and she wondered how she was going to deal with her feelings for Lester. She really wanted to say something to make him feel okay and couldn't because to say anymore would only complicate things. She still needed his friendship and his help. Knowing how she managed *affairs of the heart,* she decided not to give him hope that she couldn't afford to give.

Then Lester stared at her for three seconds, his fingers circled around her chin. "Maybe I'm chasing a dream that has no legs," he stammered. His expression stilled and it grew serious.

"How are things with your divorce?"

"There's nothing new to report, sorry to say," she replied.

"With what you know, can't you fight this thing with Mario?"

"I'm considering my options."

"Do you need my help?"

"Maybe, I'll let you know." She got up and raised the window and breathed the fresh air.

He stood, walked to the door, and turned around to look at her. "Well, my lines are always open to you, Cara. You've got the power and it rests in the keypad on your telephone."

She turned around and walked toward him thinking, why does loving someone have to be so complicated?

Suddenly, he pulled a white envelope from his shirt pocket. "I almost forgot. This is something I promised you."

Cara took the envelope and swallowed the lump in her throat. She offered him a polite smile. She realized it was the final note from Jennifer.

"Oh, my goodness!" she exclaimed. She stood there, amazed and very shaken. She couldn't help but to search his face for a hint about the contents.

"It's a copy. The original belongs to the C.P.D. According to the autopsy, her blood alcohol level was .31. Added to that were traces of an antibiotic. It's the primary diagnosis in twenty percent of the cases where suicide is the cause of death."

She thanked him.

"You're welcome. Oh, don't breathe a word about this," Lester added.

"My lips are sealed." A pulsating knot within her demanded more. She wanted him to hold her so she could tell him that they could probably work through their problems and it would be okay between them again. But, she just breathed deeply and waved him good-bye as she stood at the door.

She laid the envelope down on the coffee table waiting for a calm moment to open it. She paced the floors and said, "I'm sure I've traveled this road before, and yet nothing is looking the least bit familiar."

Chapter 36

Behind the scenes, Naomi and Mary Lee had both been busy, trying to prevent a life-altering calamity in both families.

It was Mary Lee's turn to head it off. She'd talked to Mario last night and she remembered his exact words, "Mother, I'll agree to your demands, only if Cara shows me the proof."

An hour later she called Naomi again.

"Hello," she answered. She had set the table for dinner before the call came in. Frank checked on Ashley's temperature.

"Mario won't bulge unless he gets some information. Is Cara willing to talk to him?" Mary Lee panted.

"I don't see why not."

"Then call and ask her. Let me know her answer right away."

"All right. I know it wasn't an easy thing for you to do. Thanks, my friend." Naomi replied and hung up.

———

Naomi called Cara at 6:15 p.m.

"Hi, dear. How're things going with you?"

"Okay, considering." Cara replied. Actually they weren't, but she wasn't about to reveal the reasons to her mother. She asked about Ashley instead.

After Naomi assured her Ashley was going to be fine, she relayed Mario's message.

"I won't do it, Mom. The proof I have is not for Mario's eyes or ears. He's created a brick wall between us. Mary Lee will have to be the one to talk to him."

"I was afraid you'd say that. Okay, I'll give her your final answer."

"Please do, Mom. I'm tired of this merry-go-round."

"I'm sorry if this frustrates you. I promise it will end once and for all."

After Cara hung up she opened the envelope and braced her back against the back of the sofa to read Jennifer's note.

Cara, this is good-bye. My life has come to nothing and it's not because you didn't try to save me. My deepest dark secret I couldn't admit to you or anyone was that Duncan and Cecil are lovers. I know because I caught them at the house one day when I got home early from work. Yeah, that's right. He is sleeping with other women and this man, too. Don't tell anyone, please. Love you, Jennifer.

———

Mary Lee reached Mario at exactly 10:15 the next morning. A woman answered and said he wasn't home.

"This is his mother calling. Ask him to call me ASAP."

Mary Lee's next phone call was to Giles. She told him they had big problems and that he had to face his brother.

"It is the only way you can avoid political shame," she blurted out.

"Mother," he uttered hesitantly. "What went wrong?"

"Everything. Besides that, Cara knows too much about your past and your true heritage. That's not all. She knows you framed her."

"You have any idea how she discovered the truth?"

"Yes, I'm afraid so."

There was a long pause. All too quickly he had run out of diversions. Giles knew his world was about to explode, and he knew it was time to stop hiding. "Are you disappointed?"

"I'd be lying if I said I wasn't, Son. However, I'd like to believe you had a good reason. Please tell me you did."

"There's much more I want to tell you. I'll have to explain later, okay?"

"Well, I know one thing for sure. You didn't know Mario was your brother before this happened. Otherwise, you wouldn't have done it. Right?"

Deliberately, he avoided her question. She gave him Mario's phone number, just in case.

"Oh, by the way, I tried reaching Mario before I called you."

"And?" Alderman Bennett asked.

"A woman named Paula Coles answered. I'm sure it was her."

It was unmistakably all the encouragement he needed, because after he hung up from talking to Mary Lee, he picked up the phone and dialed Mario's number.

He heard the faint voice say, "Hello."

Alderman Bennett sighed loudly, clearly anxious about deciding one way or the other, what he would say.

Chapter 37

Cara had a difficult time sleeping the night before. Recurrent dreams of Jennifer had traumatized her. She began to remember the images, vivid and disturbing, which had formed in her mind. She remembered Jennifer calling out her name, smiling the entire moment as she waved from the clouds, softly repeating the words, *I'm happy now. Don't worry; you be happy.*

Once she was fully awake she turned the lamp on. She rolled her body across the bed and reached for her Bible. She read a few verses from the book Ecclesiastes. She started to accept what had happened, but was not exactly okay with Jennifer's decision.

Then she turned on the television in her room. A late-breaking news story interrupted the morning weather report on Channel 5 News.
Alderman Giles Bennett was a victim of a drive-by shooting last night outside his ward office. According to police, he sustained multiple gun shot wounds and was rushed to Hyde Park Hospital where he's heavily guarded. No word on his condition or motive for the shooting. His deputy chief, Joe Michaels was with him and luckily escaped injury.

"Oh, no!" she gasped. "What? How did this happen?" With shivers of panic, she paced the floor. After failed attempts to reach Lester, she realized it was a workday and figured he might be in the shower. Although she had the day off, she got busy going through her daily routine. She made coffee, toast, and a poached egg.

At 6:45 a.m., she sat down at the table and suddenly pushed the toast and boiled egg to the side. A quick and disturbing thought entered Cara's mind. *What if he doesn't make it? Who would want him dead?* She bowed her head prayerfully.

Afterward, she took a big sip of coffee. Then she speed dialed Naomi.

"Mom, it's me. Someone shot Alderman Bennett last night."

"My Lord, is he going to make it?" Naomi asked.

"I'm not sure. The news report said he is at Hyde Park Hospital."

"I'll call Mary Lee," Naomi said, and paused for a moment. Oh, one more thing; sit tight and leave the police work to the professionals."

"I will. Talk to you later."

Cara hung up and immediately reached for her cellular. She called Lester again. This time he answered and he knew about Bennett. To her surprise, Lester was unofficially involved. It was commonplace among police friends to help each other on the side. Although he was not assigned to the case, luckily he was granted permission to give undercover assistance to Bennett's case.

"I'm glad you're involved," she breathed a sigh of relief. "What is his condition?"

"He just got out of surgery. It's too early to tell," Lester replied. "It's a madhouse here." The area was filled with several police investigators and anxious news reporters with cameras and microphones, some holding small reporters' notebooks taking notes.

"I'm all right. Hey, there's something you need to know. I'm getting a strange feeling about the shooting. Mario's mother leaked the family secret to my mother. They're aware of how much I know, which is basically everything except why I was framed. Together, they decided to use that as leverage to convince Mario to drop the charges against me. Mario agreed to the deal, providing that I give him the proof that I never cheated on him."

"This thing with Bennett can't get any worse," Lester said.

"I don't know. I'm thinking that someone forced him to frame me. The person felt threatened in some way. It's the only logical answer.

A dead man can't talk, right?"

"Right, Miss Detective." He couldn't quite halt the chuckle that escaped him. "I'm just kidding. You got any ideas about who we should be looking for?"

"Well, I've given it a lot of thought since my meeting with Loretta Bennett. It's a long shot, but it's worth it. Can you do a background search on someone named Odessa Grant?"

Lester remembered reading the name from Cara's printed chat session with MattIwas. "She's the ex-prostitute who gave the alderman shelter during his teen years. What specifically are you looking for?"

"Her family tree, mostly her sisters' and brothers' names, where they reside, stuff like that."

"I'll get someone on it right away," Lester promised.

"Thanks."

"You're welcome. Just stay inside and keep your cellular on. I'll call you later."

She said good-bye to Lester and decided to do something she had wanted to do for a long time. Mario had obviously been checking on her indiscreetly and following her around lately.

She decided it was time to return the favor and surf the street where Mario lived. Although he lived on the third floor, she believed it would help her in some way to drive by and take a look at where he lived. Just by chance, she might spot the rat.

Shortly after she defrosted a pork chop, and finished her third cup of coffee, and cleaned the breakfast dishes, she left the apartment.

Twenty minutes later, she arrived in Hyde Park. She turned off on Fifty-second and Vernon. The street was mounted with a few high-rise complexes, a renovated mini-shopping center, offices and restaurants.

Five minutes passed before she figured the way to Mario's street. She slowed to pinpoint which building fit the number jotted on her notepad. She drove too fast to get a good look and decided to drive around a second time. On the return trip, she slowed, stopping in the middle of the street momentarily. The sun flickered on a man's blond hair as he jogged on the sidewalk. A blue jeep turned the corner. It moved slowly up the one way street, then found a place on the other side to park. She had noticed the same jeep on her tail a while back. She remembered how Lester's watchmen would signal their presence. She decided the driver was someone else.

Nervously she glanced at each car parked near Mario's building. She looked carefully and noticed the Thunderbird was missing. Soon she saw a red Camaro that had a Tennessee state license plate. She memorized it quickly, by saying it over and over out loud, and drove off.

Once she'd stopped at the traffic light on Fifty-third and Lake Park, she scribbled the number on her notepad and drove back to her apartment.

She walked inside and sat down on the sofa to think, trying to figure out who had followed her. Her thoughts went rampant. *Whoever it was, the person knows every move I made today. I won't let it scare me.*

Her cellular rang and she was glad that it was Lester.
"Hello."
"Cara, hi. Are you staying put?"
"No, I drove by Mario's place. I had a hunch and it panned out. A red vehicle with a Tennessee license plate was parked in front of his apartment." She gave him the number.
"We'll run a computer check. The license bureau will have a picture. I'm sorry I forgot to mention someone new has been assigned to cover you today. It's for your own good, you know."
"Oh, my! That's a relief." She sighed. "Did you learn anything about Odessa?"
"Yeah. Here's what we've found. Ms. Grant never married, grew up in Tennessee, moved about a lot and is currently living in Detroit.

She's got a sister, Paula. No brothers. Odessa has a long arrest record for prostitution, but no convictions."

"Now we're getting somewhere. Clearly, Paula got Alderman Bennett to set me up. She wanted Mario free. The one damaging piece of evidence was my birthmark. Mario had to mention that to Paula. There's the motive and thanks to you, we've linked her to the alderman. But, how do we prove it? If Bennett dies, she'll get away with her crimes."

"Not if I have anything to do with it," Lester replied.

Amazingly impressed, he realized how bound and determined Cara was and there was no stopping her once she'd made up her mind. And, he wondered what he would have to do to keep her from making another move that would surely put her in harm's way. But in truth, he believed her theory was right on.

"Let's see what comes back on this license plate number," he said. "Talk to you later."

"Sure. I'll be waiting for your call." She paused for a little while. "You're such a good friend and I won't ever forget that."

Being quite adept at reading between the lines, Lester sensed she still cared for him. And, as encouraging as the thought was, he was sure Mario would soon realize he'd made the biggest mistake of his life. Although his grounds with Cara were shaky at best, for some reason, Lester believed the future still belonged to him.

Chapter 38

Precisely at 11:32 a.m. the next day, Mario picked up Mary Lee from O'Hare. During the drive to the Ramada Inn on Lake Shore Drive, they rode in almost complete silence. As hard as he fought it, he couldn't help but remember their conversation over the phone the night before. *Mario, I'm flying to Chicago tomorrow. I need to talk with you face to face. My plane lands at O'Hare at 11:05 in the morning.*

He drove them from the airport in forty minutes. She hardly said anything while she checked in. Finally, they entered her room and while he placed her baggage carefully on the floor inside the closet, she plopped down in one of the wicker-backed chairs, with both hands clutching her purse.

"Since I can remember, I've never seen you like this, Mama," he said, as he walked over and knelt on the floor in front of her. "What is this about?"

She became afraid and wondered what Mario would do, what he'd say to her. Would he still adore her like most sons do their mothers?

"It's about a family so dear to me, that my heart is going to break telling this story to you. So here goes.

"Once upon a time, thirty years ago to be exact, a certain man and his wife were raising their family in Mississippi. There were two sons; one had just turned five years old, and the baby boy was only four months old. Happy to have beautiful boys, they gave them names beginning with the same initial as their mother. Their lives were complete. But one dark day in September in 1969, something dreadful happened to the oldest boy. The mother took him with her to the grocery store and then to get some gas for the car. She locked the door and left her son inside the car while she went in to pay for the gas. When she returned, her son was gone and was never seen again. The man and wife were devastated. The man nearly lost his mind. Somehow he decided that to keep from destroying himself and others around him, it was best to cut their losses and relocate to another state. As crazy as it sounds, this man figured the only way to do that was to put the lost son out of his mind, acting like he had never existed. So, the man swore his wife to a lifelong secret. And, like an obedient wife, she kept the secret. To this day the younger son has never been told."

Mario stood up and sat down on the bed. "Mama, for some reason I get the feeling this story is about us. Is it?"

"Shhh! Don't interrupt." By now, she'd imposed an iron control on herself. No longer able to sit comfortably, she stood and walked to the window. The sun was still high in the sky. Boats sailed far out on the lake and cars were speeding along the outer drive.

She turned to look at him again. "Since I've gotten this far, let me continue."

"Okay, I'm listening." He got up and joined her.

She took a deep breath. "Remember the old cliché, "What goes on in the dark, must someday come to light?" she asked in a deep husky voice.

"Yeah."

"Well, something miraculous happened: The wife, with extraordinary luck and help from someone close to her, found the older son over the Internet. To make this long story short, they reunited and got to know each other. Again she wanted to tell the younger son he had a brother. Above all else he deserved to know."

"Why didn't she, Mama?"

"For reasons unknown to the mother, her older son made her promise never to reveal his existence. Seems he has a somewhat shady past. He managed to put it behind him. He started a new life and a respectable career as a politician. He feared losing everything he'd worked so hard to accomplish. The mother was again held to the secret, and so the lie continued."

He shrugged to hide his confusion. "Is that it? Why was it so important to come here, look me in the face and tell this story to me, Mama?" He panted in terror hoping his fears were premature.

She looked him directly in his eyes. "Because the mother can no longer keep quiet. You're the younger son."

His dark brown eyes showed the tortured dullness of disbelief, and he refused to register the significance of her words. Since he'd never in his life uttered a word of disrespect to his mother or father, he found himself saying instead, "I…I can't find the words to respond to that." He turned away from her.

"Oh, Mario. Say something. Say anything. Curse me if you will, I'll overlook it." If only he knew how much she wanted him to do something…anything.

For a moment Mario stammered around in bewilderment and then he plopped down on the bed and bowed his head to his opened legs. Nearly five minutes passed before either of them spoke.

Finally he raised his head when Mary Lee got up to turn on the television. He appreciated that the volume was reasonably low.

Then he slowly stood up, stumbled over to the mini bar, and pulled out a tiny bottle. Just as he tore off the top, he looked back at Mary Lee and let his eyes drop in shame. Then he stomped off to the bathroom and without hesitation, flushed the contents. Deep down he'd realized something he'd known for a long time. Drinking wouldn't cut it this time. Seconds later, he came out and as he approached her, she stood with her arms opened wide. He grabbed and held onto her tightly and they both cried openly.

Finally he spoke again. "I have a brother! I've always wanted a brother," he said, pulling away. "What is his name?"

"Matthew is the name we gave him."

"Where does he live?"

Just then, late-breaking news interrupted the Jenny Craig talk

show. They sat down alongside each other on the bed facing the television. The news reporter said, *Although Alderman Bennett was heavily
guarded by the police and the media, he is missing from the intensive
care unit at Hyde Park Hospital.* Then a scene with a male reporter talking to the attending nurse was shown. She stated how baffled everyone
at the hospital was that such an important patient could be removed without so much as a whimper.

The news anchor continue: *Hospital administrator, Shayia Glass,
has assured us that everything is being done to locate the alderman.
According to police officials, it's their belief that the popular alderman
was removed for safety reasons, in which case no one knows where he is.
Stay tuned for updates as we will bring you more information as soon as
we receive it.*

"What a mess," Mario said, feeling unnerved by the tragedy. "I
hope the guy makes it. He's one hard-working politician."

"I hope so, too," she said, returning to her seat and moving her
head from side to side. "I hope and pray he makes it."

"You seem awfully concerned, Mama."

"Yes, and for good reason. He's your brother," she told him, gently holding his hand. "Alderman Bennett is my son, too."

"I don't believe it. How can that be?" At that moment, Mario
leaned his head toward her and gazed into her eyes, not trusting himself
to speak and lacking the strength to sit still.

Pacing the floor like a crazy man didn't help either. He asked her
to turn off the television. Then he let his body drop down onto the bed
in a straight position and he stared around the room. He'd heard more
than he cared to.

"Mario, are you okay? Talk to me, Son."

He finally opened his mouth. "But his name is Giles. Did he
change that too?" While he lay there, she told him the rest…the little she
knew about the people who raised Matthew, his life growing up as a
Bennett, the sordid lifestyle he led, the prison term, and that he turned his
life around and made something out of himself.

"Does my brother know our father died?" He eased his body back on the bed to hear some more.

"Yes, he was too afraid to come to the funeral. But he came to the hospital the day after you. It was sad for him. He took pictures of Bradley lying there unconscious. And, he asked me to take a picture with his face cheek-to-cheek with your father. In case Bradley didn't wake up, there would be a picture to hold onto forever."

"What about Daddy? Did he know, too?"

"I convinced your father to call Alderman Bennett and he did. Bradley suffered the heart attack shortly afterward."

"Wow! What about me?"

She searched for the best way to tell him. "Many times he talked about how he wished you could be told the truth. He'd even worked out a plan to meet you, hopefully for the two of you to become the best of friends. He would've treated you like a brother."

"How touching, except I would've still been in the dark," he replied, shaking his head in dismay. "But, Mama, once the secret was out between you, surely in time I could've understood his plight just as you did. There was no reason for him to fear me."

"Right, and I guess it's time you know the rest. It's about the proof your wife has." He flopped back on the bed and closed his eyes waiting for the ton of bricks to fall on him. "And," she continued, "some-one did frame her and somehow she traced it all back to Alderman Bennett. She feared hurting our family and decided to sit on it. Now you see why I pleaded for you to let her have Ashley?"

"You got some aspirin? My head hurts." It had all started to make sense: The anonymous phone call. Why his brother feared the truth. Of course, why else would his brother need to keep their family ties a secret?

By then, it was nearly four o'clock in the afternoon.

"I'm sorry," she began crying again. "My heart aches for you right now."

"It's okay, Mama. I just need some time to digest it all."

"You must be starving. Can I get you something from the diner?"

"No, thanks. I'm not hungry," he answered. He hunched over and rested his arms on his thighs. "You remember how I yelled to the top of my lungs and said those awful things about Cara?"

Mary Lee sat quietly and nodded.

"Now, I know why you defended Cara. Why couldn't I have done the same thing? What she must think of me?" He willed himself to his knees and stood up. "Right now, I'm worried about my brother. He could die and I'll never come face-to-face with him, never get to say hello. Mama, why do you think he lied to me about Cara? He knew nothing about our family or that he belonged until you discovered each other. So who the hell put him up to do such a dastardly thing?" Mario asked, sounding desperate.

"I have no idea."

Then the thought occurred to him that the person who shot his brother might try again. "Mama, did Matthew ever mention he had enemies or that he feared for his life?"

"Never. He didn't talk much about his life or his work."

"It's now that I realize how precious life is. Maybe I haven't been spending my time the way I should have."

He got quiet again and stayed that way for a few minutes.

"What're you thinking?" she asked.

"Oh, just that I don't have a prayer to lean on this time. It just so happens, I was thinking about Cara, the divorce. By the way, I promised to get back to my lawyer."

Mary Lee stepped to the bathroom, giving him privacy. He sat up on the side of the bed and reached for the phone to call the lawyer. He agreed to meet the lawyer the next day.

When Mary Lee came back and sat down, she said, "I'm proud of you. Hope you did the right thing, finally."

On those words, he let his body drop back on the bed, thinking that his mother had been so right all along. "Don't go giving me too much credit. I haven't behaved like a gentleman. I pushed my wife out of my life and for what, a damn lie?"

Then she sat next to him on the bed, and asked, "Be honest with me, how do you feel about Cara now?"

He realized it was time to face the truth about his feelings. "Of course I still love her and I can kick myself for pushing her into the arms of another man." His voice was weak and shaking.

"You're kidding! Who?"

"Somehow she met my best friend, Lester Miller. He's a homicide detective. She doesn't know it, but I've been watching her."

"This friend, could it be that he was just helping her? Maybe that's all it is."

"I don't think so, Mama. Anyway, I'm just as guilty," he said, sounding desperately unhappy.

"Since you can't be sure she's fallen for him, remember, it's not over until the fat lady sings."

Mario told Mary Lee about his one-time affair and how it almost ended his marriage. Then, Mary Lee understood Cara's motivation to leave him this time.

Mario adjusted his body to face the wall. "I hurt her real bad this time. She'll never forgive me."

"Maybe you should tell Cara how you feel," Mary Lee pointed out. "I believe she'll come around, if you prove your love for her and that you are willing to change."

"I can't face her." Suddenly Lester and Cara started to wear on his mind.

Oh, my God, Cara! What have I done to you?

Chapter 39

Lester arrived at his condo around nine that evening. He was satisfied that everything had been done to protect Bennett. Calling in bigtime favors, he convinced Michaels to take Bennett to a secure room at the University of Chicago Hospital. Getting him away from Hyde Park Hospital had been extremely difficult. Without disrupting the alderman's I.V. and his heart monitor, undercover officers dressed in hospital garb eased him out, through a rear entrance and into a private ambulance.

By now, Lester was exhausted and he soaked his tired body in the tub for almost an hour. He thought about his next move as he dried his body and changed into his robe.

Then his cellular rang.

"Hello."

"Lester, I need to talk to you."

"Hey Mario. What's up?"

"My mama is in Chicago. She told me everything."

"Everything?" Lester asked, voice lowered.

Mario always hated fake I-don't-know-what-you're-talking-about tones. He felt like yelling at Lester, *I know about you and Cara. How could you do this to me, you son of a bitch?* Instead of doing further harm, he said, "You heard me man, and don't act like you don't know what I'm talking about."

"Okay, I see you're upset," Lester replied. "Maybe now is not a good time to talk about this."

"I know about Alderman Bennett. He's my brother. Where is he, Lester? Surely you'd know."

"Someone did try to kill him. It's possible this person will try again," Lester replied.

"How much do you know about my family's situation, and when did you find out about it?" Mario barked, sounding as if he would strangle Lester if he could only see him. "I need information. I need to know how my brother is doing. Surely the police have some idea. Doesn't our friendship mean anything, anything at all?"

"What kind of question is that?" Lester asked. Mario's tone aroused and infuriated him.

"It's a simple one," Mario said, trying to calm down.

"The answer is, yes. I'm still your friend. I'll tell you, but you have to promise not to tell another soul. I'm sure you know why."

"All right, I promise," Mario said, calmed down.

"The alderman is barely holding on and hasn't regained consciousness. I'm truly sorry."

"Thank God, he's still alive though. When can we see him?"

"I'll call you tomorrow. Can't promise when you can see him. But I'll try," Lester said.

"Okay. Sounds good. I'll tell Mama he's still alive."

"And no one else, remember?" Lester insisted.

After Lester hung up the phone, he thought about how he would implement his plan. He had expected Mario to say something altogether different. On the other hand, he believed Mario when he said he knew everything. He had to. So, Lester adopted a new policy: *You don't ask; I don't tell. I can play this game, too.*

Before he called it a night, he called Cara and told her what was going on.

———

At exactly 10:30 that same evening, Mario held the phone between his shoulder and head while he made a cold bologna and cheese sandwich. He waited for Paula to answer. The phone continued to ring. *She must be out somewhere or asleep,* he thought. Maybe it could wait until morning. No. He wanted to find out now. What made her leave the other night before he got home? She'd promised to cook dinner. Why hadn't she called him?

Mario remembered his promise to Lester. Certainly, it didn't pertain to Paula. Why would it matter? In no mood to play games, still he needed to talk to Paula. He left her a message, "Hey Paula, what's up? Answer the phone."

Fifteen minutes later, when his phone rang, he answered.

"Hi. I bet you're wondering what happened to me."

"Where were you? Out messing around, I bet."

"Oh, no, that's not it," she said with deceptive calm.

"What's the problem then? We had plans for yesterday. When I got home, dinner was missing and so were you."

"Well, to tell you the truth, I started to think you could get too comfortable with things the way they are. I... I don't want to live like that ever again, Mario."

"Whatever," he snapped.

Paula sensed something was wrong and knowing Mario like she did, a bad mood left undressed could harden into a bad attitude.

"Let's change the subject? I was just being silly," she said. "Come to my place. I'll fix you that dinner I promised. Then we can make love all night long. Please?"

"Paula, I'm not in the mood," he quickly replied.

"Why not?" She got the feeling that he had a serious matter on his mind. "Can't you tell me what's wrong?"

"I'm not sure if I should," he spoke louder, letting out an audible breath.

"Fess up, Mario. It's me you're talking to."

"It's top secret. You really shouldn't know. But I know you. I won't get a moment's peace if I don't tell you. You might recall hearing on the news someone tried to assassinate Alderman Giles Bennett."

"Yeah, I heard about it."

"Today, my mother told me that he's my older brother."

She didn't respond.

"Are you still there?" he asked.

"Brother? How can that be?" Her voice was shakier than she would have liked.

"It's complicated. But what she told me all added up. I've got a brother."

Oh, no. This can't be true. Can it? Paula thought and hung up on him.

———

The next day, Cara arrived home from the Laundromat at 1:15 p.m. The phone rang.

"Hello, Ms. Fleming," Attorney Garnell said. "Seems your husband has stopped the divorce proceedings. I thought you should know right away."

Immediately, she thought, *I don't believe this. What am I supposed to do now? I wonder what Mario is up to? Anyone else would've called his wife and discussed such a decision. Idiot!*

"I take it you're in the dark about his decision."

"That I am, Mr. Garnell." And she decided it made no sense to inquire about Mario's reasons. She would probably be told about client confidentiality or some legal mumbo jumbo that she didn't quite understand.

"I'm glad I called as soon as I did," Garnell added.

"Now, what am I supposed to do?" Care whined.

"Call him and ask for an explanation. You deserve to know why."

"I was afraid you'd say that. What if I want to proceed?"

"Then we'll file the petition this time. Give it some thought and when you've talked it over and decided what you want to do, give me a call."

After she hung up, she called Naomi.

"Mom, Mario knows everything about his family's secret."

"You don't say! Well, we're getting somewhere with this mess. Has he called you?"

"No, you'd think he would have, especially since he's decided to call off the divorce." Sensing that Naomi was about to respond, she said,

"Wait. I've got more news. I know who got the alderman to frame me."

"Who?" Naomi's breathing had become erratic.

"Paula Coles. She had an affair with Mario when we lived in Memphis. She obviously did it to ruin my marriage. This time she's playing for keeps."

"Who told you? I mean how do you know it was her?"

"A background search was done on Paula. She's the sister to Odessa Grant. Remember the alderman's prostitute friend in Detroit?"

"Now I get it. My Lord! Wait until I tell Frank. Since I filled him in on everything, he's worried about you. If you get the time, call him this evening. He needs to hear your voice."

"Okay. I need to hear Ashley's voice, too."

"How do you feel about Mario withdrawing the divorce petition?" Naomi asked.

"I don't know. Mostly, I'm concerned why he hasn't picked up the phone to tell me. I don't like being left hanging."

"Mary Lee is in Chicago. Has she called you?" Naomi asked.

"No."

"She's staying at the Ramada Inn on Lake Shore Drive."

"Oh, I see." Cara said, while thinking of her next move.

Almost instinctively, Naomi said, "Remember, it's time to stop playing cops and robbers. I mean it, Cara. Let the big guys do the work for you this time."

Cara let out a sigh of relief. "It seems I don't have a choice in the matter."

———

After Cara hung up the phone, she started the shower. Minutes later, she stood under the shower massage and the hot water came pouring down heavily. She lathered Irish Spring soap all over her body and washed with a soft towel until she felt clean and her tired, tensed muscles were relaxed.

When she had finished showering, she put on her bra and opened another drawer and pawed through the panties, looking for a red pair to match her slacks. She checked her appearance and brushed her hair into a ponytail.

Seconds later she thought she heard a noise. Then she heard sirens. At first she didn't pay much attention, thinking they were from the news clip flashing across the television screen. She clicked it off to be sure. The sound became increasingly louder. She'd become used to emergency sirens, fire, police and ambulances in Chicago and wouldn't have paid much attention, except this time, it sounded like it stopped directly in front of her building.

Chapter 40

Cara dashed to the living room window. No mistake about it, an ambulance and two police cars were parked in front of her building. Lights flashed. People lined the sidewalk.

Soon, two white paramedics pulled a stretcher from the rear of the ambulance. Moments later, two more squad cars arrived and parked in the middle of the street.

Cara wondered if it had to do with Mrs. Walker, as she watched them walk up the front entranceway. She grabbed her keys and walked into the hallway. The men hurried past her apartment door, headed to the floor above. She ran down the steps. As she was about to knock, Mrs. Walker stood in the doorway, peeping and trying to listen.

"Hi." Cara gasped for breath. "I was afraid you were ill or something. I'm so glad you're all right."

"I'm glad you thought to check on me. Won't you come in?"

The smell of collard greens cooking filled the air, and voices streamed from the television. Cara turned around to face her. "What do you think happened to Louis?"

"It's not him," Mrs. Walker said. "He left a week ago for Florida."

Mrs. Walker walked back to the door and carefully opened it. Cara followed her. A police officer was walking down the steps with white gloves and a mask on.

Cara spoke first. "Excuse me officer, what happened up there?"

"We got an anonymous tip to check out the top-floor apartment. Apparently gun shots were heard."

"That's odd," Cara said, giving Mrs. Walker a quick glance. Then she looked at the officer who seemed to be in a hurry. "Did you find anyone up there?"

"Yes, I'm afraid so. A young woman was shot to death. That's all I can tell you, ma'am." The officer turned around and walked out of the building.

"Did you hear what he said? That's terrible. Who would do such a thing?" Cara asked.

Mrs. Walker didn't answer and quickly locked her door.

"I can't believe it," Cara said, managing no more than a hoarse whisper. "It's the first time I've been this close to death."

"Come, let's sit," Mrs. Walker said. "It's times like this that my legs fail me."

Cara followed Mrs. Walker and sat down on the sofa. She wished she'd thought to bring her cellular along. She couldn't afford to miss any calls.

"Do you think it was gang related?"

"Probably. It's not uncommon around here. I'll make us some tea," Mrs. Walker said.

Ten minutes later, they sat for a while talking about the situation. Mrs. Walker watched Cara with a keenly observant eye.

Later on, they heard sounds from the hallway. Both ladies rushed to look out of the living room window. They stood baffled and mostly in silence watching until they saw two officers move the body out of the building.

"I wonder who they found dead up there," Cara said. "Louis had so many women. Maybe it was a girlfriend."

Mrs. Walker explained, "I had a hard time keeping track. Mostly they'd come and go. But my guess is that the dead woman was the one who stayed with him off and on. She'd come over whenever her husband beat her up. Louis gave her keys to the place. And, when he got tired of her, he'd put her out."

"Why?" Cara asked, sipping some of her tea.

"She was a heavy drinker."

"That's a sad way to live, don't you think?" Cara asked with thoughts of Jennifer.

"Yes, it is. You feeling better now?"

"Yes. And, thanks for the tea."

"It's understandable that you would be frightened. I've seen so much crime in my lifetime. But then again, you never really get used to it. Each time is like the first time all over again."

Cara nodded. "Mostly, I'm worried."

"What would you have to be worried about?

Mrs. Walker knew all too well about Cara's regular male visitor. Once he'd worn his uniform. And, she'd noticed men parked on the street watching the building and often wondered why.

"Can I ask you something totally unrelated?"

"Sure. Why not?" Cara replied.

"The man who comes to visit you, is he a policeman?"

"Yes, and to be more exact, he's a homicide detective. His name is   Lester Miller. He works out of Area 2 on Wentworth Avenue. He's been a really good friend, looking out for me."

"You aren't in any trouble, are you?"

"No. Compared to most, I'm straight-laced. I go to work every-day, pay my bills, mind my business and try to stay out of other folks' business. What I'm worried about has to do with matters that I can't talk about right now. What I can tell you is that the reason I'm living alone is because I was set up to look like I was cheating on my husband. We're separated and soon to be divorced. My friend is doing what any good male friend does. He's making sure I'm not in any danger."

Instantly, Cara thought about Lester and how he really felt about her. Did he love her the way she needed to be loved and trusted? Was he the type of man who would love a woman enough to get her and then change to his old ways later?

"I had no idea," Mrs. Walker said. "That explains it. I could never figure out why someone so attractive and nice as you had to live alone. For what it's worth, I hope everything turns out okay for you."

"Me, too," Cara said.

"You mind if I give you some old folk wisdom?"

"No, I could use some more."

"People who live the longest are independent minded. They don't pound themselves fretting about other's opinions. They do what's right for them."

"I appreciate what you just said. It couldn't have come at a better time." Cara stood up from the sofa. She dangled the door keys. "I guess I'll go home now," she spoke loudly. "I'm expecting some calls."

"Okay. I'm so glad we had this talk. I'm here if you need me. Remember, you're not alone," Mrs. Walker said.

––––––

Once Mrs. Walker was sure Cara was inside her apartment, she locked her door and sat down to re-think everything that had happened that morning. It was around ten that morning when a strange man and woman had pulled up in a red car and parked across the street three apartments down from the building. The woman sat inside the car while the man got out and entered the building. He was short and of medium build and wore a cap pulled too far down on his head. Mrs. Walker heard footsteps through the building entrance. Looking through the peephole, she got a good look at his face. She heard him tiptoe up the steps. Then, she opened the door and saw the man go into the third-floor apartment. A few minutes later, she heard muffled sounds and she closed her door. She eased back to look through her peephole and saw the man darting out of the building. She made the anonymous phone call to 9-1-1.

––––––

Around five that afternoon, Mario got a call from Mary Lee. He had just arrived home in time to prepare to meet with Lester.

"For God's sake, Mario, don't mention this call to anyone. It's a matter of life and death," she said, breathing out of control.

"Whose life are you talking about?" he asked.

"Cara's," she said. She got him to think about whether he could've slipped and told Paula about Cara's birthmark.

If his life depended on it, he could not explain how Paula would know about Cara's birthmark. But every nerve in his body was rattling, telling him he must have told her. "Oh, my God! It's possible, but I didn't mean to." He felt as if his breath was cut off. "Are you suggesting Paula got to my brother and forced him to frame Cara? How could she? Giles and Paula don't know each other."

"Oh, yes they do." She gave him all of the details.

At that moment he wanted to strangle Paula. His chest felt like it would burst. "Well, I'll be damned, he said, seething with anger. "I'm headed out the door to meet Lester. I'll call you later, Mama."

———

Lester was waiting at a small table in the corner when Mario stepped in. He was prepared to tell Mario what he wanted to know, hoping Mario would help nail Paula. Uncertain of what to expect, he braced himself for the fight of his life.

Mario went straight to the bar and after a few words with Freddie he joined Lester. It surprised Lester that Mario didn't order something to drink.

Lester stood up to welcome Mario with his hand extended for a handshake. A wave of apprehension swept through Lester, but his fears were premature. Mario sat down across from Lester and he had the strangest look on his face. He seemed calm and he smiled easily.

"Hi. Thanks for meeting with me," he said to Lester.

"You're welcome. How are you doing?"

"I'm hanging. It's just that I never expected things to end up like this. I've known about you and Cara a short while, but since yesterday, even that has taken a backseat in my mind."

"You're being too kind," Lester answered quickly over his choking, beating heart. *This guy sure isn't slow to spill his guts*, he thought. "If you don't mind, I'd like to explain a few things about me and your wife."

"Go ahead," Mario said.

"Man, I didn't go searching for her. She found me. You want to know why? She was having a hard time dealing with not knowing what the caller told you. I listened and asked questions. Anyway, after we talked, I had doubts about who to believe. Strange men started to follow her around the city. I traced the license plate to your brother and another one to his political chief, Joe Michaels. I even broke department rules to keep her under surveillance. I took time off to go to Detroit to check Bennett's background. One thing led to another. I found the woman he referred to as mother. Loretta Bennett is her name. But it was Cara who took everything I learned, added to what she'd discovered over the Internet and put it all together. Then without telling me, she took off to Detroit and talked to Mrs. Bennett and that's how she learned the alderman was a Fleming. The rest of what happened is history. She never gave up trying to prove her innocence."

Mario sat without moving an inch, his head bowed at times.

"Sad to admit, but in the midst of all this, things changed," Lester added. "We got closer. If you will recall, you made it clear that it was definitely over between you two, no matter how many times I tried to get you to reconsider. I hate that it happened. Now, if that makes you my enemy, then I'm sorry. I'm so sorry." Lester kept all expression from his voice as he apologized.

"Okay, okay, I hear you," Mario said and paused. You were a good friend to Cara, even when I was too stubborn to be that for her. And, you acted out of friendship to me. So, instead of acting like a jerk, I can honestly say that this whole situation has brought about a new attitude in me.   It's hard to explain to you, Lester. What's not hard to say is, thank you and that I forgive you. Thanks, for being a friend to Cara. As far as what happened between you," Mario said and paused for a minute. "I'm glad it was you and not some other man."

Suddenly, Lester noticed that the tension between them had started to melt. He moved his head closer toward Mario. "Are you sure you're all right? Can it be that a new Mario has really emerged?" Lester asked.

"Yeah, and I feel better inside. And now, I want to clear the air with you and make things cool between us."

"I'm glad. Are you ready to help me nail the real culprit?"

"I'm ahead of you on that one."

"How did you figure it out?" Suddenly it hit Lester that Mario hadn't reached for a cigarette.

"Let's just say that I was hit with a wake-up call. Mama laid it all out for me like she's never done before. I'm so ashamed that it took everything she had inside of her to get me to see the light." Mario replied. "She called me before I left to come here. She forced me to think about the one person outside of Cara's parents, her doctor and me, who could've known about the birthmark."

Lester looked at Mario. "I got a question for you. Can you account for Paula's whereabouts the night Bennett was shot?"

"No. I figured she was home," Mario said. "Can you take me to see my brother?"

Less than ten minutes later, the two men drove in their cars to the University of Chicago Hospital, with Lester in the lead.

Just ahead of the rush hour traffic, they arrived fifteen minutes later and entered through a rear door. They took the stairs to the fifth floor. To the right was a room with double doors. Inside, it was semi-dark, cold and quiet and there was mostly discarded equipment; copiers, inoperable patient beds, weigh scales, chalkboards and sealed boxes stacked ceiling high along the walls.

Lester walked through the organized clutter and Mario followed him inside the adjoining room that had a sign on the door in red letters: No Admittance.

Inside, the room was dimly lit and the hum of onlookers had been smoldered behind the closed door with a dark window. A black nurse sat alongside Bennett's bed reading a book. She lifted her head, revealing a face that was more interesting than attractive, with strong cheeks, a square jaw and a wide mouth. Lester waved a hello and she continued reading.

"Why don't you have a few moments with him alone?" he said, looking at Mario.

Mario eased to the bed. Bennett's breathing was labored and his face was ashen, and it was there that Mario saw an image of his mother...her facial shape, mouth, contour of her eyes and he looked older than Mario imagined, considering they were five years apart. He held the alderman's hand for a few minutes. Then Mario silently spoke to God, promising he would change his ugly ways and be the man their father had wanted him to be.

Finally, he opened his mouth and whispered, "I'm the baby brother you didn't get to know. Stay alive and come back to me from wherever you are."

———

Still very afraid, Cara sat in her apartment around eight that evening, frozen in time, thinking about the dead woman and the fact that she had been murdered in cold blood. Would the police return to ask more questions? If so, she had none to give. She figured Mrs. Walker had all the answers and that she knew everything that went on in the neighborhood.

She thought about Loretta Bennett and realized that she needed to know that her Giles had been shot. She placed the call.

Chapter 41

It was a little after nine that evening and Paula had given up trying to reach Mario at home and on his cell phone. She figured that by
now the news of Cara's death had reached him. Even so, why hadn't he
called to notify her? She let her mind drift back to that day she had
accompanied Ralph, the assassin, to the building on Exchange. He came
cheap. A crack cocaine user for years, he was hard up for money.
Although he had botched the assignment to kill the alderman, this time
she believed themission was a done deal.

She remembered lifting Cara's address from a pad on Mario's
dresser: *7714 South Exchange, 2nd floor. Ralph said the woman was
dead when he left the apartment.*

Still, the thought occurred to her to get in contact with Ralph to
be sure. She reached him at his low-income housing apartment on State
Street.

"Hello," the husky voice answered.

Loud rap music was playing in the background. She wondered if
he could hear her. "Ralph, this is your little friend in the red Camaro."

"What's up?" His voice was higher than needed.

"I was thinking about …would you turn down that music?" She
spoke in a loud, sarcastic tone.

A few seconds later he returned to the phone. "What can I do for
you this time?"

"It's about the woman you took care of. Do you remember what
apartment you went to?"

"He cleared his throat. "Yeah, I remember. Why?"

"Good," she spoke eagerly, taking half breaths. "So it was the second floor you went to, right?"

"Lady, whatcha trying to do to me? I heard you say the third floor."

"You motherfucker. You shot the wrong woman. I don't believe this!" Paula screamed.

"Oops, seems I forgot to mention I lost my hearing in the right ear from a gang beating three years ago. What you want me to do about it now? I can use another five hundred."

"I'm broke, you fool," she uttered with quiet emphasis.

"Hey, whatcha you want from me? I asked you to go with me."

Chapter 42

Shortly after midnight, the clock found a twenty-fifth hour.
Hours had passed and Cara hadn't eaten all day. She rushed to the bathroom thinking she was going to be ill. Sitting down on the floor and leaning against the tub, she wondered about Mario and Lester. Had they forgotten she existed and needed answers? Calling Naomi or trying to reach
Mary Lee was useless.

A few minutes later, Cara thought she heard noise around her
apartment door. She pulled herself up and quietly eased to the door. She
looked through the peephole. At first she didn't see anyone. She continued to watch a few seconds longer and decided it was just her imagination.

Then she stretched her body on the sofa facing the door. She
noticed the doorknob turn one time. She looked around the room. The
walls seemed to be caving in. Deep down she'd always been afraid. Now
it gnawed away at her courage to keep a brave face. Immediately she
reached for the cordless phone and dialed 9-1-1 and whispered, "Send the
police to 7714 South Exchange now. Someone is trying to break into my
apartment. Please help me."

Although she had, two double locks on her door, she searched for
some kind of weapon, a knife or a hammer to grab onto, while forgetting
she had mace hidden in her purse. She rushed to the kitchen and grabbed
a knife from the silverware holder, and then walked back to the living
room. She prayed that the police would respond to the call as fast as they
had yesterday. Suddenly, she heard two knocks at the door.

She dashed back to the door and took another peep. This time a rough looking black guy, with huge eyes and wearing a long bibbed black cap, stood there. His eyes darted around the hallway in frustration.

"Who are you? What do you want at this time of night?"

"Oh, hello ma'am. You don't know me. Your husband, Mario, he's been shot. You need to come before it's too late."

"What did you say your name was?" Cara asked.

"That's not important."

"Where is he? How did you know where to find me?"

"I can explain all of that, if you would just open your door."

"I'm not going to do that, so just tell me," she snapped at him.

The cordless phone in her robe pocket rang. She walked away from the door and answered.

"Hello," she spoke in a suffocated whisper.

"Cara, honey, this is Thelma Walker. I saw a thug-looking man coming up there. Don't let him in. He's the one I saw in the building the day that woman was murdered."

"Oh, my God! No."

"Listen, your detective friend knows about him."

"He does? When …" She'd known fear before, except this time it was as bad as it could get. She thought about the police. "What's keeping them?" She accidentally pushed the off button as she rushed back to the door. *I'll call her back later*, she thought.

Leaning on the door and still holding the phone, she put her right eye to the peephole. Her eye was eyeball-to-eyeball with his. Afraid he would shoot a bullet straight into her, she jumped away to the left side of the door and ran toward the sofa.

Just as she moved away, she heard, "Bang! Bang!" Balls of fire pierced through her door. She thought the shooting would never stop as a third gunshot went off. The sound of feet trampling down the steps made her gasp. Her mind swirled, causing her to drop the knife to the floor. Then there were sirens from both directions on the one-way street.

The sounds grew louder. There were persistent knocks at her door.

She heard a male voice. It was familiar. "Cara, open the door.
It's okay. It's me, Mario."

"Mario?" She ran toward the door and looked through the peephole. Instantly she wondered what was he doing outside her door and
why. She opened the door and when she saw him, she was relieved and
his eyes told her that he felt the same way. "Mario, I'm so glad to see
you," she cried, as he held her close to him.

"Thank God, you're okay."

He walked with her toward the sofa with his arms still around her.
Cara started rattling off the sequence of events that had just taken place.
Mario carefully put his gun on the end table. "He won't get too far. One
of my *bullets* hit him."

Hearing the word bullets, she lost consciousness in his arms.

Twenty minutes later, Lester had knocked at her door and Mario
let him in. He stepped inside. Cara was lying on the sofa as though she
was in a peaceful sleep and Mario sat down beside her.

"We got him in custody." Lester tried to steady his breathing. "Is
Cara okay?"

"She fainted in my arms not long after I got inside the apartment.
I guess the drama was too much for her. The hit man tried to get her to
open the door. Told her some lame story about me being hurt. Of course
we know how he knew my name. I can't think about what would've happened if she had opened the door. Anyway, she refused to let him in. It's
my guess the man shot his gun thinking she was still at the door."

"I once remember that you said Cara stayed miles ahead of everyone."

"Right, and this time it saved her life."

"The guy was carted off in one of the squad cars. Soon he'll be
singing like a bird down at the station, if not before," Lester said with
authority.

Mario exhaled deeply while he continued to look at Cara. "Good.
It's what we need to haul Paula in."

"His name is Ralph and he's a first-class hoodlum. The kind that comes cheap," Lester remarked as he ran his fingers across the two bullet holes in the door. Lester walked over to the sofa and gazed down at Cara again. "Are you planning to stay with her?"

Mario spread his hands. "Absolutely. I won't leave her like this. Where will you be?"

"I'm headed to Ms. Coles' apartment. Undercover surveillance should be in front of her place as we speak."
Mario walked him to the door.

"Talk to you later, buddy," Lester spoke, with a settled calmness.

"You bet. Call me here."

Mario locked the door and returned to Cara's side. Only now that he was finally alone with her did he dare to relax. He dropped his head down wishing she'd wake up. When she didn't, he started to hum a familiar sweet tune, while he gently rubbed her forehead and around her face.

In a matter of seconds, Cara woke up bringing her arm up and above her head. "Mario, you're still here. What happened?"

She blinked, feeling light-headed, and her lips were dry.

"How you feel?" His dark brown eyes softened, watching her with concern. She sat up. He gently grabbed and held her. Willingly she let him hold her for the second time.

"I was so scared. Did they catch that man?"

"Yes, and now you're safe," he said, pushing loose strands of hair away from her cheek.

"Tired. I haven't slept or eaten since yesterday."

"Can I get you something to drink or eat?" He pulled slightly away from her. His stare clung to hers, analyzing her reaction.

"Thanks. Just some water."

He returned with a tall glass of water from the refrigerator. She straightened her body, letting her feet fall to the floor and she drank all of it.

"Feel better?" he asked.

"Yes, I do." Cara gave him the glass and she slowly curled her body back on the sofa. "I...thank you for saving my life." She didn't want to appear ungrateful, and she wondered how Mario, of all people, managed to be the one outside her door to protect her. "Were you working with the police? How did you know I was in danger?"

"It's a long story. During the last twenty-four hours, I learned a lot from talking to Mama and Lester. It was Mama who helped me realize that it had to be Paula who knew about your birthmark. I also know that Alderman Bennett is my brother, but we don't know how she got him involved in planting the evidence against you. You need to know that Lester explained his involvement and that he apologized for his one time indiscretion with you. I accepted his apology and thanked him for being there for you."

In her mind, she knew he was totally up to speed. Finally she spoke. "The footsteps I heard coming from the third floor must've been yours," she said. "I didn't know what was going on. All I know is that I was totally afraid."

"Yes, it was me keeping an eye on him from a short distance. If you only knew how much I wanted to let him have it when I saw him turn your doorknob. Lester advised me what to do. I had to play it by the book. He said if I had to shoot him, I should try not to kill him."

"Really?" she asked, sitting up. "How did you and Lester know my life was in danger?"

"Lester filled me in on the urgent call he got from Mrs. Walker, your downstairs neighbor. We all have her to thank for saving your life. Apparently, she traced Lester to the 2nd District station. He went to her apartment to talk to her one day while you were at work. They decided you needed protection and devised the plan. In the meantime, Lester had a hunch and put a wiretap on Paula's phone. That led the police to the hit man. The rest is history."

"You did this for me?" She hesitated, her brow lifted. "I don't know what to say." Cara lowered her voice for dramatic effect.

"Say nothing, except..." He froze, letting long hot tears roll down his cheek. "I hope, someday, that you can forgive me for not believing you. Mama told me everything, Cara." He fought to control the tears. "I know how you risked your life to prove your innocence, and how rough things must've been for you. I'm so sorry." His head dropped and his body slumped. Then he paused for a moment. "I just needed to say that and it's okay if you can't find it in your heart to forgive me. As it is, I'm finding it hard to forgive myself."

She sat up and put her hand on his shoulder. "You came to rescue me," she said, making an effort to soften her voice. "I'm so grateful for that." *What she wanted to tell him was that she still carried the pain inside because of what happened between them. She felt uncomfortable because she couldn't yet separate the fact that he'd just saved her life from the pain he'd caused her in the past.* "It means a lot to hear you ask me to forgive you. It won't erase what happened between us, but you know me, I don't have it in my heart to hold grudges. You have to answer to the God you believe in, not me. It's for that reason that I can once again forgive you. That's about all I can promise, Mario."

Mario sat up straight and nodded. "Oh, I understand and I can accept that you need time to deal with the rest," he said. "Honestly, it's eating my insides raw looking at you, being so close to you, and yet knowing how much I hurt you. You've always been the brave one, Cara. Outside, you are strong, patient and reasonable. But deep down, this must be ripping you apart. Believe it or not, I feel your pain."

Cara exhaled long and deep. "Really?" She stopped to look at him, wondering if this was her husband or some clone. "Paula's revenge definitely wrecked our world and affected so many people. After I left you, it was really tough for me, but thanks to your brother I got a better paying job. I questioned his motives and it wasn't until later on that I realized he meant me no harm. He's got a good heart and that's why he did it." She breathed and smiled. "You should focus on him now."

"I'm sure you're right," Mario said, gently touching her hand.

Little by little, warmth crept back into her body as the tears blinded her eyes and captured her voice. They were tears of pure nostalgia.

The life and times they had together brought on a sorrow that seemed to weigh her down.

Leaning forward, she peered at him. "Now, do this one last thing for me. Forgive yourself."

"I'll try."

The phone rang and she answered. "Hello?"

"It's good to hear your voice," Lester said. "How are you?"

"I'm alive. And, I want to thank you for everything you did to help me."

"No problem. I couldn't desert you. Can I speak to Mario?" She glanced at Mario and passed the phone to him. "It's Lester. He wants to talk to you."

"Hi, Lester, I hope you're going to tell me Paula's been arrested." Mario stared at Cara.

"No, it's just a matter of time though. I'm calling about your brother. He's out of the coma and resting comfortably. He's asking for you and your mother."

"That's great news. I'll go see him tomorrow. I'm staying here tonight."

"Okay," Lester replied.

"Thanks again. I'll never be able to repay you."

"Don't mention it," Lester said.

While Cara listened, her eyes were misty. By Mario's reaction and words, she knew the alderman had regained consciousness. She was glad for Mario and his family.

Mario clicked the phone off and put it down on the cocktail table.

"According to Lester, my brother is going to be okay. Will you come to the hospital with me?"

She was caught off guard by the sudden vibrancy of his voice. "Oh," she cast her eyes downward for a moment. "Under the circumstances, it might be too overwhelming for him. You and your mother should see him first. I... I'll go with you on the next visit, if that's okay," she answered.

More than anything he wanted her by his side. She was the half that could make him whole again. "I understand, but know that I want you there with me whenever you can come." He paused, looking deeply into her eyes. "Mama asked about you."

"Good. I hope to see her before she goes back to Memphis." Cara smiled at him and looked at the clock on the wall. It was three in the morning and daylight was just a few hours away. She was glad it was Sunday and had counted on sleeping later than usual. She wondered what he would do, leave her alone or sleep over. She was still afraid, but would never admit it.

They both sat in silence for a while and he watched her lean back on the sofa. She started to yawn a little and her eyes drooped some. He was still watching her.

Mario drew his lips in thoughtfully. "Why don't you go and get some sleep? I'll sleep out here on the sofa until morning."

"Good. I'll feel better with you here."

She got up to get the spare comforter and pillow she kept in the linen closet and came back to the living room holding a pink fluffy pillow and a solid magenta comforter. She placed the linen at the end of the sofa.

"This should help you get some rest."

"Thanks, and don't worry. I'm just here to protect you."

She stood motionless in the middle of the room. He sensed her disquiet. "By the way, we've talked a little about everything and nothing about our daughter. How is she doing?" Mario asked. He seemed really upbeat this time.

"Yeah, you're right. This situation has kept us from Ashley far too long. She's getting over a terrible cold. The other night when I called down there, she was playing with Chantiera, a little girl that lives four blocks down the street."

"That's good. I'm planning to go and see my baby real soon," Mario said and smiled.

"I meant to thank you for the child support. Most of it is going to a special college fund for her. The rest, I send to my parents to help with expenses."

"I'm not surprised that you would do that. You're just the type of woman who would use her support money to help her child." Mario fluffed his pillow and opened the comforter. He wanted to say something. He even wanted to beg her to give him another chance.

"Thanks for saying that." She slowly got up and looked back at him. "Good night."

As someone who hated to lose, Mario was determined to find a way to fix the damage he'd done. *There has to be a way,* he thought.

Finally, he kicked off his shoes and stretched out on the sofa. While still fully clothed, he pulled the cover over his body. Within minutes, he broke into tears the same as he had on the day his father died.

Chapter 43

Less than five hours later, Cara woke up to the sound of the phone ringing and she reached out groggily, unaware of what she was doing.

"Hello."

"Did I wake you?" Naomi asked.

Cara paused just for a moment to check the time. "Yeah, Mom, it's good you did. How are you doing?"

"I had a dream last night that you burned in a fire."

"Not quite. Something did happen here last night. Mario rescued me from some gunman that Paula hired. Mario also slept on the sofa, and don't go getting any ideas."

"My Lord! Are you all right?"

"Yes, we're safe now. Good news, Mom. The alderman regained consciousness last night. Mario wants me to go with him and Mary Lee to visit Bennett, but I declined. It'll be too awkward being there. They need time alone. Can you imagine the things they need to say to each other?"

"Yes. You're right. I hadn't thought about that. How're you and Mario getting along?"

"Okay. Actually, we're doing okay under the same roof and he was a total gentleman last night."

"I hope they catch that Paula soon."

"Me, too. They say it's just a matter of time. Mom, I need to shower and get dressed for church before he wakes up. I'll call you later. Give Ashley and Daddy my love."

She hung up and jumped out of bed. After throwing on her robe, she slipped into the bathroom and turned on the shower.

Meanwhile, on the sofa, Mario had heard the phone ring. He worried that it might've been another call from Lester. Just yesterday he asked Lester point-blank where his relationship with Cara was going. He recalled Lester's words, *Mario, it should be no secret that Cara is one hell of a woman. You'll be glad to know she never said she loved me. Quite frankly, I don't believe she ever will.* The sound of the shower became clearer and Mario continued to lie there wondering about Lester. *Was Lester being diplomatic just to get my cooperation to save Cara's life? Or did something go wrong between them? Cara hasn't actually given me reason to believe she wants me back,* he thought.

He got up and made a pot of coffee thinking she'd appreciate the gesture. He helped himself to a cup and admired Cara's flair for maintaining a lovely and clean kitchen. Some things never change, he thought.

Suddenly he heard the bathroom door open. Cara dashed out, hurrying to her bedroom properly clad with a blue beach towel around her. She'd always been self-conscious about exposing her body, even to Mario.

Fifteen minutes later, she appeared before him looking incredible. She wore an olive green two-piece skirt suit. Her hair was down her back and 14-carat gold earrings were looped in her ears. As usual, she applied just the right amount of makeup.

"Good morning. How you feel?" he asked.

"Hi. I'm better. I smell coffee." Her eyes brightened with surprise.

"That it is," he beamed as he stood up and motioned for her to sit down. He quickly filled the yellow mug to the rim. "One sugar and no cream, right?"

"Yes." She grinned, easing the tension.

He set her coffee on the table before her. She took two sips and smiled. "It's actually good. Thanks."

She sat down at the table facing him. "Have you thought some more about your visit with your brother?"

"Yeah, I did. I did what you always do, I prayed and the answer came to me. I know exactly what I should do," he said.

"Good for you. I'll send up a special prayer for all of you."

Shortly afterward, Cara walked him to the door. He turned to face her. "By the way, I called off the divorce. I meant to talk about it last night, but I just couldn't find the right moment."

She blinked and then focused her gaze down. "I know. My lawyer told me."

———

Mario had left to go home and Cara finished her coffee. Then she thought about Mrs. Walker, realizing she owed her a world of thanks. She called her neighbor and they spent time chatting about the whole ordeal. Cara learned how Lester and Mario had entrapped Ralph, the gunman. As she listened to Mrs. Walker talk further, Cara came to realize why no one told her about the plan and she understood why Mario agreed to position himself on the floor above her apartment.

"I can't thank you enough, Mrs. Walker. You've been more than a good neighbor. You were like an angel on my shoulder." Cara wanted to reach through the phone and hug her.

"I'm glad to know I was able to do some good," Mrs. Walker boasted.

"And as long as I'm living in this apartment, I'll be your guardian angel," Cara said.

They talked some more and then Cara glanced at the clock on the kitchen wall. "I've got to leave for church. See you later, after I get back."

"Oh, yeah that reminds me, I met your husband. How will you ever choose between them?"

Chapter 44

Around 9:30 that same morning Lester and a slew of plain clothed cops had Paula's apartment surrounded. Lester had been there since day-break. He climbed the steps to her third-floor apartment and knocked on her door twice. He waited a few minutes and knocked again, calling out her name. "Ms. Coles, this is Detective Lester Miller, Chicago Police Department."

After waiting for five minutes, he walked halfway down the steps. He connected with a cop waiting in the alley. "Detective Miller here. There's no answer; apparently she's out."

"I can see why," the officer replied. "She's pulling out of the garage as we speak, and I'm on her tail."

Immediately, Lester scurried to his unmarked car and drove off behind three squad cars down Seventy-first and Cornell. Paula was able to get slightly ahead, driving faster than the speed limit allowed. She managed to avoid colliding with the cars in her path. She passed through two traffic lights in the nick of time, crossed the railroad track and drove west to Jeffrey Boulevard. She nearly hit a car speeding through the light when she turned right on red.

On South Shore Drive, luckily the traffic on the four-lane outer drive was light. Passing every vehicle ahead of them, Lester could clearly see Paula's car. Soon he realized that she was about to approach the dangerous curve near the Museum of Science and Industry. By then, the speedometer in his car had reached 80 miles an hour.

Traffic from Fifty-seventh Street poured onto the Drive at normal speeds. A driver of a gray SUV was aiming to turn left and the black sports car veering to the right on swerved in the same direction heading south on the Drive.

Suddenly Paula veered her car toward the lake. Instantly, she plowed into the cement wall, flipping over into Lake Michigan. Sounds of steel banging and tires hugging the street brought a line of southbound cars to a standstill. One vehicle burst into flames and drivers close by scrambled to get out of their cars. Some rushed over to the embankment.

Lester pulled over a few hundred feet away and parked in the emergency lane. Within a matter of minutes, three fire trucks, four ambulances and more police cars appeared on the scene. Several tow trucks arrived shortly afterward. Gapers were then ushered away from the area.

Once all unaffected vehicles were out of the way, Paula's car was lifted up from the water. The windows were rolled down. Soon the paramedics rolled the stretcher down the pavement. The body was covered with a white sheet. He wanted so much to bring her in alive, but in this case, he didn't seem to mind that they didn't get to her in time. Bennett's anonymity would be preserved. Case closed.

Lester soon pulled off and merged southbound onto the Drive, letting the area police handle the matter and wondering how Mario would react.

————

People waiting to enter the church started to pour in and fill scattered vacant spaces on the pews. It was during the morning hymn and everyone stood singing robustly *My Faith Looks Up to Thee*. Cara rejoiced, feeling grateful about the sudden turn of events in her life. Mostly she was happy to be alive and she sensed that a suitcase of emotional baggage had been lifted from her mind and her heart. As she sang, she thought prayerfully about Mario's family.

As more people scurried to find a seat, she caught a peripheral glimpse of Barbara, who was dressed in the navy blue usher's uniform. She stopped in the aisle directly alongside her pew. Suddenly, Cara looked up and saw Mario coming toward her wearing a warm smile on his face. Before he could ease past her to stand to her left, Mary Lee scrambled to stand on the right of her. Cara stopped singing and hugged her mother-in-law.

"Hi, Mother Fleming. What a surprise to see you guys here," Cara softly whispered.

"It's so good to see you," she whispered in Cara's ear. Mario couldn't sit still to do anything today. He just had to come to your church."

"I'm glad you're both here." She continued to hold Mary Lee's hand as she started to sing again. Then on impulse, she looked at Mario. He gave her a quick glance and he reached out and clutched her hand, singing the words like he meant them.

After the song ended, they sat down. Mario leaned over and whispered, "Hope you don't mind that I'm here. I asked the usher to take us to where you were sitting."

Cara smiled demurely, thinking Barbara ought to be happy with her church guest this time. "Don't be silly. I'm glad you wanted to come to church today. You'll like it. The choir will rock the church. And, the sermon is always good."

He gently withdrew his hand and folded both hands down to his lap, apparently braced to enjoy the service.

Fifteen minutes later and during the sermon, Mario's pager pulsated inside his shirt pocket. He waited a few minutes, slowly pulled it out, and pushed the message button. *Been trying to reach you. Paula drowned in Lake Michigan trying to flee the police on the Outer Drive. More later. Lester.*

Mario dropped his head for a moment and then he looked at Cara, thinking the nightmare was finally over. He nudged his hand against hers. When he got her attention, he slid the pager into her hand. She looked at him and glanced down to read the digital readout. With a stunned look on her face, she shook her head and watched him press the pager button off and return it to his shirt pocket.

Chapter 45

Cara stood outside the University of Chicago Hospital thinking she wasn't ready to face Alderman Bennett in his hospital bed. Mario had persuaded her to come with them. Once inside the double glass doors, they approached the reception desk and Mario gave their names and relationship to the patient. The clerk issued them guest passes.

When they arrived at Alderman Bennett's private room door, Cara followed Mario and Mary Lee inside.

Bright sunshine streamed in through the big windows in his room. Bennett was awake, and his bed was tilted slightly upward. Bennett's eyes sparkled with pleasure. He folded his hands peacefully.

"Come in. I was hoping you'd come to see me." He smiled, looking first at Mary Lee, then Mario and finally at Cara.

Mary Lee took a few steps to his bedside and bent to kiss him on the cheek. "Hello, my child. Don't ever give me a scare like that again. I thought I'd lost you all over again." He wrapped his arms around her and held her for a few moments.

"For the second time, Mother, I'm glad to be back." She smiled at the alderman. Then she looked at Mario. He was standing on the other side of the bed.

"Hi, big brother. I'm Mario." He leaned his head down low and their faces touched. "I'm so glad to finally meet you. Thank God, you're alive," he said, holding his brother's hand.

"Likewise," Alderman Bennett whispered. He breathed in shallow, quick gasps.

"Try to take it slow for now. I'm not going anywhere. We got nothing but time to talk," Mario assured him.

Bennett paused to breathe deeply until he calmed again. "You were just a baby when I last saw you. It seems that all my prayers have finally been answered. There's so much I want to say to you. I'm so sorry. I didn't know you were my brother. Paula threatened me with everything I worked so hard for. Can you forgive me?"

Mary Lee couldn't resist rubbing his shoulders gently. She looked at Mario seemingly anxious for him to say something.

"You bet I can. And, this time I want the world to know you're family. No more hiding, no more secrets, okay?" Mario said proudly.

"Okay, it's a deal. That's a mighty big load off my shoulder," Alderman Bennett said and smiled.

"You must know I'm not angry with you. Mama told me what happened two days ago. So, yes, I can forgive you." They gave each other the thumbs up gesture.

Cara stood more than a few feet away from his bed, watching everything. Perhaps, it was simply her uneasiness. Then Bennett gave a slight nod at Cara and smiled.

She took that as encouragement to come closer. She'd heard and seen it all and she smiled back at him. Slowly she came closer and stood alongside Mario. Amazingly, being face- to- face with Bennett remind-ed her that she knew him on four levels – a chat room buddy, a politician, a church member and now her brother-in-law.

"Hello, Alderman Bennett. I'm Cara. How're you feeling?" she asked, gently.

He had glanced at her for a sign of objection. "Better now," he said, taking a deep breath. "Seeing the three of you together like this has given me all the reason to want to get well and get out of here."

Alderman Bennett reached out and softly held her hand in a gen-tle grasp.

"I can't help wondering what you, of all people, must think of me. I know I caused you pain. For that, I'm truly sorry."

"It's okay." There was a faint tremor in her voice as though some emotion had touched her. "Please, try not to worry about that now. You've more than made up for the harm you caused me. I'm praying you get well soon and get back to helping the people in your community."

"I'll hold that close to my heart, sister-in-law. You're as smart and optimistic as you are beautiful. I'm grateful for your understanding."

Cara noticed that he appeared drowsy and that he wanted to say more. She looked at Mario and whispered in his ear, "Why don't you stay with him? He'll appreciate the company. Besides, it'll be a good time for you to talk, ease his mind some. Tell him Paula won't be black-mailing him or anyone else ever again."

"Okay, whatever you say. Can Mama come with you?" Mario asked. Before Cara could answer, she noticed that Bennett was even more awake than before.

"Stop whispering, you two," Bennett joked. That brought some laughter to the room.

He looked at Mary Lee and asked her to sit down and relax. "I've got one more thing to beg for." He folded both hands with his head bowed and eyes closed. When he opened them, a smile found its way through the mask of uncertainty as to how he would speak words of wisdom to Mario and Cara. He needed to be sure his bad deeds wouldn't keep them apart forever. *The time is now or never*, he thought.

"Giles, go on. We're listening," Mary Lee said.

He looked at Cara. "Remember what I wrote you in my last e-mail?"

"Yes."

"You didn't know who I was at the time yet I knew you. It's just that I needed to say something to give you hope and belief in yourself. It went something like this: There's hope when something has died; there's hope when you think you're down and out and have no where to turn; There's hope when you've been lied on and had to give up your happiness and peace of mind." He unfolded his hands and gazed his eyes up into hers. "Did it help you?"

"Yes."

"Good. Now, I'm moved by the spirit to say this to you and

Mario.

People are sometimes mean and difficult; forgive them anyway. If you're successful, you will win some false friends and sometimes enemies; succeed anyway. What you spend years building, someone could destroy overnight; build anyway. You see, in the final analysis, it's between you and God; it was never between you and them anyway. God put you together; let no man keep you apart.

Bennett looked at them, one by one, smiled happily and closed his eyes.

———

Mario sat quietly by Alderman Bennett's bedside that afternoon, thinking profoundly and dreamlessly this time, with no thought of the future and no fear of the past. There was only the present. He tried to cope with the idea that he might lose Cara. For a man who was fighting an uphill battle for his marriage, he might as well have been clinging to a straight pin. He was tired, discouraged and needed a whole day of sleep.

Then he remembered unfinished business about the case. *Did Lester locate Paula's sister in Detroit? Other than her girlfriend in Memphis, there was no one else to call, that someone had to make arrangements for a funeral and burial.* At no time had Bennett sat up in bed and opened his mouth to talk again, so Mario eased out of the room to call Lester on his cellular phone. Lester sounded groggy from only four hours of sleep in two days. Mario was relieved to know that Paula's body was at Jackson Funeral Home on Cottage Grove. Her sister Odessa was on a Southwest Airline flight to Chicago to make arrangements to have Paula's body prepared and shipped to Detroit for the services. And, most disturbing was that Loretta Bennett had called and asked for Lester's help to arrange a private visit with the alderman.

"Does Mrs. Bennett know my mother is here?"

"Yes, and she backed off," Lester replied.

"Good. For once she made the right decision."

Mario couldn't begin to imagine what meeting the woman, even by accident, would do to his mother. He was all too aware that the woman who kidnapped his brother had, in the end, helped Cara find the needle in the haystack. He owed Loretta Bennett a debt of gratitude.

Chapter 46

Cara had decided on a complete take-out meal from Kentucky Fried Chicken. While driving to her apartment, she and Mary Lee talked about Giles, and she apologized to Cara for having to lie about needing Matthew's screen name.

"Don't worry, Mother Fleming. No need to apologize. We should count our blessings for the good that came from it," Cara replied.

"What did you think about Giles? He wants you and Mario to work things out, you know?"

"Yes, that was quite clear. What he had to say was touching. I can see that he's your son. I'm so glad he came back to you."

"Except for a different name and a new life, he's back in the flesh, mind and soul. I just wish Bradley could've lived to see him."

They both got quiet and Cara tuned the radio to a station that played gospel music. Mary Lee took comfort in a song by Yolanda Adams.

Cara thought about Lester and how he'd removed himself to help everyone. It hadn't mattered so much now that he had been deceitful. He was above that, a good man and a good friend to her and Mario. She loved him in a special way and could never forget him. As it turned out, he was the wrong man at the right time in her life.

Oh, sure he'd reminded her about passion and romance and he had given her the best sex she'd ever imagined was possible. He had taken her to the mountaintop. She'd seen what was possible, yet she knew he was not the man to share the view with. To do so would have been nothing less than going from a frying pan to an inferno. She'd learned enough to fill a lifetime. She felt a gap in her heart wider than the Grand Canyon.

Cara pulled up in front of her building and Mary Lee helped her take the food inside. While she changed into a pair of jeans and a yellow V-neck sweater, Mary Lee put the large box of chicken, mashed potatoes, biscuits, coleslaw and greens inside the fridge. Mario was expected to come over later and dine with them.

Then Cara took Mary Lee downstairs to meet Mrs. Walker. The two older ladies liked each other right away and surprisingly Mary Lee took her phone number and promised to keep in touch.

Before Mario arrived, Cara and Mary Lee talked and reminisced about the good old days in Memphis, how Ashley was growing by leaps and bounds, and finally about Mario. Mary Lee was careful not to push Cara's feelings or plans about her future.

———

Mario arrived at 4:30 p.m. They got the food ready and the three of them sat at the table. While they ate, Mario gave them a glowing report about Giles. The two brothers talked for a long time about the years he had spent away from home. They promised to start acting like brothers. There were reporters waiting outside the room, and he also received a surprise visit from Joe Michaels. Giles introduced them and Mario left shortly afterward.

After the meal, Mary Lee insisted that Cara and Mario take a moment to talk alone in the living room. She cleared the table and made the kitchen tidy again. Mario pulled out his cellular and called Ashley. They took turns talking with her, Naomi, and Frank.

Cara looked up fifteen minutes later as Mary Lee entered the living room holding two glasses of white wine. Cara gently took a glass.

"Thanks, Mother Fleming. Sit down and relax."

"Did I hear him call out Ashley's name?" Mary Lee asked in amazement and passed a glass to Mario.

"Yes," Mario answered.

"What has Ashley been saying to you guys?"

"Oh, just that she loves us and how she can't wait to come to Chicago and be with us." Cara wondered how her father must've reacted when he heard Ashley say that. She figured that Naomi had somehow persuaded Frank to stop influencing Ashley. But this time, she didn't care how he would rant and rave to her about what was best for Ashley.

————

Later that evening when she was alone, Cara retrieved an electronic greeting from Lester. He obviously remembered her screen name from the investigation. She clicked on the greeting while her head started to spin. It was a happy birthday message, two days early. It wasn't that she'd forgotten; she just didn't take the time to think about her birthday. Lester's message was sweet, brief and not binding. She sent him a thank you reply.

Chapter 47

Two days later, Giles was released to recuperate at home. He could return to doing light duty at his office in a week. His housekeeper and Michaels made sure he was comfortable. The house was kept immaculate, and meals were served on time. Mario and Mary Lee were given the grand tour the same day he arrived home. Mary Lee found the photo book lying on the curio table. She explained to Mario how she'd kept pictures of him over the years.

During the ride back to the hotel, she remembered all she'd done since Sunday to plan a surprise party for Cara. It had taken some doing, but in the end she managed to convince Frank and Naomi to bring Ashley on an all-expense-paid trip to Chicago. They would come on a Greyhound bus. Expected arrival time was 5:40 p.m.

Fifteen minutes later, after leaving the hospital, Mario pulled up to the hotel entrance.

"I'll see you later, Mama."

"Okay. Try to get some rest. You want to look your best."

———

Cara woke up immediately realizing it was her birthday. The phone had been silent while she got dressed for work. She arrived at the office before nine o'clock and found on her desk a bouquet of flowers. The card read, "Happy Birthday, Cara. We wish you all the best." She smiled and was pleased that the staff thought enough to remember her birthday.

Suddenly, Shirley Carr peeked her head from the cubicle a few feet away. She seemed unusually sneaky, but friendly when she greeted Cara.

"Hi, Shirley. You guys shouldn't have," Cara beamed, looking at the pink, purple and blue floral arrangement.

"It's just a little something from us," Shirley said. Dexter Grady stood close by and Shirley nudged him slightly. He appeared bashful and smiled.

"You have plans for the evening?" Shirley probed.

"No. None that I'm aware of."

"Terrific. At Mr. Dunlap's request, I made reservations for a group dinner in your honor tonight. I can pick you up around seven-thirty this evening?" she asked, eagerly waiting for Cara's answer.

"Oh, my goodness, all this for me? I'll be ready," Cara said, totally surprised. She felt like a member of the staff finally. By now, she had expected her parents to call. Surely they wouldn't forget her birthday.

―――――

Cara's parents and Ashley arrived at the bus station on Clark Street earlier than expected. It was Frank's first time in the Windy City. They waited outside the terminal for Mary Lee to take them to the hotel. Ashley was hugging the brown teddy bear Cara had bought her, Mr. Chocolate. When Mary Lee arrived in a taxi to meet and greet them, she got out and gave each of them a warm hug. Once they were comfortably seated, the driver fought to get through the Loop traffic and Mary Lee filled them in on the remaining details. Naomi and Frank seemed satisfied that Cara's nightmare was finally over.

As they rode on, Frank joked around and got everyone laughing right away. Then he looked back at Mary Lee. "You've gone to a lot of trouble. I sure hope this plan of yours works."

"So do I." Ashley had leaned over on Naomi and fallen asleep. "More than anything, it's for our granddaughter's sake that I hope Mario and Cara can work things out between them," Mary Lee pointed out.

"Here, here," Naomi added. "Ashley has talked about nothing

except coming to Chicago. She brought her coloring book to show to her mama and daddy. That child painted pictures yesterday until she almost dropped."

———

As Cara walked alongside Shirley to a private room at the Ramada Inn, she was expecting to be greeted by her coworkers.

No sooner than she opened the door and looked up, there was Mario. She looked into his eyes once again. She thought she had worked out what she'd say when their paths crossed again. He smiled broadly at her and his eyes told her what she needed to know. He was in on this plan, too!

"Happy birthday, Cara," he beamed, and stood with his arms stretched to her.

Startled, and suddenly feeling like someone who mattered in his life again and that he truly loved her, Cara embraced him without restraint.

"Thank you," she whispered while still in his arms. She pulled away slightly. "You've outdone yourself this time. In my wildest imagination, I can't figure out how you pulled this one off."

"That's for me to know and you to figure out, isn't it?" Mario said, still holding her.

As he whisked her to the middle of the room, Shirley joined several waitresses who stood near the string combo. They sang "Happy Birthday" to her as the music played softly. She slowly looked around the large room, beautifully decorated. A banner that read, "Happy Birthday, Cara, 29," sparkled in red and yellow, like a neon sign.

Shirley beamed as she snapped pictures of Mario and Cara as they danced slowly to romantic music. Cara looked at him and smiled, still baffled by his latest action.

Mario noticed that the onlookers were staring at them. They were all smiling. Mario decided, as long as he was giving everyone a show, that he might as well make it a good one.

With a deep breath for courage, he turned to look at Cara. "Remember me? I love you more than ever," he said, tilting her face toward his so that they made perfect eye contact. "Lord knows I don't deserve another chance and I am willing to do whatever is necessary to work hard to be the man you fell in love with. Even if you don't want to stay married, please believe that." Tears welled in his eyes.

Understanding softened her face. Suddenly she remembered how painful it could be when the one you really love was hurting too.

He pulled a small black box from his pocket and opened it. She stared at it, with a look of wonder as it winked and sparkled. "Cara, will you wear this ring as my wife again?"

She stared at him through a blur of tears, not sure that this was real. He was offering her exactly what she wanted all alongæ a life of love, peace and happiness with him and Ashley. "Yes, Mario. I still love you, too. It's because I love you and our daughter that I can give our marriage *one* more try." He held her tight, closing his eyes to savor the moment as everyone cheered. And, she prayed she'd made the right decision.

A few seconds later, the music stopped. Mario and Cara turned to look in the direction of the door. As everyone started to leave the room one by one, the couple thanked them. Shirley tiptoed over to Cara, hugged her and wished her good luck. She gave Mario a handshake and left the room.

Just then, a closed door opened and all the family poured into the room screaming *Surprise, Surprise!* Frank helped Giles, who was sitting in a wheelchair, into the room. Cara behaved like a starry-eyed contestant who'd just won a national beauty contest. Mario had to hold her up to keep her from falling. All together, they sang happy birthday to her.

"Ashley, Mom, Daddy," she screamed their names, bouncing around. She grabbed her daughter, taking her into her arms. "Hi, Ashley! You surprised me."

"I love you mommy. You look pretty." Ashley laid her head on Cara's shoulder. Naomi and Frank stood close by and put their arms around Cara while she still held onto Ashley.

"Happy birthday, Baby girl," Frank said.

"Are you happy, darling?" Naomi asked.

"Yes, Mom. I'm so glad you came. My God, I am so happy!" She hugged them again.

Mario stood close by and heard what they said. Cara gave Ashley to him and he held onto her. "Hi, Daddy, I missed you," Ashley said, laughing.

"I missed you, little one. This time, I promise you will stay with us."

Then Frank and Naomi joined Mario and Ashley. "Welcome back to the family, Son." The handshakes suddenly changed to warm hugs. Ashley held tight to Mario.

Then Mary Lee joined Cara, who was standing not far way. "Welcome back, my sweet daughter-in-law," she said, hugging her.

"Thanks for everything, Mother Fleming. You've been amazing through it all."

When it was Bennett's turn, he offered his congratulations to the happy couple. "Mario, I'm glad your plan worked. Let's be that big happy family now, okay?"

"You got that right," Mario said. "I've got more to do to clean up my act. Thanks for being there for me big brother," Mario said, and hugged him.

"I've got a really big surprise for you and Cara."

Mario raised his eyebrows in wonderment.

"Don't even ask. I won't tell," Bennett replied, smiling. Then,

Mario pulled Cara closer to him. All they could do was smile at each other again.

Mario looked back at Bennett. "Me and the Mrs. can't wait for the surprise."

Everyone had a good time eating from the lavish buffet of seafood and chicken. Frank and Naomi were pleased to finally meet Bradley's oldest son. Frank urged him to come to Memphis to spend some time with them, too. Alderman Bennett promised he'd come soon.

Family members talked and laughed, mostly listening to Frank talk about his first trip to Chicago and the long bus ride.

"Next time, maybe you'll get on a plane," Mary Lee quipped.

"Hell no. You'll have to sedate me before I do that." He threw back his head and laughed. He looked ten years younger when he laughed.

An hour later, Mario and Cara finally had a moment alone. They sat holding hands, unable to take their eyes off each other. Happily exhausted, the couple was still very excited about their new beginning. The others had almost vanished to their rooms. Joe Michaels had arrived an hour ago and had taken Alderman Bennett home.

Cara and Mario agreed to stay in the room Mary Lee had reserved for them. After hugging and rejoicing with their family, the couple went to their hotel room and was surprised again. A large wicker basket containing sleepwear, robes, toiletries, and clothes for Mario and Cara to wear the next day, was sitting on the coffee table.

Cara checked to see who had sent it and smiled. "Your mother is a champ, wouldn't you say?"

"Yep, that's Mary Lee for you. She's a busybody, but she means well." Mario drew Cara close and held her gently for a long time. "Let's renew our vows. I want to plan a lavish ceremony at the church with a romantic reception. Please say yes."

Overwhelmed with happiness, Cara exclaimed, "Yes, oh, yes! Let's do it again."

"Then it shall be done," he said.

Exhausted, they plopped down on the bed and held each other some more. She was a glowing image of fire, passion and love. In a raw act of possession, he grabbed her and they kissed slowly. A hot tide of sexual energy raged through both of them.

As much as she wanted him to make love to her for the first time in a long time, Cara pulled away.

"Let's savor the moment, count our blessings and..."

He interrupted her. "And, save the best for last?"

"Yes, how did you know that's what I wanted to say?"

"Because, not only do I love you, I know you like a book. You're a lady, my grand lady," he said. A smile lingered on his face.

Hearing those words, she thought, *everything is going to be okay again.*

Later, they showered and dressed for bed. They toasted each other with some of the wine Mary Lee had chilled for them. Mario told her about the inheritance from his dad's estate, the landscape business, and his decision to put most of the money in savings and CDs. All of it welled up inside him, including the desire to tell her about his surprise plan to buy them a home in Chicago. He wanted to blurt it all out, but he wanted the news to be his gift to her later.

"There's something I want you to know. I've signed up for anger management counseling and I've decided that drinking is not the answer to dealing with any problem. I've brought that situation under control."

"Really? I'm proud of you. Since your success in dealing with both problems are so important to the survival of our marriage, please know that I'll be by your side to support you."

Chapter 48

Cara and Mario were ready to renew their vows. Alderman Bennett had managed to work in secret using his political connections and got Luther Vandross to sing at the wedding. Luckily, the recording star had a three-hour layover at O'Hare for a flight to Atlanta.

Among the one hundred plus guests were Cara's coworkers, Dexter Grady, Earl Dunlap, Thelma Walker, Alderman Tucker, Renita Dates, Captain Hayes and his wife, Duncan Tate, Cecil Hawkins, Barbara Rhodes, and several of Lester's police buddies who watched over Cara. Loretta Bennett had promised Giles she'd come unannounced, but she changed her mind at the last minute. She was not ready, if ever, to face Mary Lee.

Frank made an unprecedented move at the last minute. He insisted that Lester walk his daughter down the aisle. When Frank had heard the whole story behind his efforts to save and protect Cara's life, nothing else mattered to him. Besides, he'd already given Cara away to Mario at their first wedding. Mario had been in total agreement with the decision, figuring it was a price worth paying, knowing he was going to have one more chance with Cara. But, Lester refused believing it wouldn't be the right thing to do. He knew that one day it would be his turn at finding happiness. It was just a matter of time.

With everything and everybody in place, the organist started to play soft music from a Vanessa Williams tune. Mario stood at the altar along with Alderman Bennett, his best man. They wore dark gray Gucci tuxedos. Shirley Carr, the matron of honor, walked in first. Ashley looked beautiful as the flower girl, sprinkling petals of peach colored roses as she walked down the aisle.

Then everyone applauded loudly when Luther was introduced. He stepped proudly to the microphone, dressed in a glittering two-piece black suit. When he started to sing the bridal song, *Here and Now*, everyone suddenly turned completely around to look at Cara standing at the door.

She smiled happily at Frank and thanked him for supporting her decision to stay in her marriage and for believing that Mario would treat her right this time.

"Just be happy, okay?" he said.

"I'm going to do my part, Daddy."

She wore a strapless elegant off-white gown with embroidery and crystals on the bodice and train that she found at Saks Fifth Avenue less than six days ago. Hand strung peach and blue-diamond flowers adorned her hair. She carried a bouquet of peach and white orchids and dahlias.

Twenty minutes later, Mario held her hand and looked at her. "Your love is loyal and it has deathless wings that never fail to rise to triumph. Your love has turned my heart of shame to one of honor and gladness. Cara, you make me so very happy. There shall never again be failure in my commitment to you. From this day forth and with God as the center of our lives, I promise to love you faithfully and trust you perfectly."

When he was finished, Cara recited her vows. "Mario, I love you and there's nothing anybody can do about it. Though we've walked the road that all lovers and married folk have traveled, in wild and secret happiness we stumbled. But, you're still so utterly mine. True happiness is being with only you. Yes, I can return to you as your wife, promising to love you faithfully and trusting you perfectly. Together, with God in the center of our lives, and with our little girl Ashley, we will move forward from this day, keeping the promise we made six years ago to love and respect each other until death do us part."

There wasn't a dry eye in the church when Rev. Lewis said, "On their words, and by the grace of God, I give you, Mr. and Mrs. Mario Fleming and daughter."

Less than thirty minutes later, everyone had gathered to receive the happy couple. A commercial wedding planner had decorated the church's annex in blue and peach colors. Cocktails and a three-course catered dinner of shrimp and prime rib were served. Everyone looked lovely and they seemed happy for the couple.

After the meal, a popular jazz band kept a lively mood in high gear. Mario and Cara danced to the Kenny G classic, *Forever in Love.*

Cara and Mario posed for tons of pictures and in every pose Ashley stood in the middle.

Meanwhile, standing huddled together in the crowd, Duncan Tate commented to Cecil Hawkins, "I'm glad that story had a happy ending. You should feel lucky."

"Yeah, can you imagine the political fallout that Alderman Bennett would be faced with if it hadn't? For my sake, my fingers are crossed hoping that the rest of it will stay buried," Cecil replied.

Across the room, Mario stepped away from Cara's side to speak to Lester. Then, Cara looked across the room at each person she'd met over the past few months. Her thoughts of each one slipped through her mind and she wondered what they were thinking, especially Barbara. *I've got to find the time to thank her for being my friend.*

When Mario joined Lester, he was sipping on a raspberry flavored Martini.

"Hey, we pulled it off, man. Congratulations," Lester greeted him and they gave each other a manly hug. Lester was comfortable and knew that he had done the right thing helping his friends reunite. *If only I knew how Cara really felt about me, I would have given Mario a run for his money,* he thought.

"Thanks. You're the best friend I've ever had. It took a lot for me to realize that," Mario said.

"Don't ever forget it." He nudged Mario to look at Duncan and Cecil. "That's the couple I told you about. The one with the straight hair was the *anonymous caller.*

"Oh yeah? Any other time, I would have called him a you-know-what," Mario chuckled.

They both laughed. "Seems like old times, huh," he said, putting his arm around Lester.

"Yep, that it appears," Lester replied and sipped some more of his drink. "Aren't you going to have at least one drink?"

"Nah. I don't need it. I'm cool. The only thing I'm concerned about now is that my brother's past stays out of the press. His career depends on it," Mario said firmly.

———

An hour later, Mario, Cara and Ashley had changed into traveling attire. Good-byes and hugs to everyone were exchanged. Then Cara stood and embraced her parents for a few moments.

Later she joined Mario at the top of the steps and he reached out to take her hand. "I'm ready." Mario took the small bag from her hand. The rest of their luggage was already in the limousine trunk.

"Then let's go and start that life we always wanted," he said.

Amid rice throwing and hand-blown kisses, Mario ushered Cara and Ashley down the steps and into the limo parked in front of the church. Ashley sat between her parents on the back seat. They turned to face the crowd and waved good-bye. The driver would take them to

O'Hare to board a plane to the Cayman Islands. Mario had secretly made the plans right after Cara agreed to stay with him. They would spend the Christmas break on a real honeymoon, but not without their daughter. It was the way Mario and Cara wanted it. Helping things along, Mary Lee would fly there the next day to keep Ashley occupied.

As for Frank and Naomi, they would take the bus back to Memphis later that day and they seemed satisfied that Cara and her husband were happy and were now able to take good care of their granddaughter.

As the driver was about to turn the corner, Ashley turned and looked at Cara and then Mario. "Mommy and Daddy, that was fun. What's next?" Mario and Cara laughed heartedly.

Mario sat Ashley on his legs and she faced them both.

"We're going to get on an airplane and fly up and away to a beautiful island where there's a lot of water, beaches, sun, trees, peace and happiness," he replied, smiling.

"Oh, boy! I can't wait. Can you Mommy?" Ashley's eyes sparkled as though she was playing a game. Funny, how at that moment, Cara's mind flashed to just yesterday when she realized that her period was a month or so overdue. She couldn't remember exactly and pushed it completely out of her mind thinking it had been because of the whole ordeal surrounding the attempt on her life, discovering that Paula was the culprit, breaking things off with Lester, and having made the decision to give Mario another chance. It had been more than any woman could reasonably expect to handle in a lifetime.

She looked at Ashley, planted a kiss on her cheek and said, "No, honey, I can't either."

Once they were on the Ryan Expressway headed straight to the airport, Mario looked at Cara and said, "I love you. I promise, this time we're going to make it, " he said with much emotion and a special gleam in his eyes.

"I hope so, too, Mr. Fleming."

Discussion Guide

1. After reading *Anonymity*, did you immediately believe in Cara's innocence or did you think that maybe she indeed had an affair?
2. Adultery is said to be an act committed by one out of every five American men and half as many women. Has adultery become commonplace? Why do you think society is so forgiving of adultery?
3. What were your thoughts about Mario? What were his positive attributes? What did you dislike about him? Do you think someone like Mario can learn from his mistakes?
4. Was the outcome of Paula's life a matter of "what comes around goes around"?
5. Did Lester really fall in love with Cara or was Cara yet another name to add to his list of women?
6. Although Jennifer appeared to be a pillar of strength, she was actually dealing with issues in her own marriage? Do you think there was more that Cara could have done to help Jennifer? Do you know anyone who has experienced the same illusion of powerlessness as Jennifer?
7. Do you think Alderman Giles Bennett (AKA Matthew Fleming) should have refused to do Paula's dirty work? What do you think would have happened if the Alderman's past life were exposed to the media?
8. Do you know anyone who has experienced the loss of a child through abduction? If so, what was the outcome?
9. Were you sympathetic to the manner in which Bradley dealt with the loss of Matthew and later with the knowledge of Matthew being alive?
10. Mary Lee was a matriarch who loved her family and took care of business in her own way. What do you think of the way she handled Bradley? Mario? Matthew?
11. Do you think Cara, Mario and Ashley will live "happily ever after"?